DISCARD

A
RELIABLE
WIFE

ALSO BY ROBERT GOOLRICK

The End of the World as We Know It

A
RELIABLE
WIFE

A NOVEL BY

ROBERT GOOLRICK

ALGONQUIN BOOKS
OF CHAPEL HILL
2 0 0 9

Published by
ALGONQUIN BOOKS OF CHAPEL HILL
Post Office Box 2225
Chapel Hill, North Carolina 27515-2225

a division of
WORKMAN PUBLISHING
225 Varick Street
New York, New York 10014

This is a work of fiction. While, as in all fiction, the literary
perceptions and insights are based on experience, all names, characters, places,
and incidents either are products of the author's imagination or
are used fictitiously.

Library of Congress Cataloging-in-Publication Data
Goolrick, Robert, [date]
A reliable wife : a novel / by Robert Goolrick. — 1st ed.
p. cm.
ISBN-13: 978-1-56512-596-4
1. Marriage — Fiction. 2. Family secrets — Fiction.
3. Wisconsin — History — 19th cenury — Fiction. I. Title.
PS3607.O5925R45 2009
813'.6 — dc22   2008049970

10 9 8 7 6 5 4 3

For Jeanne Voltz
who was better to me than I was to myself
with eternal love and gratitude
and for my darling brother and sister
B and Lindlay.

Be not dishearten'd——Affection shall solve the problems
     of Freedom yet;
Those who love each other shall become invincible.

—WALT WHITMAN,
"Over the Carnage Rose a Prophetic Voice"

A
RELIABLE
WIFE

⚡ *Part One* ⚡

WISCONSIN. FALL. 1907.

Chapter One

It was bitter cold, the air electric with all that had not happened yet. The world stood stock still, four o'clock dead on. Nothing moved anywhere, not a body, not a bird; for a split second there was only silence, there was only stillness. Figures stood frozen in the frozen land, men, women, and children.

If you had been there you would not have noticed. You would not have noticed your own stillness in this thin slice of time. But, if you had been there and you had, in some unfathomable way, recorded the stillness, taken a negative of it as the glass plate receives the light, to be developed later, you would have known, when the thought, the recollection was finally developed, that this was the moment it began. The clock ticked. The hour struck. Everything moved again. The train was late.

It was not snowing yet, but it would be soon, a blizzard, by the smell of it. The land lay covered already in trampled snow. The land here flew away from your eyes, gone into the black horizon without leaving one detail inside the eye. Stubble through the snow, sharp as razors. Crows picking at nothing. Black river, frigid oil.

Nothing says hell has to be fire, thought Ralph Truitt, standing in his sober clothes on the platform of the tiny train station in the frozen middle of frozen nowhere. Hell could be like this. It could be darker every minute. It could be cold enough to sear the skin from your bones.

Standing in the center of the crowd, his solitude was enormous. He felt that in all the vast and frozen space in which he lived his life — every hand needy, every heart wanting something from him — everybody had a reason to be and a place to land. Everybody but him. For him there was nothing. In all the cold and bitter world, there was not a single place for him to sit down.

Ralph Truitt checked his silver watch. Yes, the train was late. The eyes around him were staring silently; they knew. He had counted on the train being on time today. To the minute, he had told them. He had ordered punctuality the way another man might order a steak cooked to his liking. Now he stood like a fool with everybody watching. And he was a fool. He had failed at even this small thing. It would come to nothing, this last small spark of hope.

He was a man used to getting what he wanted. Since his first staggering losses twenty years before, his wife, his children, his heart's best hopes and his last lavish fantasies, he had come to see the implacability of his own expectations as the only defense against the terrors he felt. It worked pretty well most of the time. He was relentless, and the people of the town respected that, feared it even. Now the train was late.

Around him on the platform the people of his town walked and watched and waited, trying to look casual, as though their waiting had some purpose other than watching Ralph Truitt wait for a train that was late. They exchanged little jokes. They laughed. They spoke quietly, out of respect for what they knew to be Ralph

Truitt's failure. The train was late. They felt the snow in the air. They knew the blizzard would soon begin. Just as there was a day every spring when the women of the town, as though by some secret signal, appeared in their summer dresses before the first heat was felt, there was as well a day when winter showed the knife before the first laceration. This was the day—October 17, 1907. Four o'clock and almost dark.

They all, each one, kept one eye on the weather and one eye on Ralph. Waiting, they watched Ralph wait, exchanging glances every time Ralph checked his silver watch. The train was late.

Serve him right, some thought, mostly the men. Some, mostly the women, thought kinder thoughts. Maybe, they thought, after all these years.

Ralph knew they talked about him, knew their feelings for him, complicated as they were, were spoken aloud the moment he had passed, tipping his hat with the civility he struggled so hard to show the world day after day. He could see it in their eyes. He had seen it every day of his life. The chatter of deference, the inevitable snicker at what they all knew of his past. Sometimes there was a whispered kindness because there was something about Ralph, even still, that could stir a sympathetic heart.

The trick, Ralph knew, is not to give in. Not to hunch your shoulders in the cold or stamp your feet or blow warm breath into cold palms. The trick is to relax into the cold, accept that it had come and would stay a long time. To lean into it, as you might lean into a warm spring wind. The trick was to become part of it, so that you didn't end a backbreaking day in the cold with rigid, aching shoulders and red hands.

Some things you escape, he thought. Most things you don't, certainly not the cold. You don't escape the things, mostly bad, that just happen to you. The loss of love. The disappointment. The terrible whip of tragedy.

So Ralph stood implacable, chest out, oblivious to the cold, hardened to the gossip, his eyes fixed on the train tracks wasting away into the distance. He was hopeful, amazed that he was hoping, hoping that he looked all right, not too old, or too stupid, or too unforgiving. Hoping that the turmoil of his soul, his hopeless solitude was, for just this hour before the snow fell and shut them all in, invisible.

He had meant to be a good man, and he was not a bad man. He had taught himself not to want, after his first wanting and losing. Now he wanted something, and his desire startled and enraged him.

Dressing in his house before he came to the train station, Ralph had caught sight of his face in one of the mirrors. The sight had shocked him. Shocking to see what grief and condescension had done to his face. So many years of hatred and rage and regret.

In the house, before coming here, he had busied his hands with the collar button and the knot of his necktie; he did these things every morning, the fixing and adjusting, the strict attentions of a fastidious man. But until he had looked in the mirror and seen his own anxious hope, he had not imagined, at any step of this foolish enterprise, that the moment would actually come and he would not, at the last, be able to stand it. But that's what had occurred to him, looking at his collapsed face in the spidery glass. He could not stand it, this wrenching coming to life again. For all these years, he had endured the death, the hideous embarrassment. He had kept on, against every instinct in his heart. He had kept on getting up and going to town and eating and running his father's businesses and taking on the weight which he inevitably took on, no matter how he tried to avoid it, of these people's lives. He had always assumed his face sent a single signal: everything is all right. Everything is fine. Nothing is wrong.

But, this morning, in the mirror, he saw that it was impossible, that he was the only one who had ever been fooled. And he saw that he cared, that it all mattered.

These people, their children got sick. Their wives or husbands didn't love them or they did, while Ralph himself was haunted by the sexual act, the sexual lives, which lay hidden and vast beneath their clothes. Other people's lust. They touched each other. Their children died, sometimes all at once, whole families, in a single month, of diphtheria or typhoid or the flu. Their husbands or their wives went crazy in a night, in the cold, and burned their houses down for no good reason, or shot their own relatives, their own children dead. They tore their clothes off in public and urinated in the street and defecated in church, writhing with snakes. They destroyed perfectly healthy animals, burned their barns. It was in the papers every week. Every day there was some new tragedy, some new and inexplicable failure of the ordinary.

They soaked their dresses in naphtha and carelessly moved too close to a fire and exploded into flames. They drank poison. They fed poison to each other. They had daughters by their own daughters. They went to bed well and woke up insane. Ran away. Hanged themselves. Such things happened.

Through it all, Ralph thought that his face and body were unreadable, that he had turned a fair and sympathetic eye to the people and their griefs and their bizarre troubles. He went to bed trying not to think of it, but he had gotten up this morning and seen it all, the toll it had taken.

His skin was ashen. His hair was lifeless and thinner than he

remembered. The corners of his mouth and his eyes turned down-
ward, engraved with a permanent air of condescension and grief.
His head tilted back from the effort of paying attention to the bodies that stood too close and spoke too loudly. These things, borne
of the terrifying stillness of his heart, were visible. Everybody saw
it. He had not covered up a single thing. What a fool he had been.

There was a time when he had fallen in love on every street corner. Chased so tiny a thing as a charming ribbon on a hat. A light
step, the brush of a skirt's hem, a gloved hand shooing a fly from a
freckled nose had once been enough, had once been all he needed
to set his heart racing. Racing with joy. Racing with fair, brutal ex-
pectation. So grossly in love his body hurt. But now he had lost the
habit of romance, and in his look into the mirror, he had thought
with a prick of jealousy of his younger, lascivious self.

He remembered the first time he had seen the bare arm of a
grown woman. He remembered the first time a woman had taken
her hair down just for him, the startling rich cascade of it, the smell
of soap and lavender. He remembered every piece of furniture in
the room. He remembered his first kiss. He had loved it all. Once,
it had been to him all there was. His body's hungers had been the
entire meaning of his life.

You can live with hopelessness for only so long before you are, in
fact, hopeless. He was fifty-four years old, and despair had come to
Ralph as an infection, without his even knowing it. He could not
pinpoint the moment at which hope had left his heart.

The townspeople nodded respectfully as they scuttled past.
"Evening, Mr. Truitt." And they couldn't help it, "Train's a tad
late, Mr. Truitt?" He wanted to hit them, tell them to leave, to
leave him alone. Because of course they knew. There had been telegrams, wire transfers, a ticket. They knew everything.

They knew the whole history of his years from the time he was a baby. Many of them, most of them, worked for him in one way or another, in the iron foundry, logging or mining or buying and selling and tallying up the sales or the rents. He underpaid them, though he grew richer by the hour. The ones who didn't work for him were, by and large, not doing any kind of work at all beyond the hardscrabble and desperate labor that kept the witless and lazy alive in hard climates.

Some, he knew, were lazy. Some were cruel to their wives and children, unfaithful to their dull and steady husbands. The winters were too long, too hard, and nobody would be expected to last it out.

For some, normal lives turned to nightmare. They starved to death in the horrible winters. They removed themselves from society and lived alone in ramshackle huts in the woods. They were found drooling and naked and were committed to the insane asylum at Mendota where they were wrapped in icy sheets and lashed with electrical currents until they could be restored to sanity and quietude. These things happened.

Still, every day, more people went on than didn't; more people stayed than left. The ones who stayed, crazy and sane, all of them sooner or later had business with Ralph Truitt. Ralph Truitt, he, too, went on through the cold and his own terrifying loneliness.

"Snow coming hard," they said.

"Dark already," they said. Four o'clock and dark already.

"Evening, Ralph, Mr. Truitt. Going to be a big one, looks like. Said so in the almanac."

All the little things they thought up, to pass the time, to make some small but brave attempt to establish a human connection with him. Each conversation with him became something to be thought out, considered and turned this way and that long before words were ever said, and to be remembered and reported after he was gone.

Saw Mr. Truitt today, they might say to their wives, because few dared think of his name any other way. He was cordial, asking after you and the children. Remembered every one of their names.

They hated him and they needed him and they excused him. The wives would say as their husbands ranted about what a skinflint bastard he was, what a tightwad, what an arrogant son of a bitch, "Well . . . you know . . . he's had troubles."

Of course they knew. They all knew.

He slept alone. He would lie in the dark and he would picture them, these people. He would dream their lives in the dark.

The husbands would turn and see their wives, and desire would burn through them like an explosion. Ralph imagined their lives, their desires, kindled by no more than a muslin nightdress. Eleven children, some of them thirteen: nine dead four living, six living seven gone.

In Ralph Truitt's mind, in the dead of night, the knots of death and birth formed an insane lace, knitting the town together, in a ravishment of sexual acts and the product of these acts. All skin to skin in the dark, just underneath the heavy torturous garments in the day. Still, in his mind's eye, the husbands would race into the warmed sheets and be young again, young and in love if only for fifteen minutes in the dark, lying with wasted women who were themselves, for those few minutes, beautiful young girls again with shiny braided hair and ready laughs. Sex was all he thought about in the dark.

Most nights Ralph could stand it. But some nights he couldn't. On those nights he lay suffocating beneath the weight of the lust he imagined around him, the desires rewarded, the unspoken physical kindnesses that can occur in the dark even between people who loathe the sight of each other by daylight.

In every house, he thought with fascination, there is a different life. There is sex in every bed. He walked the streets of his town every day, seeing on every face the simple charities they had afforded one another in the dark, and he told himself that he alone among them did not need that in order to go on.

He went to their weddings and their funerals. He adjudicated their quarrels, bore their tirades. He hired them and fired them, and he never lost the picture of them groping their way through the mute darkness, hunting and finding comfort, so that when the sun came up, they could go on with their lives.

That morning, in the mirror, he had seen his face, and it was a face he didn't want to be seen. His hunger, his rapacious solitude — they were not dead. And these people around him were not blind. They must have been, all these years, as horrified as he had been that morning.

In his pocket was the letter, and in the letter was a picture of a plain woman whom he did not know, ordered like a pair of boots from Chicago, and in that picture was Ralph's whole future, and nothing else mattered. Even his shame, as he stood in the gawking crowd, waiting for an overdue train, was secondary to that, because he had set his heart on a course before he had the first idea of what the course would bring him, and because he could not, under their darting eyes, avert his gaze or turn his intention from what he had decided with his whole heart, long before he had known what it meant.

The train would come, late or not, and everything that happened before its arrival would be before, and everything that came after would be after. It was too late to stop it now. His past would be only a set of certain events that had led him to this desperate act of hope.

He was a fifty-four-year-old man whose face was shocking to him, and in a few moments even that slate would be wiped clean. He allowed himself that hope.

We all want the simplest things, he thought. Despite what we may have, or the children who die, we want the simplicity of love. It was not too much to ask that he be like the others, that he, too, might have something to want.

For twenty years, not one person had said good night to him as he turned off the light and lay down to sleep. Not one person had said good morning as he opened his eyes. For twenty years, he had not been kissed by anyone whose name he knew, and yet, even now, as the snow began to fall lightly, he remembered what it felt like, the soft giving of the lips, the sweet hunger of it.

The townspeople watched him. Not that it mattered anymore. We were there, they would tell their children and their neighbors. We were there. We saw her get off the train for the first time, and she got off the train only three times. We were there. We saw him the minute he set eyes on her.

The letter was in his hand. He knew it by heart.

Dear Mr. Truitt,
I am a simple honest woman. I have seen much of the world in my travels with my father. In my missionary work I have seen the world as it is and I have no illusions. I have seen the poor and I have seen the rich and do not believe there is so much as a razor's edge between, for the rich are as hungry as the poor. They are hungry for God.

I have seen mortal sickness beyond imagining. I have seen what the world has done to the world, and I cannot bear to be in the world any longer. I know now that I can't do anything about it, and God can't do anything about it either.

I am not a schoolgirl. I have spent my life being a daughter and had long since given up hope of being a wife. I know that it isn't love you are offering, nor would I seek that, but a home, and I will take what you give because it is all that I want. I say that not meaning to imply that it is a small thing. I mean, in fact, that it is all there is of goodness and kindness to want. It is everything compared to the world I have seen and, if you will have me, I will come.

With the letter she had sent a photograph of herself, and he could feel the tattered edge of it with his thumb as he raised his hat to one more person, saw, from the corner of his eye, one more person gauge the unusual sobriety and richness of his black suit and strong boots and fur-collared overcoat. His thumb caressed her face. His eyes could see her features, neither pretty nor homely. Her large, clear eyes stared into the photographer's flash without guile. She wore a simple dress with a plain cloth collar, an ordinary woman who needed a husband enough to marry a stranger twenty years her senior.

He had sent her no photograph in return, nor had she asked for one. He had sent instead a ticket, sent it to the Christian boarding-house in which she stayed in filthy, howling Chicago, and now he stood, a rich man in a tiny town in a cold climate, at the start of a Wisconsin winter in the year 1907. Ralph Truitt waited for the train that would bring Catherine Land to him.

Ralph Truitt had waited a long time. He could wait a little longer.

CHAPTER TWO

—◦◦◦—

CATHERINE LAND SAT IN FRONT of the mirror, unbecoming all that she had become. The years had hardened her beyond mercy.

I'm the kind of woman who wants to know the end of the story, she thought, staring at her face in the jostling mirror. I want to know how it's all going to end before it even starts.

Catherine Land liked the beginnings of things. The pure white possibility of the empty room, the first kiss, the first swipe at larceny. And endings, she liked endings, too. The drama of the smashing glass, the dead bird, the tearful goodbye, the last awful word which could never be unsaid or unremembered.

It was the middles that gave her pause. This, for all its forward momentum, this was a middle. The beginnings were sweet, the endings usually bitter, but the middles were only the tightrope you walked between the one and the other. No more than that.

The land flew away by her window, rushing horizontal flat with snow. The train jostled just enough so that, even though she held her head perfectly still, her earrings swayed and sparkled in the light.

He had sent a private car with a sitting room and a bedroom and electric lights. She had not seen another passenger, although she knew other people had to be on the train. She imagined them, sitting calmly in their seats, pale winter skin on gray horsehair, while in her car it was all red velvet and swagging and furbelows. Like a whorehouse, she thought. Like a whorehouse on wheels.

They had left after dark and crept through the night, stopping often to clear drifts from the tracks. The porter had brought her a heavy, glistening meal, slabs of roast beef and shrimp on ice, lovely iced cakes which she ate at a folding table. No wine was offered and she didn't ask for it. The hotel silver felt smooth and heavy in her hand, and she devoured everything that was brought to her.

In the morning, steaming eggs and ham and rolls and hot black coffee that burned her tongue, all brought by a silent Negro porter, served as though he were performing some subtle magic trick. She ate it all. There was nothing else to do, and the movement of the train was both hypnotic and ravishing, amplifying her appetites, as each rushing second brought her closer to the fruition of her long and complicated scheme.

When she wasn't eating, or sleeping beneath the starched, immaculate sheets, she stared at her face in the mirror above the dressing table. It was her one sure possession, the one thing she could count on never to betray her, and she found it reassuring, after thirty-four years, that it remained, every morning, essentially unchanged, the same sure beauty, the same pale and flawless skin, unlined, fresh. Whatever life had done to her, it had not yet reached her face.

Still she was restless. Her mind raced, reviewing her options, her plans, her jumbled memories of a turbulent past, and what it was about her life that had led her here, to this sumptuous room on wheels, somewhere in the middle.

So much had to happen in the middle, and no matter how often she had rehearsed it in her mind, she didn't trust the middle. You could get caught. You could lose your balance, your way, and get found out. In the middle, things always happened you hadn't planned on, and it was these things, the possibility of these things, that haunted and troubled her, that showed now in the soft mauve hollows beneath her dark almond eyes.

Love and money. She could not believe that her life, as barren and as aimless as it had been, would end without either love or money. She could not, would not accept that as a fact, because to accept it now would mean that the end had already come and gone.

She was determined, cold as steel. She would not live without at least some portion of the two things she knew were necessary as a minimum to sustain life. She had spent her years believing that they would come, in time. She believed that an angel would come down from heaven and bless her with riches as she had been blessed with beauty. She believed in the miraculous. Or she had, until she reached an age when, all of a sudden, she realized that the life she was living was, in fact, her *life*. The clay of her being, so long infinitely malleable, had been formed, hardened into what now seemed a palpable, unchanging object, a shell she inhabited. It shocked her then. It shocked her now, like a slap in the face.

She remembered a moment from her childhood, the one transfixing moment of her past. She was riding in a carriage, dressed in a plain white dress, seated beside her mother who was not yet dead. She was safe. She was in Virginia, where she had been born.

Her mother's golden hair was lit by the reflection from an elaborate lavender silk dress, her skirts voluminous and extravagantly decorated. She drove a large and simple carriage, and Catherine sat in the front seat, between her mother and a man, a military man who was not her father. In her memory, as it came to her, she could not see his face. Behind them, straight as pins, sat three other young men, cadets, smartly dressed in tight wool uniforms with epaulets and braids and stripes.

It had rained on the way, a quick, fierce downpour, and the hood of the carriage had been drawn over, and the rain fell even though the sun never stopped shining on them, such a thick rain she had barely been able to see as far as the horses' steaming flanks. Then, miraculous and beautiful, the rain had stopped and the hood had been drawn back by one of the young men so the sweet cool air had flowed around them. The hood sprinkled her mother's hair with tiny droplets, and her mother had laughed in a charming way. It was such a clear memory, the sound of it. That and the weather and the storm itself had been nice. Lovely, long ago.

The young soldier behind her had whispered in Catherine's ear and pointed as a rainbow appeared. She could still smell, all these years later, the sweet sweat of his young body in his immaculate uniform. She could remember it better than all the rest of her childhood, better than the mountains of Virginia that lay beyond where the rainbow shone. She could feel his voice vibrating against the thin bones of her chest, a deep tingling beneath her skin. He whispered something about a pot of gold that was meant to lie waiting for her, just there at the rainbow's end.

Such a miracle. The sun had never stopped shining and the rain had stopped and a marvelous sunset blossomed. The intoxicating light gave every face a beauty, and the sweetness and freshness of the air lightened every heart. She sat between her mother who was not yet dead and a soldier who was not her father in a countryside she could no longer remember on a road she hardly saw and she thought: I am perfectly happy.

It was the last time in her whole life she remembered having such a thought. She had no idea who the men were. She had no memory of where they were going or how they came to be going together or what happened to them all once they got there. Something ceremonial, the Civil War dead, the endless young boys and men whose ghosts walked the land, some memorial with rising furling flags and trumpets and a long slow beating of drums. She did not know where her father was that day, leaving her mother and herself to drive through rain and rainbows and sunsets with four handsome soldiers.

But now she remembered her lovely mother who had died when she was seven, giving birth to her sister Alice, and she missed her. She remembered the men. She remembered the way they smelled, the way their young arms filled the sleeves of the jackets and the white stiff collars scraping against their razored necks, the rasp of masculinity, and that had been the beginning, the beginning of all that had come after.

It was, she realized now, the beginning of desire. It was glory, the light, and the crimson clouds. It was the face of Jesus. It was love. Love without end. Desire without object. She had never known or felt it since.

From that beginning she had gone on and on, until her legs were tired and her mother was dead and her heart was broken. She had, no matter how impossible it seemed from moment to moment, gone on without love or money, always wondering when it would begin, the splendid end to match the splendid beginning.

She no longer dwelled on the past. She had no fond memories there, except for the single rainbow, the pot of gold. She had bitten and bludgeoned her way through life, angry, fighting in a rage for the next good thing to happen. It hadn't happened yet. So that, on the day she suddenly realized that her life was, in fact, her life, she wondered what it could possibly have been that led her forward, day after day, what events could possibly have happened to fill the hours between sleep and sleep. But at moments like this, when everything was so quiet she could notice the trembling of her earrings, she knew with dread that the answer was not nothing much, but simply nothing.

She would not, could not live without love or money.

She would remember those faceless young soldiers forever. They would be forever young. She would cherish the glory of the sun coming through the clouds, and the rainbow. Her mother's loveliness would never abandon her. But what good did it do? What use was all that to her now, sitting in front of a mirror on a train going to the middle of nowhere, on the tightrope between the beginning and the end?

There was a soft knock on the door. The porter who had brought her meals and turned down her bed leaned his dark handsome face into the compartment. "Station in half an hour, Miss."

"Thank you," she said softly, never taking her eyes from the mesmerizing mirror. The door closed and she was alone again.

She had seen Ralph Truitt's personal advertisement six months before, as she sat at a table with Sunday coffee and the newspaper:

COUNTRY BUSINESSMAN SEEKS
RELIABLE WIFE.
COMPELLED BY PRACTICAL,
NOT ROMANTIC REASONS.
REPLY BY LETTER.
RALPH TRUITT. TRUITT, WISCONSIN.
DISCREET.

"Reliable wife." That was new, and she smiled. She had read in her life perhaps thousands of advertisements just like it. It was a hobby of hers, like knitting. She was engrossed by these notices, lonely men who called out from the vast wildernesses of the country. Sometimes the notices were placed by women, who asked for strength or patience or kindness or merely civility.

She laughed at their stories, at their pitiful foolhardiness. They asked and probably found somebody as lonely and desperate as themselves. How could they expect more? The halt and the lame calling the blind and hopeless. Catherine found it hilarious.

She assumed, still, that these men and these women found each other through their sad little calls for comfort. They found, if not love or money, at least another life to cling to. Advertisements like this one appeared every week. These people didn't like the solitude of their lives. Perhaps they, at least some of them, eventually found lives they liked better.

The night before, just before she slept, she suddenly saw herself as if from above, lying in her bed, the chill of loneliness and death all around her like a nimbus of disconsolation. She hovered in the air, watching herself. She had felt, and still felt that she would die unless someone could find the sweetness to touch her with affection. Unless someone would appear to shelter her from the storm of her awful life.

It was Ralph Truitt's terse announcement, containing the promise of a beginning, not splendid, perhaps, but new, that she had finally answered. "I am a simple, honest woman," she had written, and he had answered by return mail. They had written all through the hot summer, tentative descriptions of their lives. His handwriting was blunt and compelling, hers practiced and elegant, she hoped, and seductive. She had at last sent the photograph, and he had written at greater length, as though it were already decided, the whole match. She had feigned hesitation, until he insisted and sent her a ticket for the train to come and bring her to be his wife.

The young soldier who had sat beside her in the carriage would be old himself now. She could still see the way his thumb jutted from the palm of his hand, feel the way his thigh touched her thigh as he leaned toward her. Perhaps he had a wife and children of his own now. Perhaps he loved them and treated them with kindness, with grace and affection. The world had not shown her that such things were common, but her unhappiness had been made bearable only by the certain knowledge that somewhere there lived people whose lives were not like her own.

Perhaps this Ralph Truitt was one of those other people. Perhaps this life he offered would be some other kind of life. The sun set every day. It could not be that it would set in splendor only once in her lifetime.

Half an hour. She stood up from the dressing table and stepped out of her red silk shoes, lining them up side by side. She began quickly to undo the embroidered jacket of her fancy traveling suit, discarding it behind her on the floor. Then she took off her silk blouse and the heavy red velvet skirt. She undid the laces of her embroidered corset, and shrugged it off. She felt suddenly light, as though she would rise from the floor, a pool of crimson velvet at her feet.

She watched herself in the mirror as she did these things. She saw, for a moment, the reflection of her headless body. It was not unpleasant. She enjoyed her body, the way women sometimes do, and looked at it with a dispassionate eye, as though it were in a shop window, understanding exactly the raw material from which she had produced, a thousand times, certain effects. Every day she took the raw material of her body and pushed and pulled it, decorated it so that it became a heightened version of itself, a version designed to attract attention.

No more.

She leaned over and scooped up her clothes, along with her silk shoes, and tied it all into a neat bundle. Moving quickly to the window of the compartment, she pulled it open and threw her expensive clothes into the darkness and the racket of the train's wheels. The snow was beginning now. Spring was a long way off. Her beautiful clothes would be a blackened ruin by then.

She pulled a small tattered gray suitcase from the rack above her head. She opened the clasps and pulled out a plain black wool dress, one of three just like it. She sat again at her dressing table, and ripped open a short length of hem. Taking off her jewelry, a garnet bracelet and earrings, funfair trinkets, she wrapped them in a delicate handkerchief still smelling of a man's tart cologne. Adding to it a delicate diamond ring, she stuffed the small package into the hem of the skirt.

With deft fingers she threaded a needle and quickly sewed her jewelry into the hem of the skirt. Insignificant as it was, it reminded her of the way she had once lived, her old life now hidden in the hem of a plain dress. It was her insurance, her little baubles, her ticket out of the darkness, if darkness fell. It was her independence. It was her past.

There. She stepped into the dress, buttoning the thirteen buttons. These were her clothes, the only clothes she had. She had made them herself, in the way her mother had taught her.

Without corset or stays, she felt surprisingly light. She quickly finished dressing.

She knew all the details of her new life. The details were not a problem. She had rehearsed them for hours and months. The phrases. The false memories. The little piece of music. She had so little life of her own, so little self, that it was easy to take on the mannerisms of another with ease and conviction. Her new self may have been no more inhabited, but it was no less real.

She undid her hair, the dark curls that ringed her face. She pulled it back until her eyes hurt, and wound it in a small neat bun at her neck.

She recounted her memories as they reeled into her past. A soldier beside her on a carriage seat. Her mother dying as her sister slipped from her body. The rainbow. She cataloged these memories and sewed them away as neatly as she had sewn her jewels in the hem of her skirt, needing to erase the intricacies of where she had been so that she might become the simplicity of where she was going.

She was a simple, honest woman, sitting in the unexpected splendor of a private railroad car. A child in white linen, sitting between her mother and a man she did not know.

Catherine Land sat until the last possible moment, poised between the beginning and the end. The train slowed and then stopped. The porter came in and took her suitcase from the rack. She tipped him, too much, and he smiled.

Still she stared at her face. She could not, would not live without money or love. Ralph Truitt had shyly promised in his last letter to share his life, and she would take what he had to give. She knew a good deal more about what was to happen than he did.

She got up, wrapped a heavy black missionary cape around her shoulders, and left the compartment, closing the door softly behind her. She wasn't nervous. She made her way along the corridor. She stepped down the metal stairs, taking the porter's hand in the billowing steam, and moved shyly and gracefully onto the platform to meet Ralph Truitt.

Chapter Three

She stepped into snow, a swirling, blowing blizzard that blinded her, yet dazzled her at the same time. It both darkened and illuminated the air of the platform, surrounding her with an aura of moving light. Strangers darted back and forth, greeting, kissing, hurling trunks and suitcases onto shoulders, sheltering babies from the storm. The snow moved horizontally, spiking in giddying whirls around the hastening figures, flying swiftly upward into dark nothingness. There seemed to be no end to it.

She had thought she would not know him, not until he was the last man left, but of course she did. His was the unrequited face, his the disconnection from the eddying sea of people around him. She knew him at once. He looked so rich and so alone.

All of a sudden, she was afraid. It had never occurred to her that they would have to talk; they would say hello, of course, but she hadn't gotten much farther than that. Now it seemed to stretch into infinity, the endless small talk she imagined as the daily life of married people, the details, the getting and grabbing, the parrying and accommodating, the doing of whatever it was that married people did.

Because she would marry him, of course. She had said she would and she would. But then what? How to fill the days, the endless round of meals, of chores, the endless hours in this brilliant blindness which seemed to suck out of her all possibility of speech.

The beginnings were so enchanting usually, and yet she could only stand in frozen dread at all the small complacencies that filled the middle. If she got sick, he would nurse her, she supposed. They would discuss the price of things. He would be tight with money, although he looked expensively dressed. She would ask him for money and he would give it and then she would pay for the things they needed, and then she would tell him what she had bought. They would discuss that at dinner, food she had made for him. They would discuss the weather, noting every change, or read together in the long howling evenings, by some fire or stove. She supposed they would do or say whatever it was people in their situation normally did and said but she realized now she didn't know what that was.

In the train car, on the slow ride from Chicago, the edges of things were clear and everything stood out in sharp focus. Here in the snow, in the sharp weather, everything blurred, the edges disappeared leaving only vague unknowable shapes, and she was afraid.

Still, there was nothing for them, the two of them or anybody else, nothing for them to do except go on, huddle together, wait for spring. She would do what she had to do.

She stepped toward him, his hands in the pockets of a long black coat, its black fur collar sparkling with snow. She could barely make out his face as he turned toward her, unknowing. He seemed . . . what? Sad? Nice? He seemed alone.

She felt ridiculous, with her cheap black wool clothes and her cheap gray cardboard suitcase. Just begin, she thought. Just move forward to say hello; the rest, somehow, will take care of itself.

"Mr. Truitt. I'm Catherine Land."

"You're not her. I have a photograph."

"It's of someone else. It's my cousin India."

He could feel the eyes of the townspeople watching them, the eyes taking it all in, this deception. It was too much to bear.

"You need a proper coat. This is the country."

"It's what I have. I'm sorry. The picture. I'm sorry, but I can explain."

This deceit in front of the whole town, this being made a fool of, again, in front of everybody. His heart raced and his legs felt bloodless.

"We can't stand here all night. Whoever you are. Give me your case."

She handed it to him as he took his hand from his pocket. Briefly, she felt its warmth.

"This is all. This is everything?"

"I can explain. I don't have much. I thought . . ."

"We can't stand here in a blizzard, with everybody . . . we can't stay here." He looked at her without warmth or welcome. "This begins in a lie. I want you to know I know that."

He took the picture from his pocket, her picture, and showed it to her, as though bringing it out from his pocket would somehow make her become the shy, homely woman caught there. She looked at it.

"Whoever you are, you're not this woman."

"I will explain, Mr. Truitt. I'm not here to make a fool of you."

"No. You won't. Whatever else, you're a liar."

He turned, and she followed him across the deserted platform to a carriage tied up at the side. The nervous horses stamped and blew great jets of steam from their nostrils while Ralph Truitt put her suitcase in the back and strapped it on with thick leather straps. Without a word, he handed her into her seat.

He vanished in the hurling snow, reappeared and climbed into his seat. He looked at her, full in the face for the first time. "Maybe you thought I was a fool. You were wrong."

He snapped the reins, and the horses trotted smartly into the white void. They rode in silence. The lights from the windows of the houses glowed softly, as though at a great distance. She couldn't tell how near or far anything was from the carriage, in the snow. She couldn't tell how many stores or houses there were. She never saw the turnings until they made them. He knew. The horses knew. She was a stranger here.

The snow silenced the wagon wheels. There was no conversation. She was floating in a soundless void in the middle of nowhere.

"Are there many people?"

"Where?"

"In town."

"Two thousand. About. More or less every year. Depending."

"On what?"

"On whether more die than are born."

They said nothing else. They floated through the snow, the glow of houses in the distance, each one a family, each a series of entwined lives, while they sat entirely separate and alone.

Ralph had nothing to say. He had expected things, and now she was here, whoever she was, and suddenly everything was different. In every house they passed, there were lives that were wholly known to him. In these houses, the people knew one another; they knew him as well. He had held their babies, been to their weddings, been shocked by their sudden flights into madness and rage. He was and he wasn't a part of their lives. He was there and he had done what was required of him, what was expected.

They went crazy in the cold; they went deep into the heart of their religion and emerged as lunatics. But even this was familiar. Sane, they wanted to believe that they were the sort of people whose babies had been held and cuddled by Ralph Truitt, and he found it easy enough to foster the illusion that these things mattered to him. Still, their glowing lives, their families, were intertwined in ways that he couldn't even imagine.

But this woman was not expected. He was angry. He was confused. He had read her letter until it fell apart in his hands. He had looked at her picture a thousand times. Now it was clear she wasn't the woman in the photograph, and he had no idea who she might be. His relation to every person in the town rested on the fact that he had complete control over everything that happened to him. Now this wild thing. The train late. The blinding snow. This woman.

It was a mistake. He felt it in the pit of his stomach, everything wrong, the letter, the picture, his foolish hope. It was a mistake to have wanted, to have felt desire, but he had, he had wanted something for himself. Now the object of his desire was here, and it was all, none of it, what he had wanted.

He had wanted a simple, honest woman. A quiet life. A life in which everything could be saved and nobody went insane.

He couldn't turn her away, couldn't leave her in a blizzard. He couldn't be seen leaving her. There would be talk. He would appear to be unkind. So he would take her in from the storm, give her shelter for a night or two, no more. Her beauty troubled him the most, so unexpected, the sweetness of her voice, the fragile bones of her hand as he helped her into the carriage. Who, then, was the woman in the picture? It troubled him, enough so that he was sharp with the horses and would not look her in the face.

"I have an automobile," he said, for no reason. "It's the only one in town."

She didn't know what to say.

"It's not good in the snow."

I am in the wilderness, she thought. Alone with barbarians.

They were leaving town, and the horses were skittish in the wind. He was never rough with them, and now he could feel their nerves through the leather. They just wanted to get where they were going.

Catherine saw, through the snow, the endless flat fields on one side and, on the other, a broad river, clogged with ice. So bleak and forlorn.

She thought of the lights of the city, the endless activity, the beer halls lit up in the snowy nights, the music, the laughter, the girls pinning on their hats and rushing out to find adventure. The girls would laugh in front of warm fires with men who had written them love letters. They would eat roast beef and drink champagne and rush everywhere, their dresses hiked to their knees as they ran through the snow, the laughing girls, drawn by the warmth of the gaming tables and the fires and the music and the company.

Here, out past the lights of the town, there was no sound. There was nothing except them, their carriage, the lanterns shiny on the road.

The river looked hard as iron.

She pictured the music hall girls. The men with decks of cards in their pockets and revolvers tucked in their boots. The sweetness of the languid air in the opium dens, warm when the night was too cold to move, the Chinaman waking them with tea when the storm had passed or the dawn had come or all the money was gone. The trolleys would already be running, taking people, normal people, to work. And the girls would laugh, knowing what a ruin they looked.

A million miles away. Another life, another night, a million miles down the slick black river to the bright and clanging city. Her friends were already decked for the night, seeking the heat, the music washing over them, their beautiful dresses, and laughing at her folly. She was already a thing of the past, to them. They had no memory.

The deer came out of nowhere, racing, bucking with terror, and was gone in an instant. They saw its frightened eyes for only a second, as its antlers brushed past the horses. Suddenly the world was in white chaos.

The horses leapt back in terror, charging upward in their traces, jerking the carriage sideways and almost over, righting it again as they bolted. Catherine heard a single shrill whinny, like a scream, and they were racing off, bits in their teeth, cracking ice flying from their manes, Ralph standing now, standing in his seat and pulling at the reins with all his strength. She felt the terrible chill, the awful dread of the thing she hadn't expected.

The horses veered, pulling them off the road, the wheels cracking into new snow, a sound like a blade through bone. The carriage hurtled through a thin fence and everything was noise and chaos and Ralph had one leg up on the front of the carriage, screaming the horses' names, pulling back, swearing, and the cold seemed sharper, and Catherine, terrified, holding on, rigid with fear, felt the cracking thud as the carriage hit a rut, the leftover gash of some

autumn rivulet, and Ralph was thrown into the air, the reins flying. She saw him just long enough to see the iron rim of the wheel
strike his head as he fell beneath the carriage, and then they were
off, jolting and careening wildly, the horses wild, too, off the road
now, heading toward the black river.

Catherine groped blindly. The reins whipped in the wind, but
she found them, took them in her hands. The carriage rocked in
the pitted field, but she held on. Her foolish cloak was streaming in
the wind, choking her, and she ripped it from her neck and it flew
out behind, a momentary ghost in the swirling snow.

She knew enough to let the horses run. She knew enough to hope
in their natural instincts. Her strength was no match for the terror
she felt pulsing from the horses' black rumps. She held on. She did
the only thing she could.

The horses raced on in a frenzy. They galloped down a small
bank, skimmed onto the frozen river, the carriage arcing dangerously, so that the horses were spun in a circle, leaving crazy black
trails on the powdered ice, really frightened now, aware, suddenly,
of how far they were from safety. One of the horses slipped, lost its
footing and collapsed onto the ice, which cracked and shimmered
but held. Catherine sat mute with fear, with the idea of death in the
frigid water, drowning, tangled in dying horses.

The river held. It wasn't much, but it was enough. As the horses
struggled to find their footing, she climbed the traces and lay along
their steaming necks. As the black gelding stood again she was
there, whispering in its ear, the words coming from somewhere and
lost in the wind, but enough, whispering, holding her hand gently
against the softest part of its throat.

The horses calmed beneath her hands, their panic passed. They
heard her voice, barely audible above the howling wind, and they

stood patiently as she inched her way back through the harness, her hands never leaving their flesh, never letting them forget that she was there, was in charge, promising them safe delivery.

She gently picked up the reins again and they walked, exhausted now, her eyes straining in the howling dark to pick up the ruts in the snow so she could tell where they had come from, driving them slowly back to the place where the deer had leapt out of nothing and sent the stillness flying into panic.

On the road again, the horses stood pitiful and defeated. The gelding almost collapsed, but pulled himself upright, and together the two horses hauled the carriage into the white blindness. Miraculously, the lanterns had held, and she could see a short distance ahead.

They almost ran over Ralph before she saw him. He stood calmly in the middle of the road, swaying a bit, blood streaming from a gash in his forehead, a gash deep as bone.

She jumped from the carriage. She hadn't come all this way to have him die now. Not now. She caught the hem of her skirt on the edge of the seat, heard the quick tear of the cheap material as she almost fell into his arms. The blood covered his face, mixing with the snow clotted in the fur collar of his black coat. She took his elbow. He shook her off, but then he staggered, and she took his arm again and this time he didn't push her away but leaned into her, so that she realized the size and solidity of him, the depth of his chest, even through his heavy coat the heat of his body was clear. She helped him to the seat, the blood streaming from his forehead. She found her cloak, her foolish thin cape, and covered his shivering legs.

"The horses all right?" His voice was strained.

"They can carry us." She climbed up. "Which way, Mr. Truitt?"

"They know. Just let them go." The horses moved forward, one limping and wheezing, and both blind in the night, but sure of their way.

Ralph sat as stiffly as he could, trying not to give in to the searing pain, but it was too much. He felt himself slowly crumpling, his hurt body folding in against hers. He felt it as her arm came up across him, pulling him down, pulling his head to rest against her breast, her racing heart.

Chapter Four

⸻ ⚬⚬⚬ ⸻

THERE WAS BLOOD EVERYWHERE. It was frozen into the fabric of her dress, stiff and black. It was on his head and face and clothes and beneath her frozen fingernails. Still, she was calm, determined he would not die. And then she saw the house, and a face at the window.

There was a moment of utter stillness in which she took in every detail, the weight of Ralph in her arms, the house, the face at the window, stricken with terror, the horse, its broken leg, realizing now that the cracking sound on the ice had been bone not ice. She saw herself, her hair wild around her head, her hands chill and raw, her skirt light, the hem spilling her jewels in the snow. She saw them standing in the yard, snow up to the iron wheel hubs, the horses' heads drooping in exhaustion and pain, the house itself. The house.

It's like a clean white shirt, she thought. A clean white shirt hanging on the back of a door.

A neat, columned porch, a warm rust light through drawn curtains, the turn of a chair left out long past summer. Details. She couldn't see the whole of it, couldn't see the point at which the peaked roof met. But it seemed warm. It seemed nice.

The horses stopped, the brown mare stamping its hooves, the black gelding couldn't take another step, its right front leg raised off the ground, hoof hanging dangerously. The light from the porch lit up the sweat on their heaving flanks, turned the breath streaming from their wide nostrils into bright wispy feathers.

It was trim, the house, simple without being austere, and it was bright with lights, not at all the way she had imagined it. It sat foursquare in the center of a neat lawn, steps running up to a wide porch. She had imagined something more squalid, something grown greasy through years of neglect. She had imagined a house that was desolate, an unloved structure in a bleak terrain. This was a surprise, like a crisply wrapped package, all white tissue and blue ribbon trim.

The moment ended and time began again, all in a rush. The face howled, vanished from the window and the door flew open. A woman stood dumbfounded inside.

Ralph Truitt was bleeding badly and lay heavily against Catherine. His breath was easy, his eyes were open but staring ahead without direction or focus, and the porch, the glittering door, and safety seemed miles away.

"Truitt?" the gray head thrust out, eyes peering into the swirl, voice carrying past Catherine's ears. "Is that you Mr. Truitt?"

"Help! We're here!" Catherine yelled into the wind, hysteria suddenly seizing her. "Please come! We need help."

A man and a woman ran from the house, their hair, their clothes catching the wind and flying madly. The man went straight for the faltering, groaning gelding and began to check the extent of the injuries, speaking calmly, his hand on the horse's flank as he shook his head at the pitiful leg. Catherine could see the broken bone thrust through the flesh, could feel the animal's defeat in the way the ribcage shimmered with pain.

The woman ran straight for Truitt. "Sweet Jesus," she yelled. "What's happened? What did you do?" Her brittle, bright eyes caught Catherine's, held there, accusing.

"The horses bolted. A deer . . . they bolted and threw him. I think his head hit the wheel. It wasn't my fault," she added uselessly. "It was a deer. So fast."

"Inside. Larsen!" The old man's head jerked up from the animal, which was slowly sinking to the ground. "Truitt's cut bad. Get him in the house."

So the three of them, each taking a part, carried Truitt's body into the house. He was jerking around now, wild with the pain and the blood, and it took every muscle of all three of them to get him up the stairs and into the house. They laid him on a velvet sofa, put a pillow beneath his head.

The woman said, "He'll bleed to death."

"He needs a doctor. Surely . . ."

Mrs. Larsen, she must have been, turned on Catherine. "In this weather? Not even for Ralph Truitt. It's miles both ways, and too late by a long shot when the doctor gets here. If you can find him. Drunk. If he'll come. Drunk and useless."

"Get my case, please," Catherine said. She was completely calm. "From the wagon. A gray case. And hot water. And towels and iodine, if you've got it."

The old couple stared at her, not sure. Truitt lay on the sofa, eyes straight ahead.

"Get her case," the old lady said. "And get your gun. For that gelding."

Larsen suddenly moved, leaving the room. The old woman, his wife, Catherine supposed, moved as well. Truitt came suddenly awake, eyes red with pain, and Catherine and Ralph stared at one another in the sudden quiet.

"You're not going to die," she said.

"I have that hope."

A sharp gust of wind blew into the hall as Larsen went out into the night. Catherine and Truitt waited. She felt she might take his hand, but did not.

They heard the gunshot from the yard. Catherine jumped, and ran to the window, pulling back heavy velvet curtains to see the single thrashing of the giant horse, its head a hollow of blood.

After a long time, Larsen came back through the snow, carrying Catherine's suitcase in one hand, the pistol loose in the other. He laid the suitcase at her feet. He looked at her with hatred as though all of it had been her fault, and all of it unforgivable.

She clicked the rusted cheap clasps and opened the suitcase, rummaging around in her black clothes and plain underthings to find her sewing case. Turning, she stepped on the hem of her skirt, ripping again at the tear. . . . Jesus hell, she thought, the jewelry. She knelt quickly, felt at the hem. Nothing. Christ and hell.

Mrs. Larsen came back, a bowl of steaming water in her hands, her arms filled with towels. She stared at Catherine, eyed her skirt.

Catherine rose. "It's . . . it's nothing. It tore. I lost something. In the accident."

"Well, it's gone then. Gone till spring."

"It doesn't matter." Lost, yes, thought Catherine. Lost my jewelry, and lost any way out of this place.

Catherine stared at Truitt. "This will hurt."

"It hurts now." He managed a weak smile.

"Is there anything to drink?"

"I don't touch liquor."

"It'll hurt worse."

"I know."

"Can you sit up? A little?"

He groaned as they raised him up from the sofa, enough for Catherine to sit and settle his head on her lap. The blood dripped steadily onto her skirt. She could feel it wetting her legs almost immediately.

As Mrs. Larsen held the bowl, Catherine dipped a towel in the steaming water, began gently to clean his wound. She knew it hurt, but beneath her hand his face calmed, his breathing slowed. He never closed his eyes, never made a sound, although tears streamed down his cheeks.

"I cry," he said. "I'm like a baby."

"I wouldn't have thought so. Ma'am? The iodine." She took the bottle Mrs. Larsen produced from the pocket of her apron, tipped it enough to pour a tiny stream, just along the wound that ran from his eyebrow to his hairline. She dabbed at the trickle, and Truitt closed his eyes, then winced as the sharp sting hit the bone, which Catherine could see, as the sharp smell brought to each of them a sense of the urgency of what she was doing.

That poor horse, she thought, dragging us all this way, lying now in the snow. Tomorrow, she supposed, whenever this stopped, Larsen would use the living horse to drag the dead one out of sight.

"My sewing kit, and I need you, Mrs. . . ."

"Larsen, Miss."

"Mrs. Larsen. I need you, very gently, to press the edges together, like this."

Catherine showed her, like pressing pie dough to the edges of the pan, her thumbs smoothing, smoothing the skin until the edges almost met. The cut was not clean. There would be a scar, no matter what.

Catherine found her strongest thread, dipped her needle in the iodine, and blew gently on the needle, and on the cut, bleeding harder now.

She threaded the needle. She saw how Larsen turned away, busied himself elsewhere as she took the first stitch.

"I'll get the wagon put away now. Unless . . ."

"No. We're fine." The needle pricking into and through the flesh, Catherine's hand steady and calm. The door opened and closed again as Larsen went out into the night.

Slowly the wound began to close, the flow of blood to lessen. "Are you a nurse, Miss?"

"My father was a doctor. I watched him."

It was a lie, however lightly she said it. Her father was a drunk and a liar. He had no profession. Catherine knew no more than the simple fact that she had not come all this way to watch Ralph Truitt die in her arms. If you were going to sew a wound shut, she figured, there were only so many ways to do it.

"So you never . . ."

"Never. But I watched him many times. There's no other way."

At some point she felt Truitt slip away from her, lose consciousness. His pale eyes, fixed and white with pain, finally closed, and she saw for the first time, darting her eyes from his wound, the expanse of his skin, so close it was as though she were looking through a magnifying glass. His beard was like black wheat stubble on a dry field. His skin was pale, and while from a distance he looked younger than she knew him to be, up close she could see the thousands of tiny lines across his skin. She could see the future of her own face, and she could see something else in him as his muscles went slack and his skin sagged away from his strong big bones. She could see the effort it cost him to keep his face composed, hopeful, and she could see the sadness that lay beneath the steely composure, the lack of life in him.

Her tiny fingers worked swiftly, following Mrs. Larsen's hands along the length of the cut, and finally she was done. Not too bad.

He opened his eyes.

"All done." She smiled at him, her hands still on his face, his head in her lap.

"Thank you."

"We have to get you to bed. Could you . . . it would be better if you tried to stay awake for a while. Your head may be hurt. As long as you can." She shyly reached to touch his face, but Larsen appeared, stamping, to interrupt her.

"We'll take him from here, Miss. I'll get him upstairs. Walk with him. There's no need for you, and Mrs. has your dinner. I'll take him."

Larsen reached under and pulled Ralph to his feet. Ralph swayed, but held upright, and Catherine sat as she watched the two of them clumping upstairs, Mrs. Larsen following with useless flutter.

Then they were gone, and for the first time, Catherine looked at the room in which she sat, and was startled by it. It was nice, not at all what she had imagined: very plain, very clean, and spotless. It was an ordinary square room, and yet here and there sat pieces of furniture that seemed strangely incongruous, as though they had come from some other house in some other place. Bright color. Rich fabrics. Graceful and finely made furniture, only a few pieces, standing alongside the more mundane farm things, the china press, the plain pine grandfather clock.

The sofa she sat on was one of these odd pieces, all gilded arms and carved swans and sunset colored damask, now stained with Truitt's blood. From her view, it looked like the kind of room where nobody would know where to sit, the kind of place maintained in perfect order, even though it was never used.

There was one chair, plain, strong oak, which was clearly where Truitt sat in the evenings, smoking a cigar, an ashtray and humidor on the low plain table next to it, the table covered also with farm journals and almanacs and ledgers. Next to it, a lamp that glowed with brilliant colors from a stained-glass shade, crimsons and purples, grapes and autumn leaves and delicate birds in flight. It was the kind of lamp she'd seen only in hotels. She had never imagined an ordinary person would own one, but Ralph Truitt did.

He must be very rich, she thought. The thought warmed her, and brought a smile to her face. He's not going to die. Now it's beginning. Her heart raced as though she were about to steal a pair of kid gloves from a shop.

She could hear the heavy sounds of the three moving upstairs, one boot falling on the floor, then another. Ah, they were undressing him, she realized. She had thought she had been shut out because they had not wanted her to see his weakness, but it was, in fact, his body they were denying her.

The clock ticked steadily. The wind howled without peace. Catherine sat alone, wondering if anybody on the face of the earth knew where she was, could picture how she sat, her hands quietly in her lap, her fingers touched with blood, her torn hem, her lost jewels.

She wanted a cigarette. A cigarette in her little silver holder. And a glass of whiskey, one glass to take away the chill. But that was another life in another place, and here, in Ralph Truitt's house, Catherine simply sat, her hands in her lap.

Here they were, four people, each one moving separately through the rooms of the same house. She had held his head in her lap and her clothes were wet with his blood, yet she was alone. Alone as she had always been.

Sometimes she sat and let her mind go blank and her eyes go out of focus, so that she watched the slow jerky movements of the motes that floated across her pupils. They had amazed her, as a child. Now she saw them as a reflection of how she moved, floating listlessly through the world, occasionally bumping into another body without acknowledgment, and then floating on, free and alone.

She knew no other way to be. Her schemes, she saw now, were listless fantasies, poorly imagined, languidly acted, and so doomed to failure, again and again.

She rose to her feet and wandered through the rooms of Truitt's house. There were not many of them, and they were all alike, equally immaculate, furnished with the same odd blend of the rustic and the magnificent. The dining room was tiny, but the table was elaborately set for dinner for two. She picked an ornate fork from the table; it was almost as long as her forearm and astonishing in its weight. The brilliant polish caught the light as she turned it over to read the maker: Tiffany & Co., New York City. She felt she had never seen anything so beautiful in her life.

"Larsen's with him." Catherine dropped the fork as Mrs. Larsen came into the room. "I've made supper. It's maybe not spoilt too bad, and you might as well eat." She adjusted the fork Catherine had dropped, so that it was in perfect alignment with the other, equally massive utensils.

"I was just . . ."

"Looking. I saw. Sit. It'll just be a minute. You must be starved."

Catherine sat at the table. She felt she was about to cry, for no reason except that it was a long way back and she was alone. She tried to fix her hair, then let it go.

The soup was clear and hot, the lamb cooked in a sauce that was both delicious and exotic, all of it accomplished and fine in a way that would have been admired in any restaurant in any city she had ever been to, and Mrs. Larsen served it with a simplicity and finesse that surprised and pleased her. She had thought she wasn't hungry, but she ate everything, including a dessert made of light meringues floating in glistening, silky custard.

The beautiful plates came and went, the utensils were used until none were left, and finally, Mrs. Larsen stood in the kitchen doorway and they both listened to the clumping of Larsen's boots as Truitt and Larsen walked back and forth, back and forth in an upstairs bedroom, first across a rug and then on the floor and then back to the rug.

"That was a fine dinner."

"Well, I'd hoped for more of a celebration, but . . ."

The footsteps continued.

"But there'll be other nights, I guess. Miss?"

"Yes?"

"I hope you'll be happy here. I truly do. It wasn't much of a welcome, but I do, we do, welcome you."

Catherine blushed, embarrassed. "You're a wonderful cook."

"Some people have one gift, some another." She made rough sewing gestures with her hands. "Me, I was always a mess with a needle. But put me in a kitchen, I know where I am. Even after a long while, and it's been a while, I know what to do."

Catherine stood, and they stared awkwardly at each other. Catherine was suddenly exhausted. She looked at the ceiling, the clodding boots.

"Will they be all right?"

"Larsen'll look after him. They've known each other since they were boys. Truitt's safe enough."

Mrs. Larsen began to clear away the dishes.

"I'll help you. I'm used to keeping myself."

"You should rest. Go to bed if you want."

"Where do I . . ."

"Sleep? I'll show you." Wiping her hands on a dishtowel, then licking her fingers to put out the sputtering candles, extinguishing the sparkle on the silver, she led Catherine out of the dining room, picked up her case and started up the stairs. "It's a nice room. You can see the river, and you can see over to the little house where Larsen and I live."

She opened the door to a graceful bedroom, the simple bed laid with good linens, the tester of the delicate four-poster hung with lace.

She put the suitcase on the bed, went to the dressing table and poured water from a pitcher into a porcelain bowl. She went to the bathroom and brought back a beautiful cut crystal glass of cold water, which she set neatly by the bed.

"The facilities is down the hall. Indoors. First in the county. I've tried to make it nice. I know you come from the city."

"Nothing so grand."

"You'd be surprised the number of people don't know the first thing about how to use all those forks. You can tell the places a person's been by the way he eats. You've been some fancy places."

Mrs. Larsen left her. Catherine unpacked her things, hanging her pathetic, ugly dresses in the small closet, laying away her underclothes in a bureau. This would be home, she thought. These are my things and I am putting them away in my new home. The last thing in her suitcase was a small blue medicine bottle, and she sat for a long time in a chair by the window looking at it, before she put it back in a silk pocket inside the suitcase and slid the whole thing under the bed.

She opened the heavy curtains and immediately felt the pressing cold of the air outside. Tired as she was, it was a pleasant sensation, bracing, reminding her of her own flesh. The few lights from the house lit up the constant swirl of the snow outside. She sat in a small blue velvet chair and watched the storm, and drifted in and out of a light sleep accompanied by the clumping of Larsen's boots in the room next door. Her own life was like that of a stranger to her.

Finally, the footsteps stopped. She waited until the house was completely quiet, and then she stood, and stepped out of her ruined skirt, undid the thirteen buttons of her awful dress. She could smell the hard iron smell of Truitt's blood on her clothes, on her skin, and she used a linen cloth and the warm water in the nightstand washbasin to bathe as best she could.

She stepped into a plain nightgown she had sewn only two days before, and stood, as she so often did, looking at her face in the oval mirror.

This was not an illusion, here in this house in this storm. This was not a game. This was real. Her heart felt, all at once, that it was breaking, and tears stung her eyes.

It could have been different, she thought. She might have been the woman who dandled a child on her knee, or took food to a neighbor whose house had been visited by illness or fire or death. She might have smocked dresses for her daughters, read to them on nights like this. Worlds of fantasy and wonder on a night when you couldn't see your hand in front of your face. She couldn't exactly imagine the circumstances under which any of this might have come to pass, but, like an actress who sees a role she might have played go to someone with less talent, Catherine felt somehow the loss of a role more graceful, more suited to the landscape of her heart.

Her true heart, however, was buried so far inside her, so gone beneath the vast blanket of her lies and deceptions and whims. Like her jewels now beneath the snow, it lay hidden until some thaw might come to it. She had no way of knowing, of course, whether this heart she imagined herself to have was, in fact, real in any way. Perhaps it was like the soldier's severed arm that keeps throbbing for years, or like a broken bone that aches at the approach of a storm. Perhaps the heart she imagined was one she had never really had at all. But how did they do it, those women she saw on the street, laughing with their charming or their ill-tempered children in restaurants, in train stations, everywhere around her? And why was she left out of the whole sentimental panorama she felt eddying around her every day of her life?

She wanted, for once in her life, to be at the center of the stage. The stakes therefore were higher in the game with Ralph Truitt than she had realized. Because what she was, standing before the mirror in a lonely farmhouse, was, in fact, all she was.

She was a lonely woman who answered a personal advertisement in a city paper, a woman who had traveled miles and miles on somebody else's money. She was neither sweet nor sentimental, neither simple nor honest. She was both desperate and hopeful. She was like all those women whose foolish dreams made her and her friends howl with hopeless derision, except that now she was looking into the face of such a woman and it didn't seem funny at all.

She turned out the overhead light, so that the room danced in the light from a single candle on the nightstand. She drew the heavy curtains against the storm, and slipped into the comfort of the ladylike bed.

As she leaned forward to blow out the candle, there was a sharp knock. She stepped quickly across the cold floor in the pitch-black darkness, and opened the door to find the pale, haggard face of Mrs. Larsen.

"He's very hot," she said.

CHAPTER FIVE

—◦◦◦—

I N HIS FEVER, the women came to him. They lifted his trembling body from the twisted sheets and lowered him into a
tepid bath, still in his nightshirt. His eyes rolled wildly; his
breaths came in gulping bursts. Then the chills came, and their
strong hands held him.

After a long time, they raised him again, the cooling water running in thick rivers from the nightshirt that pressed on his flesh
like a second skin. Then they stripped him, roughly toweled his
naked body and dressed him again, and helped him to freshly laid
sheets in his father's bed. They had seen his body, which no woman
had seen for almost twenty years.

He was never alone, never without a woman's hand on his arm
or his forehead or his shivering chest. They held his hand. They
made poultices of snow and laid them on his head, waiting for the
fever to break.

They held his head and chin as they tried to spoon dark broth
into his slack mouth, and he could hear their quiet voices, but as
though from far away. He was ill. He was not young, his flesh no

longer sweet. The women touched him. They saw his body. They came and went, quietly, far away, except they never left together. There was always a woman by his side, a woman's hand on his flesh.

He had not thought. Not true. He had never *not* thought of it, not one minute in all those years, but the weight and intensity of his thinking had stripped from the idea all possibility of its ever being a reality, this touch, and this faraway sibilance of the women's voices. They were real, one known to him, one unknown, and they were there at every minute. In the dark. In the dim daylight. Every minute.

Mrs. Larsen prayed over him. The other one did not.

Their fingers touched him. Their fingers lifted the hair back from his eyes, held his waist when he coughed into the handkerchief they held gently against his mouth. They heard his groans.

They held packs of ice against his head, against the back of his neck. They wrapped his long legs tightly in heavy wool blankets, wrapped his whole body until he could not move a muscle.

So long in this house, and in the fever, so many lives around him. His mother and his father. His brother. His wife—although she had hated the house so much that even her ghost would not walk the floors. His children, gone into a void deeper than the blizzard.

It had been a dark house when he was a child, when he and his dead brother had played in the attic. He was twelve years old before he realized that his father was rich, sixteen before he realized the immeasurable breadth and depth of the wealth, how far it stretched, how many lives were held in the grip of his father's money.

Yet still they lived on at the farm they began in, never changing one thing for a more luxurious thing, never painting the place, never planting a rose. They lived like poor people. It was immigrant country, and they lived like immigrants.

Inside the house, there was no mention or show of wealth. There was only God, the stern and terrible God his mother spoke of day and night, the God who burned, the God who blamed, the God who filled his mother's brilliantly focused mind even while she slept beside the husband she considered no better than a demon, his mind on sex, on touching her, on getting inside her and wallowing there like a boat in shallow water, his mind on money and how to make more and more of it.

They went to meetings, one in the morning, one in the evening. Different churches on different Sundays. The services lasted for hours. His father dozed. His mother lit up like a fire. She said her husband's soul was a lost cause.

They prayed at breakfast and every other meal. They prayed at odd times, when the children had been reckless or rude or prideful, prayed as though hell were right next door instead of far beneath the earth.

His father did not believe. His father winked. He was damned, although he didn't seem to know it, or at least it didn't seem to matter. His mother worked on him in public, and worked harder in secret, sure from the first breath he ever took that he was lost.

His mother was sewing at the kitchen table. "What is hell like?" Ralph asked her, and she paused and said to him, "Hold out your hand," and he did. He could feel the heat from the kitchen stove; he could see the deep gouges in the kitchen table from which his mother scrubbed away, every day, every trace of human hunger. His hand was steady and his trust was infinite. He was six years old.

"What is hell like?" His mother's hand flew through the stifling air of the kitchen as her son stared into her piercing eyes. She stabbed her needle deep into the soft part of his hand, at the base of his thumb, and the pain tore through his arm and into his brain, but he did not move, just watched his mother's fierce and steady eyes.

She twisted the needle. He could feel it scrape against bone. It sent a pain like nettles in his bloodstream, through every vein of his body, straight to his heart.

Her voice was patient and loving and sad, without anger. "That's what hell is like, son. But it's like that all the time. *Forever.*"

And she took the needle out of his hand without ever taking her eyes from his and wiped it on the apron she always wore except to church. She calmly resumed her sewing. He did not cry, and they never spoke of it again. He never told his father or his brother or anybody. And he never for one moment ever forgot or forgave what she had done.

"The pain of hell never heals. It never stops burning for one second. It never goes away."

He never forgot it because he knew she was right. Whatever happened or did not happen to his faith after that night, whatever happened as his hand got infected and swelled until yellow pus oozed from the wound and then got better, whatever happened as the scar rusted over from deep purple to a faint and tiny dot that only he could see, he knew she was right. And he never, for one moment, from that night on, he never breathed a breath without hating her.

Later, years later, when he was leaving the house to go to college, she said to him, "You were born a wicked child, so wicked I wouldn't pick you up for a year. And you'll grow into a wicked adult. Born wicked. Die wicked." Then she turned and slammed the door, leaving him alone on the wide porch with his new leather valise, and he wondered how she knew, for he knew she was right.

He saw women on the street, and they were not like his mother.

Their graceful necks rose from their high-collared dresses like fountains of cream; their skirts smelled of iron and naphtha and talc. When he walked downtown with his father, they would sometimes take his hand or touch his chin, and an electric current would pass through him, so exactly like, yet so different from, the pain of his mother's needle. There was a luxuriousness in this other pain, and though he was only seven or eight, he suddenly felt languid and hot and helpless before any woman, and he didn't know where the feeling came from and he didn't know what to do with it, but he knew it was all he ever wanted.

The young girls he knew and was occasionally allowed to speak to were different from these women. Once he touched his finger to the finger of a neighbor's daughter, older than he was, and he felt a sudden tingling rush to his groin, and he withdrew his hand quickly. These young girls, the ones his age, their skin was milk, not cream, and their scent was floral, without the metallic aftertaste that made the sweetness sharp, that made the sweetness burn him to the heart. At night, in bed, he kissed the skin of his own forearm, imagining he was kissing one of the women his father knew.

In his dreams, as now in his fever, the women came to him, held him in their arms. He was never apart from them. When he sat in church or ran across the schoolyard with the other boys, he knew at every minute where they stood and whether or not they were watching him.

He never spoke of it. He never talked to his brother, or his father. He knew they knew. He knew that when his mother read the long passages from the Bible which they suffered through every night and morning, he knew that his father and his brother knew as well as he what the stories were really about.

They were about how the world began with one man's hunger

for one woman, how the serpent's venom ran through every man's veins so that he could not forget himself in work or sleep, but only in a woman's arms.

Lust. It was about lust, and lust was his sin, and hell would be his natural home forever. His manners were perfect; his demeanor was calm and dignified; his longings were painful beyond endurance.

At fifteen, he would bite his pillow in the dark and silent house, and scream his muffled lust until his throat hurt. His hands were tired from groping, and eight or ten times a day he would find his hands inside his pants, his pants around his ankles, his thin hips thrusting into his fist. Afterward, more times than not, he would feel the sharp stab of his mother's needle. A pain so severe that sweat would break out on his forehead, his hands grow clammy and the small of his back damp. It was a pain that ran upward from his groin through every vein in his body, like the first sting of the nettles. And the more it happened, the more he hated God.

After that first time, he never touched a girl. He felt that the violence of his desire, the rotted malevolence of his lust would kill any woman he touched. He believed it literally, and his belief did not waver. He felt he was dying of some disease that had no symptoms and that he could not name, but he knew it would kill others as well as himself as sure as typhoid, as sure as a knife to the heart.

He was born wicked. He would die wicked. Sometimes a woman would touch him by accident, would sit with him on a step, for instance, with a thigh brushing his thigh, and he knew that this woman would die, and he would move his leg, would move away until he found himself alone in a quiet room, his pants around his ankles, the pleasure followed by the serpent's certain fang.

His father was a man. His father had touched his mother and had not died or killed. Still, he knew what he knew.

Everywhere he turned he saw evidence and heard gross rumors that what would surely happen to him was already happening to others. Women ripped out their insides with knitting needles. Men spat in their wives' faces and dropped dead of heart attacks. People photographed their dead babies in tiny coffins; the black silk dresses were stiff as dead flesh. Lust was a sin and sin was death and he was not alone, but he was in pain, constant pain, and there was no one to tell.

He was mistaken, of course, although he knew it only years later. Almost anyone could have told him he was wrong, if he had found a way to describe to anyone the terror he felt. If he had found someone to tell. But there were no words for it at the time, the sure and deadly mark of that serpent's bite.

He grew tall and handsome. His father was rich, and this he learned not from his mother or father, but from the taunting of other boys in the schoolyard, in the fact that all the boys he knew had fathers who worked for his father. As strict as mothers in the town were, any mother would have sold her daughter to Ralph Truitt for a dollar.

His mother prayed over him. His father read to him from the *Morte D'Arthur*, the old stories of the round table and the Grail, and wanted him to be educated in the city. His sweet brother had neither the head nor the blood for business, and his father demanded that the empire he was building every day must last after his death. Ralph understood he was marked for the inheritance.

Ralph didn't long for his father's life. He longed for the life of Lancelot du Lac, who woke from a sleep to find four queens under four silk parasols gazing down upon him. Lancelot's mother, the Lady of the Lake, sending him into the world to be a knight, letting him go though she loved him and feared for his soul, explained the difference between the virtues of the heart and the virtues of the body. The virtues of the body are reserved for those who are fair of face and strong of body, but the virtues of the heart, being goodness and kindness and compassion, are available to anybody.

Such is the sweetness of boys that Ralph believed these words with all his heart, even as he believed the virtues of goodness would always be denied to him, and that he would never be tall or handsome or wanted. He felt displaced in his body, homeless in his heart.

And so, Lancelot left his mother and ventured into the world, where he was strong and brave and utterly helpless in the face of women. His purity and his strength and beauty and courage were doomed to end in failure and corruption. He would never see the Holy Grail. Lancelot's helpless lust destroyed the world, not his strength, and Ralph understood all this as his father read to him. Ralph felt the hot tears in his eyes.

Lust and luxury. In the end, the virtues of the body came easily to Ralph. Believe what he might, he was tall, and good-looking and strong and rich. The virtues of the heart were unknown to him, and through his mother's incessant prayer, he knew, whatever they were, he would never have them. She sat in a bare church on a plain wooden bench and saw heaven. He sat next to her and thought of nothing but naked women and rich surroundings, silk parasols and fine carriages and endless pleasure.

His love of women, and his fear of them, of his death and theirs, grew into a hatred that never abated. It took away the sweet and left only the sharp. His childhood was desire and nightmare mixed inextricably.

He went to Chicago, to university. Away from his mother's tireless harangue, he was free to spend his days and nights in the pursuit of pleasure. He learned easily. He was popular. He despised himself when he was alone, so he rarely was. He developed a taste for champagne and the sight of naked women in hotel rooms. He saw each of these women only once; afraid of the infections his desire was seeding in them. They would have laughed at him with their cynical, musical voices. If they had known. He gave dinner parties in restaurants. He bought velvet sofas. He bought ancient paintings of naked saints, pierced by arrows. He had a tailor.

He was one of those men whose good looks are illuminated by their unawareness of them, a kind of ruddy shyness. He engaged in sex as though avoiding his reflection in a mirror, all hands and mouth, no eyes, and women found this endearing. His hungers were insatiable, his mouth sucking forward into his desire like a man's in the desert dying of thirst.

His mother never wrote and he never went home. He played cards. He read the writings of philosophers. He read French poetry aloud to uncomprehending whores. He studied charts that predicted how money grows into wealth, and he studied the tout sheets at racetracks that predicted how bloodlines could turn into a nose across a wire.

His father sent money, what seemed an infinite amount of money. Ralph stopped writing his dutiful notes to his father, stopped going to university altogether for months at a time, until he would wake, one morning, with the taste of champagne in his mouth and long for the quiet of the scholastic life, the dusty library, the drone of professors' voices. And despite this silence, every month, the same enormous amount of money would arrive in his checking account. His bankers would cluck and look at him with envy and hatred, but he was never denied a single penny.

His father was recreating him, finally taking revenge on his sour and unforgiving wife. Ralph had become reckless and wicked, and his father, if he heard of it, did not seem to care.

Ralph's brother was dull and pious. Andrew stayed home. He went to work in his father's businesses, and kept his nose to the grindstone, and never complained and never showed the slightest genius for any of it. Competency yes, but no more. He sat beside his mother in church, and his eyes were as brilliant as hers. He married at eighteen, and was dead of influenza the next winter. His wife's mother went crazy with disbelief, that her daughter had come so close to the pot of gold and seen it all go into the ground, no heir, no allowance, nothing but the bitter company of Ralph's mother, which finally, of course, drove the girl away too. Better to live with her own deranged family than her dead husband's mother, whose rectitude was unpleasant and stifling.

Ralph's father was left alone in the house with his wife. For that reason he was there less and less and went on long trips to visit his mines, his vast herds, to discuss the various partnerships involved in the creation of a railroad, and he would come home from a month or two away, richer than ever, flush with brilliance and success, to find the house dark and shabby, his wife in the same despicable dress, and still he did not say the one thing he wanted to say to his beloved older son. Come home.

Ralph had not been home in five years. He loved sex and he hated it. He loved bad women because he didn't care if he destroyed them. There was a core of hatred in his hunger for them that never ever went away, a distaste that bit like sharp teeth, stabbed like needles, and still he couldn't stop. He rented a hotel room, rich, the bed festooned with garlands and gold, the waiters silent as they brought champagne for Mr. Truitt and Miss Mackenzie, or Miss

Irons, or Miss Kenny, for singers and dance hall girls and whores and artists' models.

He thought of his brother dead beneath the ground and envied him the quiet. Death at least would end this terrifying desire.

He went to Europe. A wanderjahr, his father called it, a common thing for young men of his day. He lived in Europe the arrogant life of the newly sophisticated, his principal sophistications consisting of speaking French and knowing how to check into a hotel room with a woman who was not his wife. He was taking the Grand Tour, through the haze of London and the brilliant clarity of Paris, through the picture galleries and the racetracks and the drawing rooms of the destitute aristocracy. They pandered to him, they offered their terrified daughters like ormolu clocks, and they laughed at him the minute his back was turned. Ralph didn't mind. He could order in any restaurant, and he could always pay the bill.

In Florence he ran into a friend from Chicago, Edward, who was trying his hand at being a painter. Edward spent his days at the Uffizi and the Pitti, making hungover sketches, and lived in a state of such licentious dissolution that even Ralph was shocked. Ralph took a grand villa, and brought Edward to live with him. The two of them drank champagne from iced bottles and laughed as the candles dripped white wax on the marble floors during the nightly card parties and music parties and parties where no one wore any clothes.

Every morning, young maids would kneel and scrape away the wax while Edward and Ralph slept in their sumptuous beds with their overblown whores. Life had the serenity of knowing, ceaseless decadence.

Occasionally, in the ornately frescoed churches he visited almost by accident, Ralph would get a glimpse of a God who was, if not less terrible, at least more opulent than the God of his childhood.

Ralph had a cook, two gardeners, six peacocks, and a handsome carriage with a liveried driver. In the back of the carriage rode a second liveried servant whose function was unclear to him.

Edward knew pharmacies where furtive men would sell whatever drugs they wanted, powders to keep them asleep for forty-eight hours while the sun rose and set and rose again on the duomo, powders to make an erection last four hours. Ralph and Edward bought poisons in dark blue bottles which, when taken in tiny doses, could produce euphoria such as Ralph had never known, an ecstasy which felt like sex in every pore of his skin.

Still the money came without reproach. The terror of what happened to his body when he felt desire never went away. His heart never hardened to the pain, the hatred never ceased its relentless beat. Then he saw Emilia.

She rode by him in a shining carriage, an exquisite girl of sixteen wearing a white muslin dress with wisteria intricately woven in her black hair. Ralph never went to the pharmacist again. He never played cards, and he moved Edward and the whores and the cardsharps and the drunks into large, dark rooms on the other side of the river. He was in love.

It shocked him to wake every morning with a clear head, to find his rooms as neat as he had left them the night before, to taste the brilliant Tuscan food laid before him by the calm, dark-eyed servants. He exercised. He took boxing lessons. He took Italian lessons for hours every day from a university student, just so he could speak to her. He rode and hunted and resolved to be the kind of man who could win the heart of this girl whose name he didn't know.

His clothes were splendid, his manners good enough, his parentage unknowable at this distance. American, that was enough, he supposed. His hair was brilliantined, he smelled of cologne from the pharmacy at Santa Maria Novella and of money from America.

He was introduced to Emilia's father, then to her mother and the slow pleasantries of her drawing room where every object spoke of old, old luxury and culture. At last he was allowed to speak to Emilia herself. Ralph was more naive in his mid-twenties than these people had been in the cradle.

They were ordinary people, pretentious and penniless and ambitious for their beautiful daughter, and Ralph took them for more than they were. He miscalculated how most Italian families can drag some title out of the attic. He didn't see that they had no money, that their servants went unpaid, and that angry dressmakers went out the back door as he came in the front. He didn't see that their daughter was their only marketable asset.

He saw an exquisite beauty whose voice was music and whose manners were poetry. His Italian was, after all the lessons, the language of a child. Emilia spoke pleasant French and comical English, she blushed like the dawn as he tried to see her eyes. For months, she was sweet and charming and just beyond his reach, like the peach at the top of the tree.

He whispered her name to himself as he walked along the Arno. Absence from her was physically painful, as though his nerves were on fire. Her company was the only context in which he found his character acceptable. He lit candles for her love. He prayed for a miracle. Then finally, Ralph understood, was made to understand. Emilia was for sale.

She was sweet to him, and infinitely charming in a musical way, and Ralph, knowing so little of love, saw what he felt in his heart reflected on her face, and believed that she loved him. Her father would be saddened to part with her, but would, in the end do so because she loved Ralph and because he would, after all, be compensated for his loss.

Buying things was easy for Ralph. He had already spent three years in the silver vaults and picture markets of Europe, and he knew that the aristocracy were always reluctant to part with their treasures, and he also knew that, in the end, it wasn't the parting that was in question but only the price.

He wrote again to his father. He asked for a great deal of money. His father replied that he would send what Ralph wanted, but that he wished for Ralph to come home now, to come back and run the business. A bargain was struck. Ralph could have the bride if he would take on the responsibility he had been allowed to shirk for so long. For Ralph, the solution was a happy one. He had known for years that, no matter how long the line he had been given to play on, sooner or later he would feel the sting of the hook in his mouth and be reeled home.

All his life, he had hoped that, in the end, he would be allowed to love someone enough to speak of his fears and so be rid of them, and it was to Emilia that he told his terrible secrets, the fire in his veins, the cruel rage in his heart, and she healed him with a laugh and a kiss. You will see, she said, this is silly. No one will die.

She barely understood what he was saying. Her English was composed of manners and poetry and light, and she had no vocabulary to comprehend such darkness. All she knew was that she had been raised to be sold, and being sold to Ralph was certainly not the worst of her options.

While waiting for her elaborate trousseau to be sent from Paris and then fitted and refitted, while the endless negotiations about the dowry were being completed with such cruel acumen by Emilia's father that not a single tradesperson went unpaid, the telegrams came. Your father is ill, the first one said, come at once, but he could not leave. Your father is dying, said the second, and still he waited for Emilia to be ready.

Your father is dead, said the third telegram. So he married Emilia in haste and boarded a train and then a boat and then a train and traveled until he arrived at the farm in Wisconsin with his wife, the prodigal son come home.

Emilia was pregnant before they got home. Ralph welcomed and dreaded the birth. He remembered kneeling by his father's grave, Emilia beside him, her voluminous pearl gray skirt from Paris shimmering in the sun. Her face, so angelic in Florence, seemed merely peculiar here, too exotic for the flat landscape.

It was all so long ago. They were all dead now, his father, Emilia, the little girl she gave birth to in that first Wisconsin spring, his brother. All dead, even, finally, his relentless mother, who never forgave him.

He had thought it would fade, but it never did. For twenty years not one soul had touched him with affection or desire, and he had thought his need would fade, and he was amazed, at the turning of every year, how the lust that had gripped his youth gripped him still in all its ardor, all its rage. It had hardened around his heart, more every year, and it never let him go.

Yet he leaned away from the soft voices of the few women who spoke to him, knowing he could have any one of them, yet choosing none. Instead, he chose solitude, or he was chosen by it, and it was horrible and unbreakable. For still, at any moment, every night and day, his flesh itched with desire, his mind turned constantly on the sexual lives of the men and women around him, and this turning caused him to loathe and cherish other people in equal measure. His love died with Emilia, and with the child, but his desire flourished in the barren soil of his heart and its soft whispering never ceased in his ear.

In his fever, now, the women came to him. In his fever, they touched him. Their touch both burned and cooled.

CHAPTER SIX

—◦◦◦—

I T SNOWED FOR THREE DAYS. Catherine was so bored she
was sometimes afraid she would lose her mind, or at least
lose her way. In the midst of this crisis, she must not lose
sight of her plan. Every night she turned the blue bottle in her hands
and watched the blizzard through the liquid. Like a scene in a snow-
globe; she saw it unfold. Every night she prayed he wouldn't die.

When she wasn't nursing Ralph, she roamed the rooms, looking
at everything, touching every object, every piece of furniture. She
turned over every plate, picked up every piece of silver to see the
hallmarks stamped there. Limoges, France. Tiffany & Co., New
York. Wedgewood. She calculated the worth of each piece, the
value of the whole.

The few conversations she had with Mrs. Larsen either concerned Ralph's treatment, or seemed to her like snatches grasped
from a dim understanding of a foreign language.

"His shoes is never there, by the door. His shoes is by the chest
of drawers. He gets them from New York City."

"I'll move them."

"No. Leave them be. I'll move them. I know how he likes things."

Deep in the night, as they sat by his side, "Sleeping like a baby now. His head is big as a watermelon. He ain't going to die."

Catherine never knew whether some response was required. She had slight knowledge of how to talk to other people.

She slept sitting in a chair in his room. She wore her plain black dress and heard the wind howling outside. She nursed him with tenderness and efficiency. Three times a day, she sat alone at the gleaming table and ate the exquisite food Mrs. Larsen brought her. A clear soup the color of rubies. A meringue with chestnuts. Duck in a mustard sauce. Things she had never seen, foods that frightened her with their beauty. She asked Mrs. Larsen if she and her husband didn't want to eat with her, or have her eat in the kitchen with them. That, apparently, was not part of the plan, and so she went on in solitude at the head of the enormous table.

She ate with an appetite that excited and appalled her. Rich foods so at odds with the bleak country, so suitable for the comfort of the cold. Her hunger was fueled by boredom and anxiety, and it never went away, no matter how much she ate.

At night, she stood for hours at her window, watching the snow fall, longing for what she had left behind. During the day, the whiteness was so bright, she had to shield her eyes from the glare. She could not keep the curtains open for more than a few minutes.

She thought of people, ordinary people, moving through the streets of the cities, and she marveled at the commonplace of their lives.

She thought of the rooms she had left behind, the rooms in which she waked and breathed, the way they were furnished, the way voices carried in through the open windows, the way she walked and wept in them. She stared down at the stupid and listless people who had somehow managed to achieve in a flawlessly easy way those dear little things that eluded her.

They owned plates. They all had socks. The world was filled with people, and she thought with derision of the extraordinarily few she had known, really known, in her life.

And as much as she might sneer at the emptiness of their lives, the stupidity and the boredom, she had ended up in this house, soundless in the relentless snow, and she gladly would trade places with any one of them.

In the life behind her, she would smoke cigarettes and drink liquor and take drugs and grab what she could get out of the sea of people around her. Men wrote her letters. They had seen her at the theater, high up in a box, and they would write and she would answer. So delicate. She would find forgetfulness for an hour or a summer or a night with any one of them whose letter amused her, a man with blue eyes or green eyes or brown eyes, their faces so close, pleading for what she could not imagine, and eventually the tremor would pass and the luxurious beauty of it would fade and she would see only the stupidity and the foul odors and the hatefulness of her own heart, a hatefulness which told her every minute that the pleasure these people obviously found in these simple moments would be forever denied to her. And then she would move on.

She itched for a cigarette. She would wade through drifts over her head for the escape of opium or morphine. But she was far away from all that. She would not even take a glass of sherry. She would follow her plan and her plan would work, if, of course, Truitt did not die.

"How is he, Miss?"

"He's restless. And hot."

"Tough old bird. Don't you worry, he'll make it."

When I have his money, she thought, I will go far away, I will go to a country where I don't know anybody and I don't speak the language and I will never talk to anybody ever again. But no, that wasn't the plan. She must remember the plan. When she had his money, she would marry her useless and beautiful lover and they would live a life of such extraordinary delight. Oh, yes, that was the plan.

In every one of the cities where she haphazardly had landed, when anxiety and dissatisfaction engulfed her as they eventually did, she found the municipal library and spent hours there, reading descriptions and guides to other places she might eventually go. She knew the street plans of Buenos Aires and Saint Louis and London. She knew in intimate detail any number of places she had never been. Like a studious schoolgirl, she sat in the waning light of a vast municipal library, and she learned things.

She imagined them in Venice, herself and her useless child of a lover, sleeping until afternoon, their rooms at the Danieli a riot of half-eaten sweets and empty champagne bottles and exquisite lingerie. She had studied Italian, the light slanting down from the library's high windows.

She saw them rising languidly, the morphine a dull film across his black eyes, swathed in silks and cigarette smoke, drinking Chianti in a gondola as it moved across the black water toward the lights of the Lido, and the gondolier would sing of love and every door would open to them, revealing infinite ancient rooms of luxury and beauty and charm where aristocrats, princesses, and counts and kings would kiss them on both their cheeks and they would never grow old and they would never die. She would never be alone. She would have her lover's beauty and her own, and she would have Ralph's money, and surely the two together would be enough. That at least was the plan.

She would marry Ralph Truitt, and then, one day, almost imperceptibly he would begin to grow old and die. And then, one day, not long after, he would be dead and she would have it all.

"Mrs. Larsen?"

"Yes, Miss?"

"Where does this food come from?"

Mrs. Larsen laughed, spooning sauce over a breast of duck. "Come from? I make it."

"But . . ."

"You thought we ate beef jerky? Corned beef and cabbage? Ham from October to May? Like hicks? Well, some do. We don't. There's an icehouse where we keep most things. Some things he sends for, from Chicago. Some of it came on the same train you came on."

"You cook like an angel."

"I learned it a long time ago. I was just a girl. In the other house. It was another time. And, I have to say, it's nice to do it again. Do it properly."

"Another house?"

"Yes. It was a long time ago."

"Where was it?"

"Is. It's still there."

"Where is it?"

"It's nearby. No more than a mile. We never go there."

"What's it like?" Perhaps this other house was where the beautiful things with the names on the bottom had come from.

"It doesn't matter. We never go there. Snow doesn't stop, we'll be at the end of the fancy food soon enough." Mrs. Larsen left her alone at the long table with the gleaming silver.

Catherine knew about cooking, French cooking. She had read about it in the library. She had never actually done it, but she knew recipes for sauces by heart. She tried not to appear overly curious. It made Mrs. Larsen nervous.

It was amazing the things you could learn in a library, just by looking them up. Poisons, for instance. Page after page after page of poisons. As simple as a cookbook. If you could read, you could poison somebody in such a way that nobody would ever know.

Ralph Truitt's house had no books. There was an old upright piano covered with an embroidered Spanish shawl, and between her nursing chores, before every meal, she practiced her little pieces. Mostly, though, she didn't know where she belonged here, and there was no one to tell her. Not Mrs. Larsen, who was jolly and honest and assumed the same of her, assuming, along with the rest of it, that comfortable people somehow made themselves comfortable. She was enormous and kind, Mrs. Larsen, unlike her tiny thin husband, who watched Catherine's every move with suspicion and treated her with only barely disguised contempt.

"Oh, Larsen," she heard Mrs. Larsen say, "Leave it go. Give the poor girl a chance."

A chance at what, exactly? If only they knew, she thought. She couldn't find a chair to sit in, couldn't figure out where she was meant to stand. She looked out across the frozen landscape and could see her jewels beneath the snow. She wept for no reason.

Mrs. Larsen said to her one day, out of the blue, as they lifted Truitt's heavy body onto clean white sheets, "I couldn't bear it, Miss. I couldn't bear it if he was hurt again."

"Who hurt him?"

"Everybody. It was a long time ago. But that kind of thing never goes away. It pretty much ruined his life."

"You care very much for him."

"I respect him. You've got to respect that kind of grief. I'd have picked up a gun. But I'm telling you, if you hurt him, I'll hurt you."

"I won't hurt him."

"No, you surely won't."

Catherine was lying, but at least she wouldn't hurt him yet. He had to get well before she could hurt him. He could not die, and leave her stranded, without love or money. She couldn't bear it, the long train ride back, empty-handed.

She spooned the food into his mouth. She gently wiped the sweat from his forehead, stripped his nightshirt from him when he grew too hot. She begged Larsen to get the doctor, snowbound two towns away. Larsen figured, having seen Catherine stitch him up, that she was practically as good as any doctor he could find, and, anyway, the snow was deeper every day. It was useless to try.

She gave him hot tea. She wrapped his legs tight in heavy wool blankets, and sat up all night. She and Mrs. Larsen lifted his naked body from the bath.

She got up in the night, and stood over Truitt as he shivered with the fever. She lay beside him, and held him close to her until the warmth of her body passed through to his and the chill had passed. Her nipples rose up and radiated heat into Truitt's shivering back.

It was, she imagined, the erotic allure of human tenderness. The comfort of kindness. She had forgotten.

Her hands moved across his body as so many hands had moved across hers, and he felt no more of it than she had. When the chill had passed and he slept peacefully again, she sat in a chair until dawn, feeling a cold she thought would never pass, shivering, staring silently in the dark.

On the fourth night, the fever broke and the snow stopped falling. He would live. She had saved his life.

Catherine stood by her window for hours in the dark, the blue bottle in front of her on the windowsill. The snow covered everything and shone in the moonlight like the kind of fairy kingdom little girls dream of.

The snow was eternal, infinite. Across the yard, across the roof of the barn, down to the smooth round pond at the foot of the farthest field. There was not a footprint, not a mark in the entire landscape, only the silvered and impenetrable sweep of snow. Perfection.

You see, thought Catherine, sooner or later, everything gets a fresh start. It's not just possible. It happens.

She stood through the night, perfectly warm, perfectly comfortable in her plain dress, and waited to speak to Ralph Truitt in the morning.

CHAPTER SEVEN

—◦∾◦—

WHEN THE SUN ROSE, the snow blazed copper as a
new roof, then paled to rose, and suddenly whit-
ened into a dazzling brightness. The barn and
buildings floated in a haze of blinding light, and Catherine had to
shield her eyes with her hand.

She dressed carefully, and walked downstairs in the silent house.
She sat at the spinet, and began to play a Chopin Prelude, not one
of the most difficult ones, very softly, so as not to wake anyone. She
could tell he was behind her in the doorway before he spoke, but
his voice startled her all the same.

"That was my wife's favorite music. She played it over and over."
He looked weak, bent over as though he might be walking with a
cane.

"I'm sorry. I'll stop."

"No, no. I'd like to hear it. Please."

She played without missing a note, played with, she hoped, a
sweetness and simplicity that might seem lack of bravado rather

than lack of skill, and then she rose and sat opposite Ralph in front of the fireplace. He was shockingly pale and seemed melancholy, perhaps because his grief for his wife had been refreshed by the music.

"My father believed that music was the voice of God." Catherine spoke quietly, as she might have calmed a frightened dog. "He was a missionary for God. We traveled the world, Africa, India, China, wherever he was called to spread the word. He died in China, leaving me and my sister alone.

"He used it to speak to people in lands where they don't speak English. He believed music was universal, and he believed God spoke to people through music. He believed I played well."

She went on to describe the peoples of Africa and China, heathens who had been touched by her awkward playing, and moved by her father's sermons and had turned, in the end, to Christianity. Their souls, she said, had been saved from hell.

She made it all up, of course, made it up out of books she had read in the library, the customs of the African tribes, the strict and brilliant dressing of the women of the Chinese court, their tiny feet and birdlike voices, but she got it right, every detail, and he sat listening attentively.

When she had finished, run through everything she knew, afraid of having used up her meager store of information too quickly, he sat still for a moment, and then said, "Who are you?"

"I am Catherine Land. I'm the woman who wrote the letters, not the woman in the photograph, but I wrote the letters. I am that woman."

He fiddled with his trousers. He seemed undecided as to what he was going to say.

"I have a story to tell you. We're going to be married. Whoever you are, whoever you turn out to be. You should know."

"You said . . . I thought you weren't sure. You are suspicious. Still."

"You saved my life. That's enough. I know what you did for me." He stared into her eyes. "Everything you did. I was sick, I was almost dead, but I wasn't unaware."

She sat still, her hands in her lap. She looked into his pale eyes.

"You're not who you said you were," he said.

"My father said my face was . . . my face was the devil's handi-work. Meant to do evil. I sent another person's picture, my plain cousin India. You didn't want, or so you said . . . my father . . ." She was helpless.

"Enough. It's enough. I said we'd be married. You're here. We will be married."

They stared at each other, stared at the fire.

"Now listen," he said softly. "Listen to my life."

He sat for a long time, staring at the fire.

"Listen to my life."

He talked for hours. He told her everything. His harsh and bitter childhood. He told her about his mother and the pin and the raw scraping of his soul during every Sunday sermon, his mother's eyes on him every minute. He had believed his mother the way we all believe the people we love when they tell us who we are, believe them because what the beloved says is truth to us, and he told Catherine all of this. He told her of his dark and tortured desires, desires his mother had seen before he felt them, seen them in him as a baby, so that she would not pick him up or hold him, even then.

He told her about the death of his brother, his brother's body in a box in the icehouse, waiting for the ground to thaw before they could bury him, and told her about the women and Europe and the sensuous rambles in the palaces and the whorehouses.

He made no apologies. He never tilted his head in sentimentality, or paused for her approval or her sympathy, and she never turned her eyes from his, never wandered around the room or shuffled her feet or asked for a glass of water. She just listened. It was a life he told her, entire, flawed, scarred with indulgence and self-laceration, but brave, it seemed to her, courageous at the same time.

He had caused pain, it was true. Who hadn't? But he had suffered as well. It evened out.

He told her about Emilia, the shocking thunderclap of his love for her. He told Catherine how pale her skin was, how the flowers had trembled in her hair, how her pearls lit up her skin with a rosy glow, how she blushed when he spoke in his fragile Italian. He told Catherine that he had loved Emilia and, because of the awful profundity of his love, he had not answered his father's letters or telegrams, and he had missed his father's death and returned home only in time to kneel at his father's graveside in the cold with his pregnant wife.

He told everything. He had never spoken of any of this to anyone, but he told Catherine, because she was going to become his wife. He felt he owed her at least an album of the past. He tried very hard not to pity himself. He never placed blame, or accepted it, nor did he ever shirk responsibility. He described to her the smell of jasmine in the air, the rustle of silk in a Florentine palazzo, the dust drifting from the ancient, ruined curtains, but told her without poetry, simply described these postcards from his past, and she took in the information as though she were reading quietly in a public library.

"I wasn't a good son. I was careless, and profligate in ways I can't imagine now. And I wasn't a good husband or father, although I tried to be."

Something about his candor made her want to run away. She didn't want to know this story. She didn't want to hear the end. It made him too real. She didn't want to think of him as a person. She didn't want to hear his heartbeat.

"My wife hated this house. Well, you can see . . . It wasn't what she was used to. And she hated my mother and my mother hated her, and she was pregnant. I built her another house."

Catherine's attention had wandered. Now it shifted back.

"It isn't far from here. It took a long time. There was an architect brought from Italy, couldn't speak a word of English as far as I could tell, and he was followed by a boatload of dago workmen, and then the child was born, Franny."

His hands worked nervously. His voice caught, just for a second, but he went on.

"Francesca, my wife called her. She was as beautiful as . . . nothing. As water. As anything on this earth. Babies are, of course. She was beautiful, and tiny. My wife carried her, every day, in a carriage, over there to where this thing was being built, this palace, and they all chatted in Italian until it was dark, and then Emilia would come home and she was at least partially happy, at least for awhile.

"I wrote checks. So much money, I couldn't tell you. Money going for marble stairs and fancy china—you've seen some of it—and silverware and beds from Italy that belonged to the pope or the king of somewhere, and curtains and pictures. She was happy. Emilia was happy, like a little dog with a big bone.

"And then we moved into the house. I didn't know where to sit. I had to ask one of the maids where I was supposed to sleep. I rarely slept beside Emilia after we moved. She had her own rooms. Two years, it took.

"Franny got scarlet fever. Babies do. A lot of babies did, that winter. She was two. The fever lasted five days, and when it was gone, Franny was gone, too. Or at least her mind was gone. Her body recovered, but her mind had died. I knew that what I had always feared was true. Desire is poison. Lust was a disease that had slaughtered my child. She was sweet and simple and beautiful and blank as clear water. She loved the colored glass in the windows. She loved the way the maids would fuss over her, dressing her in these unbelievable getups. This sewing woman came from France and lived in the house, and all she did from the time the sun came up until it went down was make these costumes for Emilia and my little girl.

"The house was always full of foreigners. It made Emilia happy, and they came from everywhere. She never spent one minute with her daughter. Brought her downstairs once in a while, dressed like a princess in a fairy story, showed her off like a monkey."

Catherine saw herself wandering the corridors of the house he described, smiling at her guests, who bowed to her as she passed, dukes and duchesses and rich people and actresses, people who owned railroads and Arabian horses just for riding, just for show, touching every object on every table with the certain knowledge that she owned it all.

And somewhere in the dark the dense child, and somewhere in the light the clatter of fancy music on a piano.

"She brought a piano teacher from Italy, another Italian, I didn't even ask his name. I never knew until it was too late that it was finally one too many. We had another child, a boy, Antonio she called him, Andy. He was dark, as she was, of course, they all are, and he was like some rare bird she'd gone to the Amazon to get. A boy shouldn't be beautiful. So much black hair. So handsome, even when he was four. We lived like that, in that house, for eight years.

"Of course she was with him. Had been with him. The piano teacher. I should have known. I thought I knew everything, but I didn't know that. Imagine. The whispering and chatting and the walks in the garden, always speaking Italian, the man sitting at the table with us, every night, eating dinner like a guest, when I wrote him a check every week.

"I never saw it. Never saw it coming. She was a countess. I saw that she was happy, and it was costing fortunes. Yet my little girl, my sweet little thing, was growing every day, her hands reaching for the light like a blind person, feeling her way.

"And after Antonio . . . Andy was born, she slept apart from me, my wife. In her own rooms every night. She never came to me. I never touched her. She would stay up all night, playing cards with whores and fools, and laughing at me. Sometimes I would pass her on my way down to breakfast, just coming upstairs, a champagne glass still in her hand. Smoking cigarettes.

"Six years I put up with it. I never touched her. Then I saw them. My wife. The music teacher. I walked into her apartment. Her rooms. I just wanted to ask a question. Imagine. They didn't even look particularly surprised, and they didn't look like it was all that much fun, but they'd been doing it for years by then. Since before my boy was born, you see? It was an old routine. I remember how at home he looked, like I was the interloper and he was where he should be, between my wife's naked legs. And everybody knew. Everybody knew but me.

"I beat her, and I nearly killed him, and I threw them out. I drove them from my house. My little girl spread her arms wide and watched her mother go. I fired the servants, the maids and the gardeners and the drivers in their braided coats. I kept Mrs. Larsen, who was only a young girl then. She's not as old as she looks, I guess, but this was a long time ago, now. I kept the house exactly the way it was because I didn't want Franny to lose one more thing, but nobody came anymore, nobody was asked and nobody came.

"I hated Antonio. My own son and I couldn't go near him. He favored his mother, and as much as I tried, I saw her face and her skin and her eyes, and I only saw in him a lying, scheming memento of her. It wasn't fair, I know. I know it wasn't. I beat him and I yelled at him until he looked at me with a single hatred that never changed, and no, I don't blame him for that.

"After a long time, my little girl died. She caught influenza, and I held her in my arms and she died, and the day she died I walked out of the door of that house, and locked it behind me. I left everything in that house, all that gorgeous trash I had brought from all over the world, just to see a smile on my wife's face, and I never went back. The clothes are still hanging in the closets. I brought some of the plates, you've seen them. Some silver. Little things. Expensive things, but little. Except that sofa. Imagine. I had gotten used to it. A piece of yellow silk furniture. The feel of a fork.

"I had nowhere to go. I came here. My mother took one look and went to live with her sister in Kansas, and I never saw her again. And I lived in this house, and I beat my own boy until he was bloody, and the minute he was old enough he ran away. One minute he was here, so handsome, fourteen by then, playing those Italian things on that old piano just to make me mad. I can see where he was sitting. I told him his mother was dead, burned to death in a fire in Chicago. It was a lie, but I told him, and I told him I was glad, that the news of her death gave me the first free breath I'd had in seven years, and the next night he was gone."

He looked up at Catherine, as though he had just realized she was there. As though it took him a second to realize who she was.

"I'm sorry. There isn't any delicate way to tell it. I've never told this to one single soul. Everybody knows it, but they don't know it from me. And I'm only going to tell it once."

She looked steadily in Ralph's eyes, her hands completely still in her lap. She sat as she had told herself she would do, no matter what he said, told herself that she would not shift so much as an ankle until he finished his story. And then she would decide. Her pulse was racing. She could feel it throbbing in her wrist.

The story, she knew, was almost over.

"I have looked for him for twelve years. I have put flowers on my little girl's grave, and I have looked for my boy. And now I've found him."

Despite whatever she had told herself, she jumped.

"Where? Alive?"

"Alive. In Saint Louis. Playing piano in some whorehouse. They think it's him. The detectives. They've thought others were him, except they weren't. This time I think it is. And I want him back."

"Why?"

"Because he's my son. He's all I've got."

"I mean, why do you think it's him?"

"I heard you play that music, his mother's music. I always knew that something would happen one day to make me tell the story and the telling would make it all right. The telling would call him back. I'm not a superstitious man. But I believe that."

Tears glistened in his cold eyes. He didn't wipe them away, didn't seem to notice they were there. His hands picked at his black trousers, trembling, rose into the air to catch at a piece of dust and twist it into nothingness. He looked so ill. She didn't move a muscle.

"I have tried to lead a good life. I have tried to be kind, no matter what I felt, no matter how hard it was. You couldn't know. And I've made money. He'll need money. My son has . . . luxurious tastes. I know he does. He's his mother's son."

She looked at him. It wasn't love she felt for him; she didn't know love. But it was something equally strange to her, an undiluted desire, produced, perhaps, by the sight of his anguish. Tears in a man. It was hard for him, the telling, and the awkwardness of it made her breasts and body flush with desire.

"You must be tired."

"I'm not so tired I can't finish telling what you need to know if you're going to marry me. You saved my life. You played the music, the music my wife loved, the music my son played."

"It's a simple piece. Every schoolgirl knows it."

"You played the music. I'm not naive. I'm not very nice, after all. If telling one lie makes you a liar, then I'm a liar, because I told Andy she had died in a fire, and she hadn't, although she did die, some years later. You will marry me, or I hope you will, and we will open the house and move back into it, and everything will shine and he will come home to his own house and his own father and a mother who is far better in every way than the mother he never had the slightest idea about."

She couldn't help herself. "I have to say. It's only fair. I don't love you."

"I don't expect it."

"It's worse. I mean, Mr. Truitt, that I can't love you."

"I don't require it."

"How do you know? If it is him, what was his name?"

"Andy. Antonio."

"How do you know he'll come?"

He looked at her for a long time. The light through the windows was blinding. She could smell lunch cooking, almost ready. She could hear a clock tick. She could see Ralph in front of her, but as though lost in a dazzling snowfall.

"Because you're going to go to Saint Louis on a train and get him."

The light coming through the windows was brilliantly white. Almost blinding.

CHAPTER EIGHT

⸺⟨eνe⟩⸺

E WANTED TO TOUCH HER. He wanted to see the
exhaustion of sex in her every gesture. He wanted to
unpin her hair in a warm room, and lift a pristine
nightdress above her head. He wanted to feel the first touch of his
hand on her smooth dry skin.

He said nothing. He did nothing.

"Does it snow forever here? It seems like it just snows and
snows."

"It snows. We're almost to Canada. And, of course, the water . . .
coming across the water it gathers strength."

"And then it will stay perfectly dry, sometimes, for days at a
time." She turned her head from the breakfast table, the blinding
white washing her skin from rose to pale, then turned back to him.
"Sometimes you think it won't happen again, and then it does. It's
just . . . it's just *there*. Like that."

"Does it surprise you? It's the North. Across the lake it's
Canada."

"No. No, of course not. It's just there, that's all."

Every exchange making him feel like an idiot, making him draw his spine up straight and making him fiddle with his hair, and all he wanted to do was to see her naked on the floor. Not brutal, not unkind, enraptured. He wanted to be in love, but he knew that love, now, for him, was something that happened to other people.

"And it goes away?"

"In April. April or May."

Fool. Idiot. And the worst part of it was that he knew he gave the impression of coldness. He knew that she found him sexless, as frozen as the landscape, and he wanted to say, It isn't true, I would give everything I have to see you writhing on this floor, right now, and still he said nothing. He made no gesture that might be interpreted as leaning in to her in the slightest way.

He might have said anything. He might have said that grief had burned through him so thoroughly that it had turned his sins to ashes. That his mother had said, needle to the bone, that the way to goodness, the only way, was through pain and suffering. He could have said that grief had left him wholly good. But he said nothing. What did she care about his grief, or his sin? She had traveled the world. A missionary, she said, and there was no reason, looking at her prim quietness, her prudish stillness that never gave way for a moment, there was no reason to doubt her. She had traveled. She had heard enough about sin.

"There's so little to do. I wish there was something I could do. When you were sick, there was some reason to be here. I felt that I was doing something you needed. It's something I know, and I was glad to do it."

He touched the purple scar on his forehead.

"Now I'm better. You'll find your way."

"I could help Mrs. Larsen, but she doesn't like it. I could clean. I could visit the sick people in the families who work for you. I could come into town and help you. In your office."

"I have people for that. Just enjoy yourself. The quiet. Read."

"I love to read."

"Then read. I'll order you anything you want. It can be here in two days. Novels. Newspapers. Whatever you want."

"I'll make a list. Might I do that?"

"Of course."

He felt strangulation, a beating in his heart. "I didn't bring you all this way to be miserable. I hoped, hope, you will be happy. At least comfortable, in your choice."

"You brought me here for reasons entirely your own."

"But you came."

"I don't regret it. I won't regret it."

He wanted to hear the sounds that came from her throat when she had no breath left, when she was breathless with desire. He wanted to possess her, in all the ways his formal and distant wife had denied him, truly and deeply, in the ways of his youth. He wanted to have her in his bloodstream like a drug, to sit in his office all day making money and contemplating the rush of ecstasy in his blood.

He wanted to speak to her of his desire, of his desire for her, of the desire gripping his throat. He wanted to stand in front of her naked.

He rarely spoke to her. He never touched her, even in passing. He was no fool. He knew that she was not what she appeared to be, and he knew that what she was lay just beneath the surface of her clothes.

His loneliness was so deep. It made him feel, sometimes, as though someone malevolent were pulling on his hair. Relentlessly pulling on his hair. He wanted to touch her, and he did not. It gave him a pain like a fever.

He saw her, and he wanted to undress her. He wanted to unbutton the many buttons of her severe black dress and pull it back from her neck until he saw her white shoulders. He wanted to drop the dress on the floor, to see it lying around her feet like a pool of black oil. He wanted to see her step out of it and stand before him in her slip, a slim woman in a thin cotton chemise and dark stockings, cotton stockings he would unroll inch by inch until her delicate feet were naked on the floor. The chemise would button up the back, and so he would turn her away from him, to slip each pearl button from its buttonhole, and then the whole flimsy thing would drop, barely skimming her hips as it fell into the darkness of the mess around her feet, and so the first sight of her, his first sight of her naked body would be from the back, the wisps of hair at the neck, glowing like filaments of fire in the candlelight of a dark, cold room. He wanted to trace with his tongue the long line of her white spine, glowing in the brightness from the moon on the snow spilling through the curtains, and she would not want to move, would not turn of her own free will, and so he would grasp her shoulders and turn her toward him and then he would kiss her. The sweetness of skin. The soft touch of his lips on hers. The moment before it all began. Just pure and kind desire.

He would kiss her very lightly, and her nipples would graze his shirtfront, and her lips would graze his lips, which hadn't been kissed in so many years he couldn't count them. His tongue would touch her tongue. He would hold her face steady with both his hands as he softly kissed her.

How could he have spent his life without this? How could his youth have passed, his body have aged untouched, unadmired, unloved? His body was starting to leave him and it would not come back. In ten years he would be old.

He wanted everything. He did nothing.

One evening, a week after he had told her the story of his life, he said to her at dinner, "I thought we would marry on Thanksgiving Day. If that's all right. If it would suit."

"That would be fine. Who would come?"

"Should people come?"

"I don't know. People do. Usually. You must have friends. People you know. I haven't seen anybody."

"It seemed inappropriate, for you to go to town. People talk enough. And the weather . . ."

"There must be people."

"A few."

"So we'll have people here? There will be food, a supper maybe. A wedding."

The woman he wanted to undress, to see naked, was a stranger. Her conversation, her requests, were strange to him. Nobody had asked anything of him for so long.

"I'm not . . . I'm not pure. You should know."

He watched her in silence.

"I was a child. A friend of my father's, a fellow missionary in Africa. He came to me one night and . . . I'm not pure. Not without the sin of fornication. My father killed him. You should know."

Mercy touched at his heart. He held her hand, just for a moment, for the first time.

"That life is past. It was a long time ago. It was not your fault. Don't think about it anymore."

She looked so far away.

"It doesn't matter to me. Nobody's pure. My daughter, my Francesca was pure, but nobody else."

He passed her in the hall, they sat at dinner, and she was beautiful and unknowable. He wanted to lead her to his bed, his father's huge cherry bed with the massive carved headboard and the finely laid, perfectly crisp sheets. He wanted to pull back the coverlet and lay her gently against the cool and antiseptic white of the linen sheets, the sheets the machines in his mills wove all day long every day. He wanted with all his heart to stand in front of her as he pulled back his braces, undid in seconds the buttons and belts of his own clothes. He would lay his father's heavy silver watch on the nightstand. He would lie down beside her in his one-piece underwear, washed by Mrs. Larsen, changed every day, always clean, the buttons buttoned from crotch to neck.

Every piece of his clothing was always clean. He bathed every day before it was light, the water scalding, and the air in the room like a Turkish bath, thick with fragrant steam. He would stand in front of her and not think about how strong and solid his body had once been. He would not think about how he had thrown himself away on whores.

They would gasp, the whores, when they saw him naked. At the strength and grace of his body, a strength and grace even he could see, looking at himself naked in a long mirror. They would giggle with joy, and say things in Italian he could barely understand. That was a long time ago.

He looked at Catherine. He imagined her in bed. In his bed.

He wanted to hold her face until she finally raised her eyes to look at him. He wanted to look in her eyes and know who she was, who she was in her hidden soul. He wanted to kiss her with his hands on her cheeks. He wanted her to answer his kiss with an eager tongue. He wanted to feel the moment her hand moved beneath the cotton of his shirt and touched, for the very first time, the hair of his chest, the skin of his body. He wanted her to want all this and he wanted her to fear it, but he wanted her to submit.

Sometimes his loneliness was like a fire beneath his skin. Sometimes he had thought of taking his razor and slicing his own flesh, peeling back the skin that would not stop burning.

But he knew it would not happen, not happen to him, not ever.

"There's something I would like." She stared into the fire. It was the first, the only wish she had expressed.

"Of course."

"I want a wedding dress. I want to send to Chicago for some material and make a wedding dress. It's something girls dream of. I want a ring. Nothing large or fancy. My father told me I would never have one, and for that reason I want it. Not to spite him, but to say to myself that sometimes your little dreams come true, no matter what people tell you."

"I'll get whatever you want. I told you."

"You needn't worry. I don't expect much. Ours is an arrangement, yes? Not a childish passion. We both have reasons." And she smiled at him, the first time he had seen her smile. Her smile aroused in him a longing for something, the past perhaps, that brought him almost to tears.

"Gray, I thought. Silk, if . . . I could wear it again. After the wedding. Or I could give it to my daughter one day, if we were to have children."

"Order whatever you want. Write it down, and I'll telegraph for it tomorrow."

He thought of her standing in this house in a wedding dress she had made with her own hands. He thought of the mortal sins that raced through his bloodstream. He thought his desire had putrefied. He thought his desires would kill her. He thought, yes, they would have a child, and it would emerge, another monster.

He did not think of wanting the woman whose photograph lay in his drawer, along with the letter which Catherine may or may not have written. He wanted the woman he passed every day in the hallway, who sat across from him at dinner, who ate her food with such delicacy and charm, her small teeth sparkling, who never failed to ask Mrs. Larsen about some sauce or some ingredient he hadn't even tasted.

He wanted her teeth to bite him. To leave marks on his back, his legs. He wanted her hair to strangle him. He wanted her to tell him that his touch would not kill her.

He wanted to slice her open and lie inside the warm blood of her body.

He didn't touch alcohol. He didn't smoke. He didn't go to Chicago, as many would have, to have sex with women he didn't know. Not for a long time. None of it mattered. None of it did any good.

He wanted the moment at which he finally lay naked against her, chest to chest, her hands fluttering above his shoulders like white birds in the chill night, her frantic fingers threading invisible needles. He wanted to know that his desire was life, pure and clean and unformed and unbroken. Life as good as anybody else's. As clean as any ever known. Perfectly healthy.

In the end, such a simple thing.

In his fantasy, morning never came; they never woke to look at one another with shy eyes or bitter eyes in the blinding light. There was no tomorrow. There was only this moment, her hand sliding for the first time between his undershirt and his skin, his body sliding into the most private and untouchable parts, not just of her body but of her life, so that they were bonded together not just by the desire itself but by the burning, the ineradicable memory of the actual taste and smell of the flesh.

He remembered every woman he had ever touched. He had thought that he would forget, the way he forgot people's names or the grades he made at university or the faces of men he had gotten drunk with and told his secrets to. But the scenes of his sexual life came back to him more and more as his years in exile endured, so that he could recall their names, he could see their silken dresses and the diamonds hanging from their ears. He could remember the names of the jewelers from whom he bought these baubles for his little sweethearts.

He could lie in bed at night and see himself, as though he were a third person, making love to an English girl named Lady Lucy while his friend and roommate watched from across the room, too drunk to move or even be aroused. He could see Lucy's fingernails. He could feel her tongue on his feet. See the bow of her mouth as she slid him into her throat.

He could remember standing behind redheaded Sarah at a sink as she took a cloth and washed beneath her arms and between her legs, in a hotel room in Chicago, his kisses covering her thin and exhausted shoulder blades.

He thought of a widow in a neighboring state, a state where he often did business, a plain woman who had taken him into her bed, and submitted to him without a word, who arched her back with passion and spread her legs and opened every part of her body to him and put her tongue in his mouth and her mouth on his sex and then lay, afterward, wrapped around him, their mourning for everything they had given and lost like a blanket wrapped around their cooling sweat. They shivered in the dark.

When he left her, he had not even said good night. She had not even raised her head from where it lay in the crook of her elbow, her tears wetting the mangled pillow and her matted hair. He had left a red scarf hanging over the back of a green chair.

He had never gone back for it. His way had not taken him again to her house, nor had either of them imagined that it would. Love not worth even a scarf.

He remembered the insane trips he had taken to Chicago, after Emilia had left, to look for her and her lover. He knew then that it was not Emilia he looked for, that he wouldn't have had her back if she had crawled naked in the street and begged. He was just looking, looking for *it*, the crack between her legs, her black nipples in the dark. Her skin like oiled earth.

He passed Catherine in the hall. He watched her from an upstairs window as she wandered the road that led from the house, poking at the dirty snow with a stick, sometimes angrily, sometimes with the forlorn hopelessness of a child.

"What do you do? When you go out walking?"

"I just look."

"Have you lost something?"

"It doesn't matter. I just look."

Who was she? What did she think about all day, while he was at the office, his dark office in the iron foundry, pushing his goods around the country, digging deep into the earth to haul out its riches? Where did she go when she wandered away from the house after lunch, as he knew she did because Mrs. Larsen told him she did?

He wanted to touch her, to tear her clothes, and he did not. Instead, he gave her things. He sent for hothouse roses from Chicago that arrived blood red and sat in vases, roses that were named with the old names, French poets, English dukes. The roses, forced to lavish bloom under glass, gave no scent.

He sent for chocolates. He sent for marzipan in the shape of animals and flowers, candies for which she had no taste and which Mrs. Larsen slipped to her sweet-toothed husband in secret, until they were gone. He sent for bonnets she had no place to wear. He sent for music boxes, and sparkling ear bobs, which she would not put on. He sent for novels, and she read of the adventures of rakes half his age, of the despair of English girls wandering the moors looking for their dead lovers. He sent for a tiny bird, which sang her to sleep, which she allowed to fly at will around her room, the room he had slept in as a boy.

He would not allow her to leave the property. She had never seen the town. So, instead, he gave her trifles.

He had a taste, long suppressed, for the luxurious and the exquisite, and he knew how to pick a wine or a brooch or a bolt of silk. These things were like a memory in his flesh. The superb. The intoxicating. Every day he arrived home with something in his hand for her, little, expensive gifts that she accepted shyly, with a slight surprise. She had, he knew, no place to wear them, no place to put them.

These things, these ribbons and all this rigmarole, were his way of touching her. These things, out of season, unattainable, reserved for the few, for the rich and decadent, passed from his hand into hers every day. "Oh," she said, drawing in her breath. "Oh, Mr. Truitt, how beautiful."

He could feel the simplicity of his life fading away, like a drunk long sober about to take his first taste of brandy.

Love drove people crazy. He saw it every day. He read it every week in the paper. Every week the papers were filled with the barn burnings, the arsenic taken, the babies drowned in wells to keep their names a secret, to keep their fathers away from them, to keep them from knowing the craziness of love. To send them home to the holiness of God. He read these stories aloud to Catherine at night, after supper, and she would invent stories about the sad women and the deranged men. She would say their names over and over, until even their names became a kind of derangement.

"Why do they do it, Mr. Truitt? Why are they so sad and affected by . . . ?"

"Long winters. Religion."

"Will it happen to us, then?"

"No."

She wanted to go to town, of course. Anybody would, to walk the streets, to spot the ordinary woman who next week might drown her children, the wearied worker who would slaughter forty head of his own cattle in a single night. He would not let her go to town, even though people already knew she was in his house. *Finally,* they thought.

If love drove people mad, what would lack of love do? It would, thought Ralph, produce me. It has. His hand would reach into his pocket as she spun her stories. He would touch, lightly, the length of his own sex.

But still he did not touch her. He separated his desire for her, for any and every woman, from her actual physical self. He kept his distance. He knew neither how to love nor how to desire, in any real way. He had lost the habit of romance.

But he lay in bed every night, the sheets clean and smelling of crisp winter nights, and he thought of her, in her room down the hall. He pictured, like pornographic etchings, the hidden parts of her body. He did not touch himself. He couldn't bear it. A grown man. A man who was almost old, the stupidity of it, and her just down the hall.

His sins lay not in acrobatic visions of penetrations and humiliations. His perversion was silence. Silence and distance.

He lay, straight and sober in his bed and thought of Lady Lucy Berridge in Florence thirty years before, her aristocratic vagaries and titillations. Sooner or later, in the dark, Lucy's face, or Serafina's or even Emilia's, always turned into Catherine's. Catherine laughing at him.

He wondered, in the dark, in the latest hours, whether she thought of him in return, just down the hall, so clean, so rich, so polite. But she did not. He never crossed her mind.

She lay, Catherine, in a clean, simple nightdress, her eyes to the blinding moon and the drifting snow, and she dreamed of cigarettes. She dreamed about smoking cigarettes and about the body of a worthless man who lay next to some other woman in some other bed, in tangled sheets in a rotten town, miles and miles and miles away.

CHAPTER NINE

H E GAVE HER A DIAMOND RING. It was large and yellow, surrounded by smaller diamonds like a glittering
daisy. He kissed her hand.

He gave her a gold cross on a fine gold chain. He brushed away
the wisps of her hair and fastened it around her neck.

She thought of her pathetic baubles, buried in the snow, her
ticket to freedom. They seemed inconsequential now.

Men only give you what they give you, Catherine thought, staring out at the endless and uncontrollable snow, when they know
they can't give you what you want.

What she wanted, of course, was a quick marriage to Ralph
Truitt, followed by his painless demise. What she wanted was both
love and money, and she was not to have either except through
Ralph, except, in fact, *after* Ralph. What she wanted was some
control in her life, to get her meaningless little jewels back, something that was her own, the sparkle of her old life, to sleep once
again with her faithless lover, far away. She had had a lifetime of

filthiness and vileness and lust. What she longed for, in her heart, to her surprise, was a springtime as lush and erotic as the winter was chaste and bloodless.

The light bothered her eyes and gave her headaches that would rage fiercely for days. She had fair eyes, like her father.

"I would like some dark glasses for the sun."

"Don't you think that's odd?"

"The light hurts my eyes."

"Don't look out the windows."

"It's all there is to do."

He got smoked glasses for her, and she wore them in the house during the day. Like a blind person, she stared out into the white blank canvas that was her only pastime. She could see rabbits, frozen in the snow. She could watch the crows that descended to pick at the flesh. She could watch Larsen as he watched her staring out the window. With the glasses, the whiteness had detail. With the glasses, no one could see the glitter in her eyes.

Her package arrived from Chicago. Twelve yards of dove gray raw silk. A paper pattern. Ralph gave her the exquisite diamond ring, and the cross, which he swore had not come from his first wife. Ralph gave her a trip to see the house. The real house.

She had had presents before, of course. Funhouse bijoux, carny sparkles boys had given her even when they knew they would not walk with her beyond the limits of the fairground. But this, this was different. It was not, in the first place, a present in the actual sense, since he would not give it to her. He was merely letting her see it. He was merely letting her know that it would, in fact, be her future home, once she had done as he asked, married him and brought his lost boy home.

Yet it was a gift, she supposed, watching the house rise out of the landscape's interminable sameness, watching it take shape before her. It was his best hope he was giving her. It was his folly and his disastrous failure. It was the house he had built hoping his heart would find a home there, and it had not worked, and he had been shamed there, and humiliated. Still, he was showing it to her, knowing that he was showing her also his heart, and that was, after all, the one gift that no one had ever given her.

They crossed a field and through a wood, and entered into a long sloping rise, and the house began to appear before them.

It was splendid. It stood square and golden and massive and beautiful, and Catherine's heart took flight when she saw it. She had never seen anything like it, so alone in the vast wilderness, so regal in the midst of such ordinary land.

It took everything in her to remain calm, to rest her hands quietly on the heavy wool throw, to wait until the horse had stopped before descending from the sleigh. But it was her heart's delight, the first wonderment she had felt for so many years.

They walked up one side of the broad double staircase that led to the massive double door. Truitt pointed out a painting over the door which showed, she supposed, the villa as it must look in summer, with its orchards and its gardens and it pools and its broad long lawns leading down to the pond and the river beyond.

The doors were unlocked and swung open easily, and they walked into a broad, high central hall. Catherine couldn't stop herself. She gasped. It was so lovely, lovely despite its grandeur and its size. The ceilings were frescoed with adorable babies with wings and flowers in their hair. The room was lit by two colored glass chandeliers that hung from yellow velvet cords, each prism a different jewel, each ray of light a different soft color. From Venice, he said. They had been lowered and lit for her, ablaze with flame for their arrival. They were crystal flowers, hanging in the air, flowers that gave light.

The walls were covered in rose silk. Portraits, too many to count, looked down. The floor was marbled and patterned, covered in rich old rugs. The sofas along the sides of the hall were large and gilded. Countesses had walked here. Dukes had read poetry on the sofas. The high windows dazzled the room with light.

On either side, more massive rooms. He showed her everything, with the same slow disinterest. There was a ballroom, a music room, a library, a dining room where thirty people could have dinner. There was a glass conservatory where exotic plants once grew, orchids and palms. There were sitting rooms in many colors, filled with rich old furniture. One room was all pale yellow, like butter. One was turquoise, one green. One was trellised, painted with vines and flowers. The windows gave out onto the same interminable whiteness, but inside, everything was warm and golden.

"It's always heated. Mrs. Larsen comes over to clean. I haven't been here for years." Truitt seemed to feel nothing. He was the tour guide, pointing out a picture here or a table there, things that even still had special meaning for him.

Upstairs, nine massive bedrooms, each a different color, each warm and rich beyond anything Catherine had ever seen. The beds swagged and ribboned, the sheets laid perfectly, as though important guests would arrive at any moment.

"This was her room." It was a sumptuous, royal blue. A sitting room and a dressing room were attached to it. Her comb and brush were still on the dressing table. A cut crystal bottle was still filled with amber perfume. "And this was Franny's room." He stood at the door but wouldn't go in. They hung back and looked at the tiny bed, fancy enough for a princess, and the child's furniture and the gay curtains. A rocking horse stood beneath one of the high windows.

"She would ride for hours, back and forth. Back and forth, laughing. God, she was a delight." The slightest catch in his voice was the only emotion. "She died in that bed. I sat by her, night and day."

It was as though the child would walk into the room the next minute, pick up one of the dolls laid neatly in a row on the bed, each with its fixed expression of innocent bliss. Catherine wanted to pick one up, but she didn't go in. She couldn't. Mixed with the odor of childhood still hanging in the air was the sharp smell of death, and grief, a smell too familiar to her. The last of childhood. The end of purity.

They saw it all. Antonio's room. The guest rooms, the servants' hall, the kitchen with copper pots by the dozen gleaming on stone walls.

At the back of the house, outside, was a walled enclosure, visible from the window of Emilia's room, and from the broad hallway.

"Her secret garden. Giardino segreto. Italian foolishness. She would grow flowers there, roses and things. She said every Italian house had one, and she brought gardeners from Italy to tend it. She had trees that twined around each other, white flowers that, in the night, smelled like a woman's perfume. The small house, just there, that's where she grew lemons and oranges.

"Except it never worked. The summer is too short and she could never plant the right things. The gardeners were fools, used to a different climate, I guess. The lemons died. The flowers never came up, frozen in the ground. She sent for hothouse flowers, put them in the ground where they died. The Italians couldn't do a thing. Useless and stupid. It was an idea. It didn't work."

When they had seen it all, Catherine outwardly as sober and unmoved as Truitt himself, they went home. Home to the small ordinary house decked out with the fantastic leavings of the more fantastic empire.

Catherine dreamed of the house. She saw herself walking its broad halls, sweeping in gowns of silk and lace and embroidery down its wide marble stairs. She imagined herself mistress of the house.

Catherine began to go there every other day. When Mrs. Larsen went to clean, when Truitt was away at business, she would go and sit in every room, play the long untuned piano in the ballroom, look through the drawers and the closets. She spent whole afternoons staring at the enclosed white of the secret garden, imagining it fragrant with lemons and lilies, alive in the sunlight of August. It was a place for lovers' secret whisperings. It was in the world, but away from it, like the heart.

It was as he had said. Everything was still there. In Francesca's room, she opened the closet to stare at the tiny dresses. She touched one and felt its silken whisper in her hands.

"Her mother had a dress made for the child to match every dress she had for herself. Even made little copies for the dolls. They look old-fashioned now, but you can tell. Still. It was senseless." Mrs. Larsen was enraged by the idiocy of it. "Look at them. Are these for a child? A child who couldn't dress herself, couldn't feed herself, couldn't do anything but look with that little smile on her face? Look at this."

She pulled from the rack a white linen shift, simple and graceful.

There were words embroidered on the front of the dress, foreign words.

"She couldn't even say her own prayers. So her mother had this made, with prayers in Italian embroidered down the front. 'So she'll sleep with God.' That's exactly what she said. Franny was like a puppet to her mother, a mindless puppet. But she had a heart. She loved her rocking horse, she loved to be held, she loved to hear a man's voice singing. She didn't have the brain God gave a baby. But she was a person. A whole person. It broke his heart when she died. It broke his heart when she was alive. Like it was his fault."

"It wasn't his fault. Surely not."

"It was that woman. Was me, I'd rip every one of these dresses out of here. Make a fire. It's sad, but the child is dead. They're all dead."

"Not the son. He says. Truitt says."

"If you ask me, he's dead, too, Antonio. Dead or useless as his mother. All this chasing around, it's not going to get Truitt anything."

Catherine didn't tell Truitt she went to the house. She didn't tell Truitt she wore his wife's pearls, stuck diamond bows in her hair. She didn't tell him that she tried on the old-fashioned dresses, even though they were too small, sweeping the carpeted floor with the sweet whoosh of ruffled silk. She didn't tell him she spent long afternoons in the library, reading the romances and the plays and the poets. Mrs. Larsen kept her secret, she supposed, because life went on as before. Because she hoped for Truitt's happiness.

They ate dinner. He read to her from the newspaper the accounts of madness and true crimes, committed by people he knew. She read to him from his beloved Walt Whitman, seemingly the only thing he read. She read to him Whitman's vast throbbing hopeful despairing panorama of America, the unparticular passion for every living thing.

"Be not disheartened," she read. "Affection shall solve the problems of freedom yet / Those who love each other shall become invincible."

She didn't love Truitt, and every night the blue bottle came out from her suitcase; rage infused her as she held it in her hand. The blue bottle fueled her; it was her simple, her only plan. The house would be hers. The pearls, the books and pictures, the fancy rugs from India and the East, and Truitt would be hers, too. But there would be no affection, no ambling toward a sweet old age. One drop. Two drops. That was the future.

She roamed the rooms in secret, she wandered the secret garden, up to her knees in snow, the drifts in the corners over her head, while Mrs. Larsen scoured the copper pots and shook the dust from the heavy brocaded curtains. And all the while she did not forget. Her rage never decreased. The blue bottle was her defense, her key to the infinite splendor, the drowsy magnificence of the house itself.

She sewed her gray silk dress, according to an innocuous pattern picked from a ladies' book. She felt foolish when she looked in the mirror, as though she didn't remember what she was dressing for. The days crawled by. The snow never stopped falling.

They were married by a judge, in the living room of the farmhouse. A noonday fire burned in the fireplace. The weather cleared for the day, and two carriages stood in the yard. Two couples watched silently as they said the words. They signed their names as witnesses in the judge's book. They joined them for lunch and went away. They might as well have been strangers.

Ralph Truitt never looked at her. She was only the first step. She herself was unimportant, inconsequential to him now. That she was beautiful was both an attraction and an irritation, a detail of her usefulness. He would have his son back.

The afternoon was endless. They were both awkward. It seemed they were strangers. They didn't speak. Catherine tried to play the piano but found she was so exhausted she could barely move her fingers. The yellow diamond sparkled on her finger, the first spoils of her larceny. Ralph read by the fire, awkward in his wedding clothes. The house was cold. The sun shone off the snow. Truitt stared into the endless landscape as the light faded. They picked at supper, served by a silent Mrs. Larsen. Then they went upstairs and went to bed together.

"You'll have to help me. I'm not . . ."

He didn't, couldn't, hear her. She lay very still in his father's bed, and he entered her and almost believed she was a virgin.

She was his, she was vast, she was an empire of smells and surfaces and small sighs.

She was his wife. He touched her with his hands; he kissed her with his tongue, and she moved under him as gentle as water, as warm as a bath. The first touch of her naked skin made him gasp with all that he remembered and had denied himself for so many years.

At every moment, he asked her permission to advance, and she shyly whispered yes in his ear. He had actually forgotten the depth and intricacy of his own passion, and it flooded him with warmth and kindness.

Catherine fought her own desires. She forgot her many expert enticements. This was not about her, and that was, for once, a relief. She remembered that she was playing a part, and she played it well.

She had become used to being the woman that men wanted, and she knew that Ralph wanted to begin again, to begin with a woman who was naive and shy and giving only in small, discreet ways, and she did it well, so well that she believed her own lie. He was not the first man who wanted his own desire to be central, who thought little of her except as a necessary part of his own blind groping. She became the thing he wanted, and was surprised that she, in some way, wanted it, too.

His warmth flooded her. His mastery of the ways and manipulations of love excited her. She had expected, even after his story of youthful excess, to be bored, as bored as she always was, but the textures of his body were rich and varied and exciting in ways she felt without thought. She knew that, for now, her simplicity excited him, made him believe that he was young again, all the sweetness, the charm of blind affection at his command.

He was safety. He was security. He was more passionate and kind than she had imagined he would be, and she felt, somehow, that she was losing her footing, losing her way in the dark room under his hot hands. She must not forget. She fought against forgetfulness. She fought the desire to take his hand and kiss the palm, to skim his flesh with her tongue.

They made love every night. She no longer took the blue bottle from her suitcase, to hold it in her hand, to watch the thin liquid glitter through the cobalt. She didn't forget; she delayed.

The days seemed endless, the dinners a torture of manners and appetite suppressed. Mrs. Larsen would not look them in the eye. After dinner they went upstairs, and she went to him naked from her room and lay beside him in his father's bed. Every night they created movement and desire out of nothing but the necessities of flesh. He found her mouth and kissed her sometimes until she couldn't remember her own name; sometimes he just kissed her, and then moved his head and slept on her shoulder.

He didn't speak to her anymore of his sorrows. He rarely spoke at all, as though the sexuality between them was all the conversation they needed. She tried to tell him the story she had carefully invented of her childhood. She tried to describe the horror of her molestation, the details of missionary life on other continents, all details learned from books in the library. He was sympathetic, but hushed her with his hand softly on her mouth.

He wanted a child. He longed for grandchildren, to dandle on his knee.

Little by little, with imperceptible manipulations, she became more expert, more adept at knowing what would please him. Sometimes in the night, while Ralph slept and she stared at the ceiling, she wondered whether she didn't already have the thing she had set out to get. The love and wealth of a man who would not harm her. A man she found herself unable to find comical.

He clearly loved her. Or, if he didn't love her, he was obsessed by her. He would allow her to have whatever she wanted. She felt herself wavering, as though a new landscape were opening before her, as though she was too exhausted from the nights of passion to focus her thoughts. The blue bottle lay in her suitcase, and sometimes she willed herself to forget it was there.

She went to town. It was very ordinary, a mud track through a short stretch of dry goods stores and hardware stores and butchers and barbers. The meat looked sad and dry in the dirty windows. The people nodded at her with curiosity and thinly veiled disdain. She wore her hair more gracefully around her face. She met the Swensons and the Carllsons and the Magnussons. She looked for the insanity she read about in the papers. She found none. She looked for beauty and found little to interest her, except the untouched faces of the children. She looked for sophisticated pleasures, but there seemed to be few pleasures of any kind. Still, she wasn't bored. She wasn't restless. Every day, she waited for the time to pass. She waited for Ralph to come home.

She was dazed by the way he looked without his clothes. She was entranced by the way his hand never left her cheek as he made love to her, caressing her the way he might gentle a wild horse.

They forgot conversation. She played the piano for him, the pieces he liked, the pieces he never tired of hearing. She read Whitman to him, the electric, wounded, fruitful country spread before them, the elasticity of desire. It was all a prelude to what happened in the dark, by candlelight, in Ralph's father's bed.

On New Year's Day, in her gray silk wedding dress and her dark glasses, she boarded the train once again. The blue bottle was still in her suitcase. It waited like a serpent. The snowdrifts were as high as a strong man's shoulders. Ralph Truitt stared at her through the window, searching for her hidden eyes. He did not wave as the train pulled away.

✳ *Part Two* ✳

SAINT LOUIS. WINTER. 1908.

CHAPTER TEN

—◦◦◦—

THE CITY ENTERED HER like music, like a wild symphony. The train pulled into Union Station, that giant garish château, and she stepped from Truitt's railroad car into the largest train station in the world as though her skin were on fire.

The station smelled of beef and newsprint, of beer and iron. She had been away from this for too long. She had been in the wild white country, and her heart burned with the adventures, the friends, the food and drink, the multiplicity of event the city promised. People came here to be bad. People came here to do the things they couldn't do at home. Smoke cigarettes. Have sex. Make their way in the world.

Mrs. Larsen was to have come with her, but Larsen had burned his hand badly the day before, so Catherine came alone.

She arrived in Saint Louis with a letter of credit at a bank and a room already reserved for her at the new Planter's Hotel. It was a fine room on the sixth floor, with an austere bedroom and a small sitting room filled with mohair-covered furniture in dark colors,

with elaborately swagged velvet curtains and a small fireplace. A
fine room. Not the grandest room — Truitt would never have done
that — just adequate, and she imagined the splendor of the suites
on the upper floors, all flocked wallpaper and chandeliers and big
plants in Chinese pots; cattle barons and oil barons and beer kings,
men with money alone in hotel rooms, men who looked at city
women in a certain way, wanted certain illicit things and were willing to pay for them, and she would have moved herself and her few
belongings to something more grand, with a marble bathroom and
real paintings, but she wanted to play it out, play it right, so she sat
in her room and waited for the visit of Mr. Malloy and Mr. Fisk,
the Pinkerton agents Truitt had hired to find his dissolute, prodigal, intractable son.

She felt that she was being watched herself, so that reports might
be sent to Truitt about who this Catherine Land was when she was
away from the white wilderness. She was careful to reveal nothing,
although she didn't know whether eyes were on her or not.

The bank manager smiled and immediately gave her whatever
she asked for. He asked after Mr. Truitt's health. He offered her
tea. She never asked for too much money, never an amount that
would have been questionable. She went shopping so that she might
look more like the ladies she saw taking tea and gossiping in quiet,
birdlike voices in the hotel lobby. With Truitt's money, she walked
into Scruggs, Vandervoort and Barney, Saint Louis's largest and
finest store, aisle after modern aisle of finery and foolishness, and
she walked in with a sense of power she had never felt before. Anything could be hers. She had only to lay the hand with the yellow
diamond on any of the dozens of counters, an obsequious salesper-
son would instantaneously appear, and anything inside the display

case could belong to her. Anything that caught her fancy, even for a moment. But instead of indulging herself, she held her old hungers in check and asked only for things she needed to play a part she'd never played before.

She bought dresses for the city, simple dresses, small hats, fine and expensive, but demure. She bought a black karakul coat with a mink collar, extravagant for the country, but ubiquitously proper and anonymous in Saint Louis. She wore black kid gloves on the street. She wore white cotton gloves to take tea in the lobby, like the other ladies. She observed the women in the hotel dining room and tried to dress and behave and smile the way they did. They were all calm and glitter.

She wore her quiet dresses and her smart fur coat as she walked in the evening through the early dark and the light snow along Broadway with its halo of gas lamps, its arch that showed a portrait of every president. There were trolleys and horses, wagons filled with barrels of beer and enough automobiles to turn Truitt's foolish pride to embarrassment. In Saint Louis, Truitt would be one of hundreds of men just like him. Rich men.

She passed the fruit markets, filled with bright vegetables even in winter, and the vendors, their heads wrapped in kerchiefs against the cold, their hands in fingerless gloves, hawking their wares in German and Italian accents, assisted by wretched children in hand-me-down cotton dresses in the middle of winter. She walked without pity through the sea of destitution that washed over her.

In the country, there was insanity. There were fires and burnings and murders and rapes, unthinkable cruelties, usually committed by people against people they knew. It was at least personal. Here there was the heartless, sane, anonymous whir of the desolate modern machinery, the wheels and cogs, cold iron from Truitt's foundry. Here there was appalling poverty and gracelessness. She gave coins to the children. She couldn't look at the mothers.

She walked through the buildings and monumental statues that were left from the Great Exposition, the museum, the Japanese exhibit hall, filled with hundreds of small and delicate objects of impossible artistry and with kimonos that looked like elaborately embroidered dressing gowns, heavy and opulent.

She went to the Odeon, to the symphony, sitting alone in a box and attracting no attention. She didn't know the composers; she just liked the sweet majesty of the noise. She liked watching the crowd from above. She wore no jewelry, carried no fan. She did nothing to attract attention.

She walked through the streets at evening, hearing the music from the beer halls as the doors swung open and shut, the gay waltzes and polkas played on rattly old pianos, the laughing men and women coming and going from their pleasures. She never went in. She never thought of buying other dresses, more ostentatious, more vulgar, and joining in the laughing crowds, of being one of the laughing women. She missed her small jewels, which she might have worn, at the neck, at the wrists and ears. She might have worn perfume, scented the air as she walked. She imagined the taste of beer at the back of her throat, but found that, in fact, she didn't miss it. She thought of cigarettes, but the thought seemed far away, without magnetism. She imagined sitting with lidded eyes and hearing some tacky Negro musician play the piano and sing low down and dirty. She passed through the cold streets as inconspicuously as any other well-to-do married woman, and she was happy in her anonymity.

She ate alone in the hotel dining room, bearing the humiliation of solitude with good grace, reading Jane Austen as she waited to be served. The food was delicious, although not as good as Mrs. Larsen's, but rich and heavy so that she felt drowsy and light-headed. She ate oysters and beef and vegetables and large pale fish brought fresh from Chicago or even New York. She had dishes with French names she couldn't pronounce or understand, so that the waiter had to stand over her and patiently explain how each one was made.

In the mornings she spent long hours making herself ready for the day, deciding which of her new dresses to wear, fixing her hair in a way that was neither severe nor ostentatious. She was like an actress preparing to go on stage, and not one detail of her performance escaped her. She was used to watching everything, she needed to know what was going on around her, and she copied the manners of her fellow travelers exactly. She fastidiously pulled every hair from her hairbrush. She spoke in soft, kindly tones to the maids who came to clean and dust her room so that every day it seemed brand new.

And she thought of Truitt, of his simplicity and trust. And, oddly, she thought of his body, and the nights they had spent together. His body was not young, but richly scented and textured, and somehow familiar to her. His was a body of size without menace. He had never caused her pain. She wasn't sure the nights had been a pleasure to her, she wasn't sure she knew what pleasure was anymore, but she knew they had been something to Truitt, some kind of release from his private agony, the opening of a window kept shut for too long. A homecoming. And, as always when she had given pleasure, she was happy to have given it. She knew the cost of solace in this world. She knew its rarity.

Truitt was only the gate she had to pass through on the way to where she was going, but she was pleased that he had turned out

not to be fat or loathsome, or cruel and tyrannical, or simply ignorant, traits shared by almost every other man she had ever known.

She didn't know what she was supposed to feel for him, or even
what she was supposed to do now. She was his wife, his legal wife.
He was rich beyond her imagination. She knew the end of the
story. She knew that Truitt didn't appear in it. But she was growing foggy on how to get there, to get to the end and her rich and
spectacular reward. She forgot sometimes that she was working.
She was working a scheme the rules of which seemed no longer
clear to her.

She felt almost as though finally she were simply living life as
other people lived it, moving from event to event in a kind of haze,
a sort of questionless acceptance of the way things were. She was
surprised to find how easily it came to her. She was surprised to
find it such a relief.

She spent her afternoons in the public library, its high windows
slanting the pale thin winter light down on the long tables where
men and women, ladies and gentlemen, the latter mostly young and
handsome with glossy hair and ruddy cheeks, sat and passed an
afternoon reading novels or the newspaper, or seriously researching
things with maps and biographies and dictionaries. She liked these
people. She sat among them as one of them, a stranger to them as
they were to one another, and she was happy.

She read about plants. She read Edith Wharton about the endless verdure and pleasure of the Italian gardens and the villas to
which they belonged. "There is, none the less, much to be learned
from the old Italian gardens, and the first lesson is that, if they are
to be a real inspiration, they must be copied, not in the letter but
the spirit." She read about the singing fountains of Gamberaia, of
Petraia with its immense loggia, and the long lawns and high com-

forts of I Mansi and I Tati, and the streets of Florence and Lucca. She read about garden statuary, the grotesque and the mythical.

She imagined the secret garden, the lemon house, and in her imagination she saw them growing again, fragrant in the evening and in the day a barrage of color and foliage. She read about the hellebores, which burst with blossom through the late winter snows, the foxgloves and delphinium and the old Bourbon roses. She read about heliotrope and amaranthus and lilies. She read about the hostas that thrived in shade, and the Japanese painted fern, its delicate leaves fringed with indigo brush strokes. She said the names over and over, cataloging them: calendula, coleus, and coreopsis. She was enchanted.

She read books and catalogs about preparing the soil, how to triple dig a garden until the dirt was as fine and granular as sand, about how to enrich the soil with manure and mulch. It was not as poetic as the descriptions of the flowers, but in a way it was more exciting to her. She loved the details of things, the technique.

She was just another married woman reading about gardening. Her black kid gloves and purse lay on the long oak table beside her, the high light and the brass reading lamps making the pages bright with reflection.

She had the librarians bring her gigantic books of botanical illustrations, hand-colored etchings showing the plants she read about, and she memorized what she saw, stamen and pistil and petal and leaf. She had the beginning of an idea. It was an idea that seemed so comforting to her, so small and simple and comforting, to restore the walled secret garden, to watch it grow and make it her own. A place where she would be safe, where the world would be locked out. Giardino segreto, she repeated over and over. She liked secrets.

Her mind was on fire, and she returned to the hotel at night to lie in her narrow bed in the fresh white sheets, and she could see it; she could see clearly how it would turn out, once she learned, not just to picture it in her mind, but to make it come true with her hands. It was the first thing she had loved for as long as she could remember.

The first thing she had loved in her whole life, since the day in the carriage with her mother and the young soldiers and the rainbow. Finally she had seen the pot of gold they promised her, long ago, and now she would have it, whatever happened. She had almost forgotten about Mr. Malloy and Mr. Fisk.

And then they appeared. One afternoon when she happened to be in her room a meek porter brought a card. And then Mr. Malloy and Mr. Fisk were sitting in her small sitting room, holding their brown hats in their hands. They were of almost identical size and could have been brothers. Mr. Fisk was ruddy in the face, and Mr. Malloy was pale as winter, but both had the same steady blue eyes, and both wore brown suits of anonymous cut and color.

She offered them coffee. She offered them tea. They declined. She almost offered them a glass of beer, which they might have liked—everybody in Saint Louis seemed to drink beer all the time—but she felt it would have been out of character for her, and they might have relayed the information to Truitt.

They opened their identical little notebooks and began to reel off the details. He called himself Tony Moretti. A ridiculously thin pseudonym. His real name, of course, his true father's name, was Moretti. His given name, his legal name, was Antonio Truitt. Truitt, however, was almost certainly not his father. He had told people his father was a famous Italian pianist. Black hair. Olive skin. Over six feet tall. His shoe size. His preference in shirts. His taste in music. His disastrous fondness for women — this embarrassed them almost into silence. The drinking. The opium. His spendthrift ways with the little money he had. They had missed nothing.

He played the piano in a music hall frequented by ladies of the night, they said, ladies of the demimonde, and gamblers, probably one of the music halls she had passed. He played light classics and popular ditties, and sang sentimental songs of the moment, some in Italian, a language he seemed not to know. He didn't sing well, they said. He wasn't Caruso.

He had traveled around. He traveled the country, from San Francisco to New York, always the same, sometimes a different name, playing the piano, lazing the midnights away in whorehouses, opium dens. And each town had gone sour, each town finally had enough of Tony Moretti and he moved on.

That's why they had a hard time finding him. That's why several times they had found the wrong man. Each time they found that Mr. Moretti had just left the room, leaving only a shadow that resembled him.

"How long have you looked for him? Have you followed him from town to town?"

"Only two months, and only in Saint Louis. Speaking for Mr. Fisk and myself. Other operatives, detectives, in other cities."

They, in this case, meant anonymous men like Mr. Malloy and Mr. Fisk. The man they had found may or may not have been the man other investigators had tracked in San Francisco, or New York, or Austin, passing the information along to the home office, which sent it on to Truitt.

"He's not a good man, Mrs. Truitt." Mr. Fisk held his notebook open in his hand, as though he had recorded even the points of the conversation so that he might speak clearly, like a telegraph, not a word wasted. "He's not kind, or good, or particularly talented. He's lazy. He's dissolute. He's illegitimate."

"You perhaps set high standards for moral character. Modern people, I'm sure . . ."

"I'm afraid that is not the case, in this instance." Mr. Malloy looked at her with a seriousness that lacked the slightest trace of humor. "He's as worthless as a puppet. An exotic toy."

She was careful to make only the smallest gestures, not to show surprise at the catalog of Truitt's son's lurid life.

"He is my husband's son."

"*If* he is, you mean, Mrs. Truitt. Unlikely." As though she herself were somehow not quite legitimate. She stared at him with what she hoped was disdain. Mr. Fisk looked back down at his notebook.

Mr. Malloy paused a long time before speaking again. "Sometimes, Mrs. Truitt, we work very hard at something, we exhaust ourselves to accomplish something which seems vital to us." He chose his words with care. "Our best hope for happiness. And sometimes we find that thing, only to find it has simply not been worth the effort."

"Mr. Malloy. That is not our choice. It is my husband's wish. He is my husband's son. You're sure?"

Mr. Fisk wiped Mr. Malloy's slate clean. "He is. Tony Moretti is at least Ralph Truitt's wife's son. We have found him, Mrs. Truitt."

"I want to see him."

"And you will. We will go to his rooms."

"I want to see him before he sees me. I want to observe him anonymously, across a room, in the street. I want to measure the son against the father."

"The place he plays his music, this music hall, would not be suitable."

She had not thought. Had not thought that far. "That much is clear."

"There is a restaurant. It is frequented by the proper sort of people. You would not be ashamed. Not feel awkward. He goes there, in the evenings, before he goes to work, if that's what he calls it, to eat oysters and drink champagne. It is seemingly all he ever consumes."

"Then we will go there."

Mr. Malloy and Mr. Fisk waited, as though there were more to say. There was not a speck of dust in the room. It was a fine room, not the best, but fine. It was the sort of room in which she might have served coffee or tea, dressed for dinner or the theater, might have kept a canary, if she had lived there, but she didn't live there and no bird sang.

Mr. Fisk and Mr. Malloy waited.

"We will go there tomorrow night."

CHAPTER ELEVEN

———❦———

THERE WERE HYACINTHS, so brief and heavy with peppery scent. Jonquils. Campanula. Dianthus. There was allium, the French onion with its pendulous purple bloom, impossibly heavy, and lilac with its wafting fragrance, and violets, which young girls received as nosegays from their beaux. And the ornamental herbs, rosemary and sage.

There were tulips, which had once driven men mad with their beauty. So delicate, so rare and brief. She read about the sultan, in Istanbul, who had grown over a hundred thousand tulips, brought as favors from the wild steppes of the East. Every spring, he would have an evening party to show them off. Tulips, she read, the ones that are fragrant, are fragrant only at night. Candles would be fixed to the backs of turtles, and the turtles would crawl among the flowers, as the courtiers strolled in their jeweled clothing, whispering amidst the beauty and the impossibly delicate scent, just a hint of fragrance from the East. Catherine could see their jewelry and diadems, their clothes of the thinnest silk, could hear the murmur of pleasure, their quiet singsong voices as they floated through the flickering beauty, drinking cool minted fruit juices.

It takes seven years for a seed to turn into a tulip bulb. She wondered if the turtles that carried the candles were hurt.

There were hydrangeas, which the Italians grew in giant terracotta pots, hydrangeas which change color with the chemistry of the soil. Acid soil would produce blooms of Prussian blue. Alkaline would turn the blooms to pink, a rose that matched the ridiculous extremes of the setting sun.

Anyone can learn. Anyone can read and learn. The hard thing is to do, to act—to speak French, to go to Africa, or to poison an enemy, to plant a garden. Catherine absorbed her hours in learning, waiting for Mr. Malloy and Mr. Fisk, expanding her knowledge and perfecting her scheme, though she hardly knew anymore what her scheme was exactly. A son. The son. The son, obviously, of a harlot and a piano teacher. And Truitt, she was sure, knew this, had known it from the beginning. This extraordinary wish of Truitt's to bring him home and make him heir to all that Truitt possessed. So much. What if he should come? Yes, her blue bottle with its subtle secret medicine was hidden deep in her luggage, shining in her mind with its deep clear cobalt. But to commit such an act under the eyes of another, of a son, the risk would be too great. She couldn't inherit everything with a son in the picture. She was beginning to think she couldn't inherit anything with so little work. It should be harder. It should not fall into your lap easily. Catherine had never once in her life been confused. Now she sat and waited for her plan to grow clear once again, clear and hard and bright.

She wore a stiff black skirt and a short black jacket. She wore a hat with a veil. Although there was no reason to go anonymously, she wanted a screen between her and the man she had waited so patiently to see. She felt a deep and complex anxiety, caught as she was between her own desires and the needs of Truitt to restore some dream which would never again be made whole, no matter what. Before Fisk and Malloy arrived to call for her, she ordered a sherry, and drank it back fast, feeling the warmth and calm begin to pervade her body. She felt an almost erotic thrill, the old taste, the warmth, and she wanted another, wanted another and another, but she washed the glass and rinsed her mouth carefully until there was no trace left, and waited for the sunset.

They were unaccountably late. She walked her rooms; she tried on her hat and felt the fabric of her fine dresses. What was beneath her hands was sure to her, the things she could feel would not betray her. She sat and waited. Her gardening books, delivered to the hotel in brown paper packets from the booksellers, lay open on the table in front of the window. The illustrations calmed her, the dream of Italy.

They arrived with the dark, awkward and alert. She put on her hat and walked the streets of Saint Louis with her two watchdogs, until they came to a restaurant advertising beef and fresh oysters, lit from within by the warmth of gaslight, the sort of place with sawdust on the floor and portly waiters with long white aprons wrapped around their waists. They sat and ordered small steaks. Mr. Malloy and Mr. Fisk refused drink, and put their notebooks on the table.

He came in at seven, dressed in fine clothes, cleanly cut, spotless, carrying a walking stick and an air of insolence and familiarity. Everything about him looked clean. He had an aura of ownership that impressed her enormously. He sat without being shown to a table, and the waiters brought him oysters and champagne before he had settled in his seat.

He ate the oysters as though each were its own specific moment in time. His face and his long black hair were luxurious, there was no other word for it, and Catherine peered at him through the haze of her veil, noting every detail, the way his hair lapped over his collar as he tilted his head back to down an oyster, the way his head bowed forward into his champagne, the way his eyes closed as the liquor washed down his throat, his lashes impossibly long, like a woman's. A lock of hair fell into his eyes, and he tossed back his head. His shirtfront was sparkling, his tie of an exquisite dark silk, and he looked both artistic and antique. He was handsome, handsome in ways Malloy and Fisk would never have noted in their little notebooks, handsome in a way that could cause a woman to gasp. He was beautiful without being at all feminine, and his long strong hands hovered like great agitated birds over his food.

There was no resemblance between the son and the father. But of course, she remembered, Truitt was almost certainly not the father. Truitt was quintessentially American, good-looking without being extreme or disturbing, stout and standard and strong. The son was European, the aquiline nose, the high cheekbones, the swarthy beard, the blue hollows of his cheeks, his sharp, glittering teeth, the lidded, almost oiled eyes. He was slender. His slim frame would have fit easily inside the warehouse of Truitt's body.

His eyes were black as the ice on the Wisconsin River, and just as cold. He existed, or seemed to exist, only for himself, for that moment in time when he ate his oysters and drank his champagne, aware that he was being stared at by every woman, women who sipped the details of his face and his body as he sipped his champagne, with obvious pleasure. The men looked at him with condescension, as though he were a child's doll. He was not a person. He was an object of beauty, and he existed for that single reason and he existed for himself alone.

He ate three dozen oysters. When he was finished, one of the portly waiters went over to him and whispered in his ear. Tony Moretti smiled and nodded. He got up slowly and languidly, like a cat in the sun, and moved to a piano in the rear of the room. He didn't speak or turn around, but sat simply at the piano and stared at the keys. The room fell into a hush. Ladies put down their forks. Through the veil of Catherine's hat, he was reduced to white skin and black hair, like a photograph, grainy shadow and glowing light. Finally he lifted his hands and began to play.

He played a popular song, but he played it slowly and sorrowfully, as though it had never been played before. The notes, so light and inconsequential, took on a weight and a resonance that was altogether new, and entirely his. There was something small but magnificent about his performance, a little jewel, an invention of love. He played as though each note could be touched, could be held in the hand like mercury, touching and not touching, but miraculous in a minor way.

When he was done, there was applause, but he did not acknowledge it, merely picked up his walking stick and stood, the sorrow of the music now in his face, a self-conscious look he had probably practiced a thousand times in front of a mirror.

He felt his necktie, looked down, and looked across the restaurant floor. He began to walk slowly to the door, his eyes down. The diners went back to their food, the ladies casting admiring glances over their shoulders. Apparently there was to be no bill for Tony Moretti. Either he ran an account, or the brief music was enough. As he got to Catherine's table, he stopped and crouched to the floor, running the silver tip of his stick through the sawdust.

Catherine was panicked. Malloy and Fisk studiously looked the other way, subtly sliding their notebooks into their pockets. Tony Moretti looked up, stared at Catherine with his liquid eyes.

"May I help you?" There was no air, no air in her lungs to bring the words out, but she did, in a short, soft gasp.

"I've lost my stickpin. From my necktie. A diamond stickpin given to me by somebody I loved. I thought I saw it here. Have you seen it here?"

"No. I've seen nothing."

"Well, then. Gone. Are you in mourning?"

She was astonished at his forwardness. She glanced in quick nervousness at Malloy and Fisk. They looked down at their hands.

"No. I'm not. I am recently married, in fact."

"I hope happily. You looked like you had lost someone, the way I've lost my stickpin. I'm glad that you haven't."

"I'm sorry you've lost your stickpin."

"It's of no importance. Of absolutely no importance at all. A girl gave it to me. She means nothing to me anymore. I just hate to lose things."

He stood up, bowed slightly from the waist, and left the restaurant.

He was a calla lily, pure and white, meant for solitude and death. She turned to Malloy and Fisk. "I would never believe he's Truitt's son."

"Make no mistake. He is the man Truitt is looking for."

"He's always been Mr. Truitt's son. In San Francisco. In New York. He's a liar and a wastrel, but he's Truitt's son, or the man Truitt calls his son, and now we have him."

Fisk looked at her sadly. "He's a lost cause."

Malloy echoed the sadness. "And he won't go home. Mr. Truitt has spent a great deal of money for nothing."

"How do you know?"

"There are too many pleasures he would miss. He's entirely his mother's creation. Overly refined. Immoral in every way. A pretty nothing. Truitt won't like him. Wouldn't want him around for five minutes. They don't have anything to say to each other, no language between them."

"Nobody would like him, in fact."

"Still . . ." Her heart was pounding. She could feel the music in her veins, like liquor, warming her blood.

"Exactly. Still."

"My husband has missed the music. He has missed his son. He has an idea, a dream. We're here to make the dream come true." She was careful not to appear overly excited. She was a woman who had been asked to execute a complicated transaction, no more.

"And so we will."

"How will we speak to him? It's important not to frighten him. He must listen calmly to his father's request. There's more in it for him than he might think. Than he might think at first."

"We go on Sunday."

Chapter Twelve

She paced her rooms. She didn't go to the library. She forgot her gardens and her ladylike ways. She thought of Tony Moretti, and imagined his body in bed, she imagined being in bed with Tony Moretti, and the desire she felt for him was like a drug in her veins. He was younger than she was; he would be the last adventure of her youth. She burned with the image of Tony Moretti sitting in the restaurant with his oysters, his liquid eyes, and his long fingers playing the sorrowful, trivial tune, his eyes as he looked into hers and inquired after his foolish stickpin. She tried to find a place to sit, a book to read, and she was uncomfortable wherever she perched. In the hotel dining room, her book useless and unopened, she felt everyone was looking at her, as if they could see, not her calm manner and her proper clothes, but only her desire. She was always lying naked and wanton next to Tony Moretti, her husband's son.

On seeing him, she had felt the sexual pulse of the city begin to beat. She had not noticed. She wondered, at any hour of the day and night, how many people were making love at exactly that minute. Behind every window the sexual act was being completed second after second. The poor with their ecstatic, animal grunts, the rich with their unimaginable refinements and perversions.

She couldn't sleep. She felt Truitt was watching her, that Truitt had known all along this would happen.

Sunday finally came. It was bright, bright and hard and cold, with snow in the air. They had said two o'clock. He would be awake, he would be sober, he might be alone. She was ready. She wore her gray silk dress, her wedding dress and her diamond engagement ring, and the long fur coat she had bought. As though they could protect her. She felt she was pretending to be a proper matron going to make a call on a distant relative.

Mr. Malloy and Mr. Fisk walked her silently through bright, slick, shiny streets that led away from the hotel, from everything new and modern, and then through streets that weren't nice, that were silent on a Sunday. They walked away from the fine stores and the streets so brightly lit at night, until they came to a neighborhood of low brownstones, houses not in good repair. They were without yards or even window boxes, just dingy marble stoops. Catherine could picture the rooms behind the grimy windows, rooms she herself had lived in, low, cramped, greasy from years without care. The furniture, too, would be old and comfortless, the floors unswept, the smell of onions frying, of cheap cigars, the windows always closed, a room in the back where the mother and father slept, another for the children, no matter how many, and one thing, or two, brought from the country and cherished. Sad, hard lives, without affection, without any moment but the present and that not to be enjoyed but endured. The only rhythm of their lives was the incessant turning of the machines in the factories where they worked, and their dreams in the night were of the little towns they had come from, the sun rising and setting, the turning of the seasons, the crops planted and grown and tended and harvested.

When they woke, they would not remember the dreams, but as they stood, day after day, at their relentless jobs, their hearts would ache for something they could not name.

The faces would be as worn as the furniture, unloved and hard. Now and then, in the evenings, a look of wistful longing would come over the wives, and they would have a kind gesture for one of the girls, a kind word. The fathers would be drunk or grave or both, and sometimes violent, the children slow-witted and slothful and unschooled and uncared for, except in those few brief useless moments when the mothers could forget their hard lives. These were not the streets of the bounding ambitious muscular America, but of the tired and the lost and the dirty.

Catherine felt a million miles away, in her warm fur coat and her gray silk dress that trailed in the snow no matter how she lifted it with her gloved hands. In the country, the snow was clean as a fresh bedsheet. Here it was filthy. The cold got into her boots and crept up her legs, despite her wool stockings. She felt removed from these houses and these habits and this life. She had always been a chameleon, taking on accents and manners suited to her circumstance, but now she felt as though she had changed into something new, and she couldn't change back.

Her pulse raced. The blood beat in her ears. She was finally going to reveal herself to Tony Moretti.

They turned away from these streets and into others even more depressing. Here there was no pavement, no cobblestones, just mud tracks that ran between wooden houses, mostly unpainted, some with broken windows, all with tattered, filthy curtains hanging limply in the hard light. Linden Street, with not a tree in sight.

Malloy and Fisk looked at her occasionally, as if to apologize, but she stared straight ahead, avoiding their gaze. She was lost in her own history now. Her history was unfolding with every step.

They stopped in front of one of the three-story houses, painted a dull red, as though someone had made a brief effort, long ago, to make it look more respectable, more refined. Malloy checked his notebook. "Number 18. This is it."

She felt a chill and pulled her collar tightly around her neck. Mr. Fisk and Mr. Malloy hesitated, having come all this way with so much information at hand, and at last having no idea what to do.

"Well. I'm cold. Let's go in." It was Catherine who broke the silence. "We're here. It's time we knew. Let's get on with it." She stepped up the stairs and tried the door, Malloy and Fisk following behind. It was unlocked and opened into a dark stairwell.

"Third floor, Mrs. Truitt. It's dark. I'm sorry."

"It's hardly your fault." She stepped aside and followed the two men up the stairs. And then they were knocking on the door, and then, after beats that snapped her nerves one by one, the door opened, and there in front of them was Antonio Moretti.

He looked ravaged. He looked pure. He shone like a saint. He stood in a red paisley silk dressing gown, the front barely closed. He obviously wore nothing underneath, and he obviously didn't care.

"Mr. Moretti. There's a lady here."

"So there is. I see. I always ask a lady to come in."

Malloy took out his notebook, as though that would help them to find their way. "Mr. Moretti . . . Mr. Truitt, we've come to take you home. Your father . . ."

A shudder crossed his brow, fleeting, gone in a second. "What was that name? It's not anybody I know. My name is Moretti. Tony Moretti."

"Mr. Ralph Truitt. In Wisconsin, where you were born."

"Won't you come in? I have some brandy. It's cold outside."

They didn't want to, but the force of his eyes and the whiteness of his skin somehow drew them forward and into his sitting room. It was furnished elegantly, completely at odds with the house itself, with delicate French and Italian furniture, obviously good. The ceiling was draped with orange silk, like a tent, and Moroccan lanterns hung down, the light from the candles flickering. Probably still burning from last night. Beyond, they could see the ruin of a tented, brocaded bedroom, like a palace abandoned before a revolution.

The room was littered with clothes, and he carelessly picked up a few items, as though to make a place for them to sit. Nobody sat. He turned to Catherine and smiled.

"What was that name?"

Again, the breathlessness made her voice faint. "Truitt. Mr. Ralph Truitt."

"And you would be . . . ?"

"Mrs. Truitt. The new Mrs. Truitt."

"I hope you'll be very happy."

"Thank you."

"It isn't a name I know."

Malloy cleared his throat. "He is your father."

Moretti laughed, showing his alabaster throat, his cheeks dark with yesterday's beard.

"My father is named Pietro Moretti. My mother is Angelina. He played the accordion in Naples, where I was born. When I was three, he and my mother moved to America, to Philadelphia, to the Italian section of Philadelphia, where he played the accordion in one after another of the thousand Italian restaurants. He eventually owned one, owns it still, and my cousin Vittorio makes the food, it's very good, by the way, and my father plays the accordion, and my mother takes the money."

Malloy interrupted. "You were born in Wisconsin. Your father is Ralph Truitt."

"Who are you?" Antonio demanded.

Fisk stepped in. "We were hired by your father to find you."

"You've been watching me?"

"For several months. Yes."

"That makes me very unhappy."

Malloy and Fisk looked at their hands. Antonio turned his gaze and spoke to Catherine.

"I went to the conservatory in Philadelphia, one of those wretched snot-nosed children of the poorer classes who get to go to such places because the well-to-do public finds it costs nothing and they sleep better at night. Well, I was talented, sort of. I've played the piano in restaurants ever since. Actually, *restaurants* is a nice word for it. I wasn't talented enough for concerts, and was too talented to teach. And besides, I hate children. I like adult company. Most adult company, at least. So here I am. I don't know any Mr. Truitt. I've never been to Wisconsin, although it may be nice. It's far away."

"This is a fabrication. We have the facts."

"You can check. I have papers, documents, a checkbook from the bank. Not much money, but you can look. My father still lives in Philadelphia. My mother is still named Angelina, and she still takes the money. Brandy?" He poured himself a glass, swirled it in the dim light.

"Your mother was the Contessa Emilia Truitt. Your father was Andrea Moretti, a piano teacher hired by your mother's husband, Mr. Truitt."

"A real countess. How charming. As much as I would like to exchange the restaurant life for a royal title, I'm afraid it isn't true. Not a word. I could read you my mother's letters. She begs me to come home and find a nice girl. A nice girl like the new Mrs. Truitt, no doubt. Why would Mr. Truitt want to see me if he's not my father?"

"He feels badly."

"Because his wife was a faithless whore?"

Malloy looked at Catherine with a sidelong glance.

"Because he was, because of circumstances, because he feels he was unkind to you, and he wants to make it up to you."

"By making me leave Saint Louis and go to Wisconsin? It doesn't sound like much of a birthright."

"He's your father. He has acted as your father since you were born."

A ripple of anger crossed Tony Moretti's face. "My father has acted as my father since I was born. Would you like to see photographs? I don't have any. My baby things? They're in Philadelphia. It's simple to prove who you are. It's hard to prove you're not somebody else. I'm not this man's son, no matter how much he wants me to be. I'm sorry Mr. Truitt feels the way he does. I'm very accommodating in general. I wish I could accommodate him. I wish I could accommodate you, but hospitality is helter-skelter around here, and all I've got is brandy and you don't want brandy and I want you to leave."

Catherine sat in a chair, swept clean of clothing, among which she noticed a pair of women's dark stockings.

"Mr. Moretti," she said softly.

"You were the lady, yes? The lady in black in the restaurant. The lady in mourning."

"Yes." Her hand was trembling as she spoke. "I'm not in mourning, as I said. You play beautifully."

She pictured him in bed. She pictured him naked, aroused, lying back against silk pillows and waiting. Waiting for her. He smelled of last night's stale cologne and the warmth of his bed. She could picture it all. She knew where he had been, what he had done. She smelled the woman who had recently left.

She spoke clearly, directly to him, and he listened to her words with careful attentiveness. "You have suffered. He knows that. He knows you must be angry. He's suffered, too. His heart's raw with the nights he's spent in hurt. He knows he has hurt you. He knows he treated you badly. Now he wants to make it right. He wants to bring you home, to the house you were born in, the big house, and make it alive again. I won't say he loves you. Yet. He wants to love you. To be kind to you. To be forgiven for . . . for everything. Please. I don't know . . ."

"And what would you, Mrs. New Truitt, what would *you* do to make this ridiculous fantasy come true?"

"I have promised him. I'm telling you. He's rich. I would do anything."

"Give me your ring."

"I'm sorry?"

"I lost my stickpin, remember? I like diamonds. Give it to me. I might want to give it to a girlfriend. I might want to wear it myself, one of my extravagances. I could make it into a new stickpin. It would attract attention when I play, don't you think? The light? I may want to throw it in the Mississippi. I may swallow it. Give it to me."

"Mrs. Truitt," said Mr. Fisk in genuine alarm.

She hesitated a long moment, then she took off her yellow diamond and put it into his waiting hand.

"There. He told me to do anything. I said I would. It's yours gladly. Just come home."

"If it was home, if it had any connection to me, I would do it in a second, for you, and never need to take a ring from your lovely hand." He slipped it on his little finger. "Small, but pretty." It glinted in the light from the candles overhead, just guttering out.

"Now I want you to get out. Leave me in peace. Do you think my life is so nice? It's not. Do you think I'm surrounded by love? I'm not. But there's enough that I don't need to go through this charade." He handed the ring back to Catherine. "Or your little country diamond. Get the hell out, all of you."

Malloy wasn't finished. "Mr. Truitt, we don't make mistakes."

Moretti turned in a rage. "Don't call me that name one more time, I'm warning you. My name is Moretti. This is my day off. My hour of being nice to strangers is over. Take your insane story back to this country bumpkin, whoever he is, and tell him how wrong you were. No, better yet, get on a train and go to Philadelphia. Ask anybody. They'll tell you where Moretti's is, and ask them about their son. They don't like what I do. They think piano playing is for girls. They want me home, too. I would far rather go to a home where at least I know the people. But I have a home here. And you're in it. Now get out."

He opened the bottle and poured himself another big glass of brandy. Catherine could feel the warmth of it shooting through her veins like fire.

"We'll come back." Fisk spoke softly. There was almost no threat in his voice. Just enough.

"I don't think so. I can't imagine why." Antonio sat down in a blue velvet chair, his scarlet dressing gown falling open across his chest. Catherine could see down his long torso to his navel.

There was nothing else to do. They left, and they could hear him laughing as they stumbled down the stairs in the half-light. Humiliated, the two Pinkertons. Catherine, putting her ring back on her finger, smiled. She was somehow elated.

On the way home, through the Sunday market, through the cheap dresses and thin coats and tin rings and frozen cabbage and copper cooking pots, she passed a man who sold birds. Yellow and blue and red canaries. Little songbirds. They looked half-dead with the cold, but she bought one, and an elaborate cage, and carried both home, holding the bird in her gloved hand, blowing her warm breath on its shivering body through the frozen Sunday streets of Saint Louis.

Chapter Thirteen

—◦◦◦—

S HE WOULD WAIT for five days. Her heart was on fire, but she would wait. After that, though, she couldn't wait any longer. Not one hour more.

While she waited, she wrote to Truitt. Before she told him about Antonio, she told him of her plans for the garden. She told him about her reading, her long afternoons of research in the library. She told him about the high windows and the long quiet tables and the slanting light. She told him about the possibilities for the garden, about how she might make it bloom again. She was even tender, but no more so than she needed to be. After all, she barely knew him.

She asked if she might buy some seeds and order some plants for the spring, to welcome Antonio home. She knew what his reply would be, that she could have whatever she liked, and she smiled, knowing it was true.

She stood for hours in the Missouri Botanical Garden, look-ing at the impossible orchids, flowers white and elegant like Tony Moretti, blossoms exorbitantly delicate and beautiful. They might grow in the glass conservatory. She waited at the counters while the plant men cataloged for her what would and would not grow in the climate she described. How long was the spring? How hot was the summer? She didn't know. She imagined what might or might not be true, and she bought carefully but with hope. She paid with cash and went to the bank for more. She arranged the arrival date. She bought a small silver pen and notebook with red and white Florentine endpapers, and she carefully noted the name and qualities of every plant she ordered.

She thought of her garden. She thought of her life, her patchwork quilt of a life, pieced together from castoff scraps of this and that; experience, knowledge, clairvoyance. None of it made any sense to her.

She had no knowledge of good. She had no heart and so no sense of the good thing, the right thing, and she had no field on which to wage the battle that was, in fact raging in her.

At least a garden had order. A garden *gave* order to an untamed wilderness. She hoped for all these things. With her bird sitting on her finger, she hoped for order in her secret walled square, for some sense of what the right thing might be. Waiting was not good for her, she knew. Thinking was not good. It made her remember the past, and the past was the place she did not want to be.

Tony Moretti was like her. He was like a secret garden. He believed the lies he told. He never faltered for a moment, never wavered. And he had won.

She wrote again to Truitt and suggested that she visit Moretti alone, without the sharp intensity of Malloy and Fisk. She wrote that a gentler approach might make Moretti see the light. She was convinced, she said, that the Pinkertons were right; the man who called himself Moretti was his son. His son in masquerade. There was a feeling, she said, a tic in his eye, a curl to his lip that suggested to her that he was lying. He harbored bitterness, to be sure, and regret as well, she was careful to add, but he hid the truth behind his condescending charm and insolence, and he didn't hide it very well.

She told Truitt about Moretti's languid, luxurious ways, his velvet furniture and his silk dressing gown. She told of his piano playing. She told him about the dark apartment, the rooms that revealed such exotic elegance, such assurance of taste.

She asked if Truitt was sure, if he was certain that he wanted his uncertain son under the same roof. She knew there were parts of the past you had to let go of, certain lands that were irredeemably lost, sorrowfully lost, but, finally, lost forever. She wrote that she would wait for his answer before proceeding.

He responded that he wanted nothing else. He wanted his son; that was his only wish. She should do whatever was necessary. She should go to his rooms. She should dog him in the street. She should give him money, whatever he asked for.

Catherine herself was only a means to that end. He didn't say it but she knew; it had been clear since he first told her she was to go to Saint Louis. She was both the lure and the instrument to accomplish Truitt's deep desire. Foolish as it was.

She would always know, now, that Truitt was a sentimental fool, that he would never imagine Catherine's own desires, confronted with such a ravishment.

There. At least she had covered herself. At least there would be no question of her conduct. Malloy and Fisk, even if they followed her, would have nothing to report.

She was always and forever delighted and amazed at her own cleverness. There was no scheme she couldn't see through. There

was no outcome she couldn't shape to her will. By making Truitt
her accomplice, she made herself the heroine of her own deceptions,
and she felt a freedom and a voraciousness she hadn't felt before.
She had at first been unsure of her footing with Truitt. Now she
knew she had him.

She walked through the streets at dusk, her karakul coat pulled
tight around her throat, a veil hiding her face. She checked to make
sure she wasn't being followed, although now it hardly mattered.
She walked past the brownstones, turned into the street of dingy
clapboard houses, and stood in front of his red house.

He would be getting dressed. He would be warm from the bath,
and his clothes would be laid out on the bed. He would hear the
knock on the door and hastily put away the opium pipe, the syringe, whatever his instruments of stupor and imagination and
music, never far from his hand. He would hear the knock, and
he would be ready for her. He would know who it was before he
opened the door.

She knocked. He opened. He stared at her for a long moment,
and then his tongue was in her mouth, as slick and salty as an oyster. He pulled her inside, kicked the door shut, and kissed her with
a ferocity that was familiar to her.

He put his finger beneath her coat, just under the collar of her
dress, and touched the beating vein of her throat. She tore at his
clothes, already loose and unbuttoned, desperate to touch the
smooth white skin of his chest, of his tight slim stomach, silky
against her hand. His skin felt brand-new, as though it had never
been touched.

All the while he was kissing her, crushing her lips, his tongue in
her mouth, against her teeth, and her tongue in his mouth, gliding
over his, feeling the roof of his mouth, tasting the dissipations of

the night before, the champagne and cigars and the stale breath, tasting him, and her mind went blank, her skin turned to fire, and she was lost, lost again, lost in the brightness of who and what he was, the terror of his soul. Nothing mattered. There was no time. There was no heat or cold or past or future. There was only this, her hand against his skin, her finger in his navel, her hand beneath the waist of his pants, his finger on her pulsing vein.

Her blood was water. Her eyes were blind. She was not Catherine. She was not anybody. Nobody knew where she was. Nobody would ever know where she had been. She stood in the kingdom of touch, and it was an ecstasy to her.

They made love as if someone were watching. Uncovered, sensitive to their own movements, their own caresses, as though it were being done for other eyes, a demonstration of the effortless ways of creating the pleasures of the body. She was on his bed, her clothes in ruins on the floor, and he was naked too, she lying sideways on the bed, her bones gone, he moving above and on and at her, his tongue expertly bringing her to climax so fast and so deeply that she went on rolling with warmth and pleasure as he entered her and brought himself to coming, letting out a cry as he did so, his only sound. It was his own masculinity he was making love to, which drove him as he rode inside her, rapture at his own skill, his own pleasures, the tenderness, the savagery, ripping through her as though for the first time.

He made love to her until her lips were swollen from kissing, her skin covered with marks, her insides aching and raw. She was complete. Whole again.

"Truitt," she said in a voice she hardly recognized.

She had known so many men. She couldn't remember their faces. Moretti had known so many women. Their names were on the tip of his tongue, she knew. It hardly mattered that she was here, that she was the one, and none of that mattered.

Making love to him was not like food. It was not nourishment. It was like fire, and when she came, she came down in ashes.

Afterward she dozed, wholly unguarded. She floated in the warm waters of a foreign sea, not knowing her own name, caring about nothing, remembering nothing.

"My little darling." His voice was far away, a wind that came to her from the rain forest. "My bird. My chocolate."

She laughed softly. She nestled into him, feeling every point at which his skin touched her skin. She would never love anybody else the way she loved him, so lost, so bewildered, so helpless. Her defenses, practiced and perfected, were of no use to her now. Her mind, her speech would do her no good. She was all sensation, and hunger for more sensation.

"My music. Speak to me."

She opened her eyes. She was in the French bedroom she knew so well, tented in sky blue silk, hung with a French chandelier, in the arms of the one lover who rode her dreams, who defined for her all she knew of love. How shabby, she thought. How sad.

"Yes. What? What?"

He looked at her with his eyes so mixed with sadness and selfishness.

"Why isn't he dead?" His voice was like ice on her skin, and his eyes stared at her nakedness. She covered herself with a shawl, carelessly thrown on the bed, her beautiful black embroidered shawl left behind when she went to the north, when she changed herself for Ralph Truitt.

"He can't be. There wasn't . . . when would I have done it? How? What do you want?"

"You know what I want. You know what we agreed. I want it all. I want to share it with you."

"And you'll have it." She sat up. "How was I to know he would ask for you? How was any of this in the plan? That he would ever find you? And even then, he can't die right away, you know that. It has to go on. It has to be timed. Slow. He has to get sick, and then weak, and then he has to die, and he will, but he can't now."

He put her hand on his sex and held it there. She felt it move beneath her hand, now soft, pliant as a fish, rising and falling like breath. "Swear."

"I promise you."

He got up, grabbed a towel and began to clean himself off. There was a wet pool in the bed where he had been. He never came inside her. He was terrified of children.

He began to pick up his clothes and throw them in a corner, taking from an armoire other, equally perfect things. "As though a promise from a whore makes any difference. I have to go to work now."

She wept. He had never called her a whore before this hour, and the abrupt cruelty of it was sharp and terrible. She had sworn she wouldn't let him see her cry, no one had, but she could not help herself. She could not stop.

"What do you *want*?"

"I want him dead. I want his money. I want him dead, and I don't want to see his face. I want to hear what his face looks like when he's dying, but I don't want to see it. I want his stomach to turn to ice. I want his teeth to rot in his face. I want to live in my mother's house and have exquisite things. You *know* what I want."

"And you'll have it. You'll have it all. But you'll have it in time. You'll have it so that no one will ever know we did what we're doing." She spoke softly. "That's how arsenic works. It's slow and invisible. That's its beauty."

It was so entrancing, watching him dress, the boyish body slowly hidden away behind layer after layer of beautiful clothing, as elegant and sensuous as a woman in the way he put his clothes over the body which was her secret knowledge, her only possession, even if another had seen and held him just last night while she slept in her spinster's bed at the Planter's Hotel. No one knew him the way she did, and he loved no one but her, even if he never said it, even if he loved her only because she was the key to everything he had waited for his whole life.

He was tied to no one but her, because nobody else could get him what he wanted. They had made it up together, like the plot of a melodrama, a shocking plot, but one that was within reach, if she were clever. And she never doubted her cleverness.

"It will happen. You know that. It will."

"Tell me how. Tell me again."

"He will feel a pleasure. He will feel an exquisite longing for something he can't remember. The longing will turn to poison in his mind, and he will be haunted by nightmares. His blood will get thin, and he'll be cold all the time. No number of blankets will warm him. His hair will begin to fall out. And then he will sicken and he will die." He listened like a child at bedtime.

"Don't you have any interest in who he is? Everything I said is true. He wants you home. He wants to make a home for you more beautiful than anything you . . . than I've ever seen. But then, I forget, you've seen it."

"I've remembered every detail every day of my life. He's not in the picture."

"He loves, he wants to love you."

He suddenly turned, and knelt with one knee on the bed. He grabbed her by the shoulders and shook her like a doll. She could see his clothes all undone. She could see his white skin, feel his hot touch, even in his violence.

"He beat me. He killed my mother."

"He . . ."

"He took my beautiful mother and he beat her until her teeth fell bloody to the floor. I saw this. He took me all the way to Chicago to make me watch. He's strong. He was, at least. He took her and put his ugly hands around her throat and strangled her until she was dead. I saw this. I was thirteen years old and I saw it." He threw her back on the bed. "Why would I want his love? I want him dead."

She had heard it a hundred, a thousand times, and she had never really believed it, not once. It was assumed between them to be a truth, it was the central cause of what was happening, and she tried, she tried because she loved him, to believe it, but she didn't. And now that she knew Truitt, now that she was his wife, she didn't believe Antonio anymore.

She knew such things happened. She could picture them in the grimy brownstones and the dingy tenements. She could imagine them happening to other people. She could not imagine such a terrifying loss of sense, of restraint or reason, happening to Ralph Truitt. She had tried to see it. She had tried to see Antonio, the first haze of a beard on his cheek, watching such a thing happen, but the image would not come.

Such things happened to her, had happened to her, sudden bursts of uncontrollable fury, but they would not happen to Ralph Truitt,

Truitt who had exchanged drink for prayer the day his daughter's eyes went blank, Truitt who had seen his wife having sex with a piano teacher and closed the door and not gotten his gun.

Antonio grazed her cheek with a kiss, his dry lips like feathers on her skin. "It's our future. It's our future."

She raised herself with fury from the bed.

"And you don't have to do a single thing? Not one thing. You drink and you whore and you go to the dens and you spend every penny with tailors who will give you endless credit because it's an honor for their clothes to be seen on you, and I have to do it all."

"Me whore? What an odd thing for you to say."

"I love you. I will do anything for you."

"And you honestly think that's a rare and beautiful thing. That's what you get paid for."

"It's all I have to give."

"No. It's not. You give me my father, you surprise me with my father's death, and your love will suddenly take on a whole new value."

"I'll do it. I said I would. I will."

"Well, don't wait too long."

He was dressed. He had fully left her now, and she lay naked and awkward in the cold, wet bed. His leaving was like dying for her.

He turned to her, his eyes rimmed with tears. "I wish you could have seen her. My mother. She was so lovely, her voice so soft, her hands so small. She would take me on her lap as she played the piano, and sing the old Italian songs. She had barely left her girlhood."

He sat in a chair by the darkening window. "After she left, after he drove my mother away, after my sister died, I would sneak over to the old house, to the villa, and climb the staircase and go into her room. I would stand in her closet and bury my nose in her dresses, breathing in my mother. She smelled like another country, a country where there was always music and dancing. A country lit by candlelight.

"She was just a girl. She fell in love. People do, all the time. It wasn't her fault. Maybe Truitt is my father. Maybe not. No one will ever know. But he will pay the price for what he did to her, for what he did to me after she left.

"I have grown up, all my life, hating him. I am weary of it. I will never have a whole life until he's gone. Do that one thing for me.

"You reminded me of her, the first time I saw you. You have loved me, in your way. You open, by tiny bits, my hard heart. Do this one thing for me.

"People think I'm a bad man. A useless waste. And maybe I am. But I don't think so. I'm just a ten-year-old boy, standing in the dark of his mother's closet, smelling her dresses. I could be bad. But I could be good. I'll know when I see him in his grave."

He stood. It was almost dark. The door opened and he was gone.

She wandered the rooms. She opened the closet and saw her fine dresses, the beads and feathers, and her hats, swooping birds and jewels, and her delicate shoes, red and green and gold Moroccan leather, with pretty high heels and glittering buttons and buckles, and she suddenly wanted it to start over again. The touch and smell of her clothes, her perfumed clothes, brought it back, and she wanted to lie in bed until noon, she wanted the laughter and the dirty jokes and the bawdy songs and the sex with men she never saw again, the clink of money in her silk purse, the thrill of champagne, the cloying sweetness after the bubbles were gone, the awful mouth in the morning, opium and champagne, the nights upstairs with the women, in their silk-ribboned underwear, when they would lazily caress one another's skin and talk easily, softly all night about the things that were going to happen and less easily about the things that had happened and, somehow, it was acceptably fine. She wanted to lie in bed on a Sunday morning and laugh over the personal ads and not see the one placed by Ralph Truitt and know the name and say it aloud to Antonio Moretti and see the gleam in his eye as he grabbed the paper. She wanted not to have spent the day wondering aloud how to make use of the sad information. Ralph Truitt. Just a name, the end of an old story.

She could never get back. And if she could, where was she to get back to? Back to a carriage with her own sweet mother in a summer storm with cadets? Back to the sweetness of her little sister's eyes? Back to the moments just before any of this had happened?

She closed the closet. She washed herself carefully with water from the ironstone pitcher, and she didn't think anymore. She washed his sex from her raw skin, luxuriating in everything, regretting nothing.

She dressed herself carefully in her lady's disguise, she walked without fear through the dark streets of the parts of Saint Louis nobody went to except out of necessity, and she slept like an innocent girl in her narrow bed at the Planter's Hotel, the sound of her bird sending her to the angels.

—◦◦◦—

Chapter Fourteen

S HE COULDN'T STOP. It was like a drug she had stayed
away from for too long. She wrote to Truitt. She told
him she was making progress, but progress was slow. She
promised him that Andy, as she called him in her letters, would
come home.

She went to Antonio's every day. She was no longer afraid of Fisk
and Malloy. She never saw them. She assumed they lurked in the
shadows, but she was too far gone to care.

She and Antonio would make love, sometimes for ten fierce minutes, sometimes until dark turned to light and then to dark again,
and then she would pull a dress from the closet and they would go
out. They ate oysters and drank champagne.

Away from his singular obsession with Truitt, his charm was
childish and indelible. He made her feel like a girl again, when
everything was fresh and possible. He would tell her over and over
the story of his travels, the comic peculiarities of the people he had
met on the way, and it always seemed new and innocent, the endless adventures of a boy who never grew up. His laughter was like

clear water, sparkling with sunlight, spilling over rocks in a spring forest.

He made her laugh. With Truitt, she never laughed. Truitt was many things, solid and good things, but she never laughed.

She knew also, because he sometimes told her in the night when his armor slipped away, when he lay naked and lean and finally vulnerable in her arms, that, in reality, it was mostly a long and lonely scramble for the next dollar or the next woman, a young, broken man alone in the world with no mother or father, never a home to come home to, but when he sat with her over oysters and champagne, it was as though his life had always been filled with sunlight and clean sheets.

He would speak to her of her beauty, how he never tired of it, and she would believe him.

She went to the rude beer hall where he played the piano, and she flirted with other men right in front of him, knowing he wouldn't do anything. Sometimes there would be fights, overdressed laborers in a rage, and she wouldn't even move from her table.

Afterward, they would go to the dens, where Chinese women would undress them, wrap them in silk, massage their naked bodies with warm scented oils and feed them black, rubbery balls of opium. They would go home at dawn, and she would change into her other clothes, the clothes she had worn to come to him, and go back to the Planter's Hotel. She couldn't get the key in the lock sometimes; a sleepy porter had to help her. She slept until noon and woke to the sound of a bird singing.

She drank strong black coffee and ate almost nothing, golden toast with sweet preserves. She hardly slept, just the hours between dawn and noon. Sometimes, in the library in the afternoons, she almost fainted from hunger, her kid gloves lying by the stack of books.

She studied the horticulture of roses. She could feel the thorns prick her skin, could almost smell the blood on the back of her hand. She was not what she appeared to be to Ralph Truitt, but she was not what she appeared to be to Tony Moretti either, and she never stopped to wonder which self was her true self and which one was false.

She saw so many of her old friends. Hattie Reno, Annie McCrae and Margaret and Louise and Hope, Joe L'Amour, Teddy Klondike. She looked everywhere in every room for her sister Alice, Alice who lived somewhere in this vast city, who moved in these circles when she felt well, Alice whom she used to take to the circus and the opera. But Alice was invisible, and nobody knew where she was.

She had bought Alice books that she never read. She had bought her jewelry that she lost or gave away. She had tried, in all the world, to save one thing, to make her sister thrive, to be her friend, and she had failed even in that.

Catherine wanted to find Alice and take her to Wisconsin, to wrap her in the white gauze of the far country until she was healed and whole. She wanted to dress her in Emilia's finery and watch as she swept down the long staircase of the villa into the high frescoed hall. She would be like a child in a masterpiece, Catherine's masterpiece. She still believed she could save her.

"Forget her," said Hattie Reno. "Nobody's seen her for months. And the last time anybody did see her, she looked awful. Nobody talked to her and she didn't care. I was ashamed for her."

"She's my sister."

"And she's mean and she's hard and she's sick. She's the kind of girl don't want a roof over her head. Just runs wild. Men don't even like her no more."

"She's never had a real roof over her head."

"And you want to give her one. Before she's dead. You and who else? Who would pay for this roof?" Catherine never talked about Ralph Truitt. Her absence went unexplained. In Chicago, they assumed. They imagined they knew the reason. Fresh blood. New men with new money.

"Yes. Before she's dead."

She knew that Antonio needed her in a way that was beyond speech, and this she took for adoration. It wasn't. It was need and habit, an addiction, but it wasn't love, no matter how often he might say it.

Sometimes, sitting in the early afternoon, still in her nightdress in the quiet of her room at the hotel, the scarlet bird on her finger pecking at small pieces of a roll she held up, sometimes she knew this with a clarity that was like a knife in her heart. But he was different.

For Antonio, Catherine was the one woman who never stopped being thrilling, because her need for him was so enormous, because it made her vulnerable and willing and unprotected in ways that other women weren't. Antonio was years younger than Catherine. He was, for her, the last grasp at a youth that was betraying her.

He could do anything he wanted, love her, smack her, kiss her feet, and she would do anything he asked. She was older. She was losing her youth, and that in itself was part of her interest for him, like drinking the last of the wine. And she would kill his father and give him everything. She would do anything. She would do this. His father's death had become the bit in his teeth, the impossible, unbeatable hand at poker. He was willing to wait, but not for long.

He would fall asleep with his fingers inside her, lick the musk away when he woke up. He would have sex with her when she was bleeding, would have sex with her when she was drunk, would have sex with her when she was asleep. His appetite and her desire to be pleased were both endless. He found it exciting when she came to him in her plain proper dresses, like sex with a stranger, somebody foreign to him.

She was in a dream. She found it hard to remember where she was.

She wrote to Truitt every day. She constructed a life, and she wrote him every imagined detail. She did not want him to forget her power over him, the power to end his loneliness, to bring his son home, to make his garden grow again.

"Tell me about him," Antonio said once, after sex. His head was on her breasts, his dark hair teasing her, teasing her into a kind of stupor. She could close her eyes and try to imagine his face. She could see nothing, although she could recall with perfect clarity the faces of people she hardly knew.

"I want to know everything. Tell me again."

"He's tall. He's thick."

"Fat?"

"Not at all. Powerful." She was careful now. She wanted to please; it was her profession. She wanted to tell him only what he wanted to hear. "He's got a lot of money, I think. I know. He's got a lot of businesses. Mostly iron, for the railroads, for machinery, for everything. Everybody works for him. A lot of money. I don't know how much. He's got a railroad car. He thinks it's remarkable to own an automobile. And there's the house, but you know it. There's his silence. He reads poetry. I read to him at night. He's very sad. He's sad in himself, in his heart."

"Imagine when we live in the house. Imagine the parties." He could see the parties; she didn't have to describe them. They were like his life now, but with more people and more money and more champagne and more everything that might, in the smallest way, give him pleasure. There would be women to wait on him, to pick up and clean his ruined clothes. There was his father's grave, next to his sister's. He would spit on it.

Where would the people come from? They would bring them in the railroad car, from Chicago, from Saint Louis, an endless succession of people who would do anything for him because he could do anything for them, if he chose, at his whim. He would have sex with somebody else while Catherine watched. He would shave his face in a gilded mirror from France. Sleep in the golden bed his mother had brought from Italy. They would take drugs from Chicago and walk down the middle of the streets of the town laughing at nothing, and nobody could do one thing about it. And the money would never stop coming in. There would be no end to the luxuries.

"Your toys are still there. Your sister's dresses hang in the closets. Your mother's, too. They are beautiful."

"You'll wear them."

"I've tried. They're too small. They would fit Alice. They're hopelessly out of fashion, like in a museum. A box of jewelry is in her dressing table. Pearls and emeralds and rubies. Bows made of diamonds to wear in your hair. A diamond watch. Things she forgot to take, or couldn't take, when she left."

"He beat my lovely mother. He beat her until she bled. She

hardly knew what she was doing. She left with the dress that was on her back, nothing else."

"It's all still there."

"And I don't want Alice. Not anywhere near me."

She tired of telling the story. Tired of comforting him. He was still a boy, a little boy who was frozen in childhood, and who could never get it back. She knew this. She knew the father's death and the diamond bows and the callous, lascivious disregard would never restore to him what he had lost, because what he had lost was time and what he had left was rage.

He knew it, too. He tried to remember. He tried to remember his sister, or his mother, and nothing came to mind. His anger was the hot still point on which his life was impaled.

"He misses you with all his heart. He's sorry for what he did. The pain of it never goes away."

"You think my pain goes away? You think I like this, this ignorant life?"

She had to be careful at every step, a tightrope walker in the circus.

He couldn't sleep at night. His heart pounded and the blood raced at his temples. He felt a pressure in his body and he tossed and turned until the light was too bright outside to stay in bed. When he couldn't stand it any longer, he settled for unconsciousness, the morphine, the opium, the wine, but he woke up and he didn't feel rested.

He felt that his soul, his rage, showed on his face. He imagined the skin of his face splitting open and the pus of his rage sliding down his fine high cheekbones.

He ate only enough to stay alive, and then only foods of the most rarified kind. Oysters and champagne. Quail and caviar. Melons that were brought up the river from South America out of season. Ham from Parma. Foods that passed for a caress from a woman long dead, a woman he imagined had loved him as a child.

He had sex because he was beautiful. It was beauty's burden to be made available. He had sex because there was a moment during the act of love in which he forgot who he was, forgot everything, forgot his father and his mother and his tiny idiot sister, forgot the beatings and the curses that Ralph had hurled against his flesh, and Ralph cold sober, sober and cold, over and over, willing him to hell and he a child of eight, when it began. In sex, he ceased thinking and became only being, all movement and pleasure and expertise. He lived in a sexual frenzy because sometimes, afterward, he could sleep for an hour or two.

"Don't tell me about it. Don't talk about him."

"Whatever you want."

Catherine was an exception, the woman he came back to again and again. The woman who was all he understood of love. She had been savaged by her life and her face was still beautiful, her body untouched by disease. She knew what she was getting into; she saw into his soul and wasn't burned by the fire.

Alice was another exception. He had gotten drunk one night when Catherine was away marrying his father, and he had spotted Alice as he staggered home in the dawn. She was standing, standing as though frozen, on the corner of a dark street, and he had approached and said two words to her. They had had sex in less time than it would take to play the first movement of the Moonlight Sonata. They had not said a single word, as though he were too bored and Alice merely mute.

"I know where she is."

"Who?"

"Alice. She's in Wild Cat Chute."

Catherine turned away and covered her face with her hands. Tony Moretti smiled.

Chapter Fifteen

——◦◦◦◦——

ALICE.

When Catherine Land was eight years old, after her mother had died of influenza and Alice was just old enough to walk, her father lost all reason. He couldn't bear the sunlight, couldn't bear the feel of clothing on his skin, couldn't bear the taste of the saliva in his mouth when it wasn't being burned by cheap liquor. He lost his business, he lost his friends.

One day, they had no money. One day, they had no house. Their furniture, her mother's furniture, lay in a pile of snow in the street.

And then he died, too. It took six years. Catherine never went to school, because they never stayed anywhere long enough to go to a school and because there was no one to watch after the baby.

Her father died of drunkenness, of course. He drank himself to death, but Catherine secretly knew he died of a broken heart. It happens. She knew it and she watched it, and it wasn't pretty or romantic and sad. It was pathetic and ungainly and hard as horses pulling a wagon through the mud.

And then they had nobody. Then they had nowhere. Catherine was just fourteen, Alice seven.

They went to the poorhouse. Catherine marched them across the docks until they came to the grim warehouse that hid the poorest away from the eyes of the less poor. Alice went to a little school, a charity inside the charity, and she taught Catherine to read. Catherine did whatever chores she was given, washing clothes, cleaning floors on her hands and knees. She took on small bits of charity sewing, and she became expert at it, the first thing she could do with pride.

While Alice was at school, Catherine sat in a small park near the harbor and watched the water sparkle in the thin sunlight, and she sat there, just staring, until one day a man came and sat beside her and touched her hand and asked her to his cheap hotel room, and she found what she was to do with her life, what was to become of her and how she was to save Alice.

She didn't know what she was doing. She didn't know why he asked or why she did what he asked her to do. It meant nothing to her.

She realized that her body was her bank; it was all the money she had. It was all she would ever need.

She worked, she learned to read, and at night, before they locked the doors, she wandered the docks and made small bits of money the only way she had available to her, sex in doorways, in huge shipping crates, on a pile of coats in the back room of a bar.

Sometimes Catherine stayed out all night, moving from man to man as the hours moved relentlessly on, returning in the morning when they unlocked the big double doors. Her body ached, as though she had been scrubbing floors all night.

While Alice learned her letters and numbers, Catherine tasted power in the hunger of men. Power over them, over their desires, power to save her sister. She knew now she could keep Alice safe, could get her away from the rats and the lice and the small-mouthed halfwit children who were abandoned, too. At least she and Alice had been loved, once, in a place that seemed like some country in a dream.

She lay in strange beds and imagined the house in which she and Alice would live when they had money. And there they would be perfectly happy and complete in themselves. The house would be clean all the time, and sunlight would stream through the windows even in winter.

She was sixteen. When there was enough money, she moved them to Philadelphia. They moved into a room in a shanty on the Schuylkill. Catherine would come home late and sleep in the same bed with Alice. She was always there in the morning to wake her with a kiss. They hadn't come a single step from their days in Baltimore, but Alice went to a proper school, a charity Catholic school with strict rules and dirty windows. Alice hated it, but every night, before she went out, Catherine helped her with her homework, and so Catherine began to learn little bits about little things.

Alice dressed in real clothes, which Catherine made for her. She had a warm coat in winter, and Catherine would go to the market and wander through the bolts of cloth, touching every one. She sewed, and she discovered the big library. She remembered her mother telling her that the library housed all she would ever need to know, about history and art and science.

It terrified her at first. On her initial visits she could only stare, not knowing what to ask for or where to turn. Finally she asked for a book, a book on sewing, and she read it, sitting at the long tables, taking notes with a pencil she had stolen from one of the stalls in the market.

Learning became her. She loved the smell of the books from the shelves, the type on the pages, the sense that the world was an infinite but knowable place. Every fact she learned seemed to open another question, and for every question there was another book. She learned the card catalog. She never learned more than she needed to know.

She read romantic novels, and she imagined that the men and women at the reading tables around her were the subject of those books. Happy and passionate lives, so simple it seemed for others. She read Jane Austen, Thackeray, Dickens, stories in which the lives of the tattered poor turned out to be blissful in the end.

She read about the capitals of the world, the cathedrals and minarets, the broad avenues, and the volatile and ever-expanding world of science.

When she was eighteen, she was the kept mistress of a married man. She was grown; Alice was still a child. She lived near Rittenhouse Square, in real rooms on a real street. These were the rooms she had dreamed of in the hotels. She learned the art of pleasing a man without having sex with him, sitting on his lap, making small talk, cutting his cigar. She was intelligent, she realized. From the library, she had many topics she could discuss with ease and charm. Men enjoyed these things. She was like the geishas she read about in the library, like the courtesans, the mistresses of the great. She dressed beautifully, silk dresses she made herself from pattern books, dresses from Paris he bought for her, wrapped in grosgrain ribbon from fancy stores in Broad Street. She entertained his friends when he had card parties, telling amusing stories, pouring them wine, laughing at their crude jokes.

She was astonished at how simple it was. He came on Sunday afternoons, and he always brought some little gift, a token of his gratitude that such a lovely young girl would allow him to touch her, to put his hand on her breasts. Then he went home to his wife and his own children, to other rooms she was never to see.

Alice had no patience or aptitude for learning. She was a bitter child, bitter and recalcitrant and selfish, and there was no reason for it. Everything had been done for her. Catherine had a lot of time on her hands, and she would sit for hours, trying with Alice to figure out her lessons. Alice was all feeling, a being without reason or intellect. Finally she refused to go to school at all. She loved pretty dresses and walking out in public in the finery Catherine's protector bought for them, and she loved him, solid, red-faced Uncle Skip, as she called him. After a year, Catherine found them in bed together. Alice was twelve.

It was not a shock. It didn't surprise her that Uncle Skip, having bought two women, would want to enjoy two women, but her rage was uncontrollable. She stole and sold everything she could from their fancy rooms, and Catherine and Alice got on a train a second time and went to New York.

It was a new city, vast and filled with possibility, a blank canvas. But it was the same story. Catherine would sew and whore and spend her days in the library. Alice looked like a little princess and yearned for freedom. She loved to make men look at her and then turn away with a scornful laugh.

Alice told Catherine she hated her. She said she had been in prison all her life. Catherine wasn't surprised. Alice said that, as soon as she had someplace to go, she would leave Catherine and never look back. Catherine was twenty-two and she felt like she had been on the planet for a hundred years.

Then Alice was gone. Catherine found her in Gramercy Park, walking a little white dog, a fifteen-year-old girl on the arm of a forty-year-old man, and Catherine gave up. There wasn't any more she could do.

Now she had become the thing Catherine had wanted to save her from; she had become Catherine, only worse, because for Alice there was no reason. It was not a thing she had to do; it was what she wanted. The empty attention of stupid, lonely men. It was beyond thought.

Catherine left New York and went to Chicago, where she lived for years with no further word from Alice.

Then she began reading in the newspapers about the Great Exposition to be built in Saint Louis, and she decided to go there because she knew there would be a lot of men, laborers from Italy and Germany who had left their families behind and come to Saint Louis to make money. She had not one ounce of kindness left in her heart.

And then one day she saw Alice.

She approached her gently.

"Alice. Sister."

Alice turned. The shock of recognition turned instantly to bitterness.

"What are you . . . ?"

"Same as you. The Expo. The men. The money." Alice laughed.

"What happened to New York? To Gramercy Park?"

"The dog died. William hit me. I came here. A long time ago, I don't remember when. The Golden West."

"I . . ."

Then Alice had slapped her face. Had left a welt on her cheek and run down the street laughing.

Catherine never saw her again, had not tried to find her. Now it burned in her like a fire. She had money. She had a place to take Alice. She wanted to save her sister. It was not a kindness. It was a desperate hard unbreakable need to create some order out of the chaos of the past. Alice might find peace in white Wisconsin. The blindingly pure snow might wash away her bitterness and her cruelty and the hardness of her soul.

Wild Cat Chute was a bad place. It was the place you went to when you had run out of other places that would let you in. It was crawling with rats and garbage and diseases and the diseased. It was just a place on the way to the river, a runway once used to bring cargo up into the city, but now it was filled with shacks and people who didn't even have shacks, people who were no longer able or fit to sleep indoors, in the prison of a room. People who heard voices. People who died.

Still, as Catherine turned the dark corner into the mud track, all she could see were the children. They were herself. They were her childhood and her past and the hunger and the fear and the loss, and no coat could have kept out the chill of that. They had no names. They had no light in their faces. They had no one waiting for them and nowhere to go.

Alice was nowhere.

Some said they remembered a girl like her, a girl who had gone away with a boatman. Some said they remembered a girl who had gone to the hospital, dragged kicking and screaming, maybe to a loony bin, maybe to a hospital where you came back better. Catherine searched the hospitals and found nothing. You sink to a certain level, you don't have a name any more. You don't have a history or any particular features or friends, and Alice had reached the Chute, the end of the line, the end of hope, the end of whatever it is that makes a person particular in the world.

"Where is she, Tony?" She begged him. He was supposed to know. He had said he did.

"Things change. People move. People are always moving around down there, sleeping in each other's beds, beating each other's children. She's there. Just keep looking. Hurt yourself if you want."

"I'll go again tonight. Every night. Now."

He was naked in front of her, the last sun glowing on his shoulder blades as he washed himself, his exquisite clothes laid out on a chair. He threw down his towel and turned with sudden exhausted fury, "Why do you care? People lose things, Catherine. It happens. People lose what they love all the time."

"I care about her."

"You don't care about anything. You care about getting back something you've lost. Like an umbrella on a trolley. Like a locket in the street. That's all. But I'll tell you this. She's not the thing you lost anymore. She's a hag, she's *nothing*. She's got no face, no name, no place to live. And this pathetic attempt to find your sister isn't going to change anything. You're still going to kill my father, you're still going to live in his palace with me and all that money."

His beautiful clothes. His beautiful hair, his hands holding a silver hairbrush, his handsome face in a cracked silver mirror. The way he cared for her and didn't all at once.

"Your cruelty is astonishing. Alice——"

"Was sweet and cute and fresh and not very bright, but she could sit in your lap, just sit in your lap, and make you come. She didn't have a shred of a soul even then. And she's dying because she's not cunning and careful and smart like her big sister and she wants it that way. You disgust her. Your name enrages her. You think she's not down there? You've left your name with every drunk in the place and she's still not there. Because it's the place you go if you don't want to be found. Ever. There's only one way in, and there's only one way out, so leave her in peace. Just leave. Go back to Wisconsin. Forget Alice. Do what you promised. It's what you were born for."

But she couldn't forget Alice, and, in the end, she found her. She stood in her new fur coat against a wall and howled like the wind. A solemn little girl took her by the hand and led her to the end of the street.

She was finishing off a drunken sailor under a streetlight at midnight in the snow while people passed by and threw pennies and nickels on the cobblestones. When she was finished, she spit on the street, on the sailor's shoes, and he staggered away without even closing his pants. Alice looked up and saw Catherine, then calmly leaned over and began to pick up the change in the dark.

"I don't want you here."

"I've come to take you . . . to take you someplace nice."

"I don't want to hear about it. I don't want to know."

"I have money. I have money for you." She reached into her purse.

"I don't want it. What would I do with it?"

"I've come here for you. Let's go to your . . . to where you live so we can talk." She looked at the row of shanties, lean-tos with candles guttering out in the late dark. "Which one?"

"Whichever one's empty. I don't want you here." She was counting her money. "Some rich man, I guess."

"Yes. He's rich."

"In here." Alice ducked into an empty shanty, no more than boards stacked against a wall. Catherine ducked and followed her in. Alice reached in her pocket, pulled out a two-penny candle stolen from a church and lit it with a trembling hand. "There. Home."

In the flickering light, Alice's face looked girlish again, softer, golden. The skin across her cheekbones had the tightness of somebody who was going to die. It didn't matter from what.

Catherine thought of the sweet dresses she had made, the smocking and the lace and the long pleated hems. She thought of the homework, Alice's beautiful and careful penmanship, the safe rooms of Philadelphia. She remembered the tiny dog in Gramercy Park. All lost. So much losing in this world. So much loss.

"I'll get you doctors. I'll take you home and . . ."

"Oh. A home. I bet you got a lot of money in that purse."

"I'll give you some. I'll give you anything to come with me."

Alice leaned back against the wall of the shack and rolled a cigarette. Her hands trembled with the cold. She lit the cigarette and looked at Catherine. "You know, I feel so lazy. I work so hard all the time and I don't feel tired, I can't sleep at night, but I feel lazy. Like you could do anything to me and I'd be too lazy to care. But I can't go with you. I don't know where it is, but I know it's too far."

"I'd take you on a train."

Her face turned hard again. It was just a flicker, her hope, and then it went out. Her cigarette sparked in the darkness. "Catherine. Try to understand something. I never liked you. I told you once. I'm telling you now. Not ever."

"I . . ."

"You could take me away, you could take me to Paris, to some spa far away and make me well, and I'd still be bad."

"There was never a moment when I didn't love you."

"Like some little doll baby."

"You were all I had in the world. All I loved. I wanted things to be different for you. Sweeter."

The candle flickered out. They sat in darkness except for the glowing tip of Alice's cigarette. Catherine wanted to reach out to her, but she didn't. "Isn't there anything I can do for you?"

Alice hesitated, then grabbed Catherine's hand, caressed Catherine's silken skin with her own rough, dirty fingers.

"Sister, sit. I'm sorry. I'm bad and I'm sick and I say things. But just sit by me. I'm never alone, but I always feel so lonely. So far away from everybody. Nobody holds me. Nobody touches me or calls my name. Sit with me until I sleep. That's all I need, all you need to do. Please."

"Can't I take you somewhere? Out of here? To a hotel? A hot bath? Clean sheets?"

"You know, it's funny. Even if I were well and clean and dressed in a hat and a fine silk dress, I would never leave here. This is all my life is about. I finally found a place I belong."

Catherine stood, took off her fine fur coat, and laid it over her sister's body.

"That's nice," said Alice. "You always looked out for me."

"I tried."

"Why were you so good to me? I didn't deserve it."

"You were all I had. I tried to save you from some of the misery."

"You can't save anybody. You know that by now."

Alice closed her eyes, smoothed the fur of her sister's coat. "I re-member the boats. On the river in Philadelphia. The beautiful men rowing, like spiders skating with the tide, the sun on their strong brown shoulders. So quick they were, here and then gone. You think I've forgotten, and I've tried, but I remember. The beautiful dresses you made, they must have been beautiful, everything you did was beautiful. And the little shoes, the buttonhook. Where are they now? What happened to those things? You were good to me. So good and kind."

"I haven't been good or kind. What a pair we are."

"When I close my eyes, when my head is clear enough, I think you did your best, and I hated you and I was hateful. You were the last nice thing, and I may never see you again and so I say thank you. I've never said thank you to anybody, for anything, but I'm saying it to you now."

"You're welcome."

"As though it were ever enough. You should go now. It's late. It can get pretty rough. Go back to your nice hotel and your rich man. You tried to save me and you didn't. It wasn't your fault."

They sat until the cigarette was gone and Alice was asleep, her money clutched in her hand. Rats crawled around them once the light was out, and the cold came in and the snow came down harder, and Catherine looked at the slim outline of her sister's face, and she thought her heart would break.

Then she saw it. She saw something descend, an angel was all she could call it, grace made visible, like a mist, like a fog. With golden wings and white hair and white skin the angel floated down, like out of a child's picture book, like a book of stories from the library, this creature of light and air wafting down from the sky as quiet, as vaporous as breath. She knew this angel, this answered prayer had

come to her, and to Alice, and the boards would part and the angel
would take her sister in his arms and fly with her around the world,
to London and to Rome and to the mountains of South America,
the whole brilliant gracious blue spinning mother, and lay Alice
softly into a clean white bed with clean white sheets, wholly safe
and completely healthy. The angel drew closer. She could hear the
soft whoosh of wings, and no other sound but that, the whooshing.
She could see the angel's pure white transparent feet, could feel his
warm breath on her frozen cheek.

Then Catherine watched the angel rise into the dark night sky,
his arms empty. Alice lay unredeemed, as inert as an abandoned
doll. Catherine knew it was too late; there was an abandonment of
hope. Her sister couldn't be saved.

And she knew she couldn't kill Ralph Truitt. She knew she
couldn't bring harm to one living soul. Not anymore.

The angel was gone, the whooshing only the icy wind off the
dirty frozen river, trailing up and into Wild Cat Chute, where
Alice Land lay dying.

The snow was falling harder. The cold got through Catherine's
skin and into her bones. She shivered. She opened her sister's hand
and curled into it all the money she had, dollar after dollar, crum-
pled bills, whore's money, dirty money, and she closed her sister's
hand around it. She kissed her on the forehead, wet with the sweat
of disease, of dissipation and despair. She wiped a wisp of hair out
of her eyes. She watched the snow fall through the open roof and
onto her fine new black fur coat over her sister's sleeping body,
knowing the money and the coat would both be gone before her
sister woke up.

These were the lives they had made, she and Alice. Such things
happened.

CHAPTER SIXTEEN

WHEN IT WAS FINALLY CLEAR to her that Alice was gone forever, had been within reach and had slipped away to despair and death, she lay on her bed in the hotel and wept for two days. She was undone with grief. She wore the plain, austere dresses she had brought from Wisconsin. The maids brought her broth and worried for her, asking if she were sick, changing her sheets, drawing a hot bath for her in the afternoons, plumping her ruined pillows. They fed the bird.

Alice had been her child, her darling. She had lived a part of her life in the hope that things would be different for her, that she would find a nice man and a little house, something normal, nothing grand, and she would be industrious and motherly. She was prepared not to see her; she was prepared for their lives to become unmanageably distinct; but she had never imagined this.

She went to church. She didn't know how to pray, and she asked one of the fathers to help her. She knelt down, her face pale, and she asked for forgiveness, she asked for some reason to go on, and none came. God, as he had always been, was silent. No angels descended, no honey-haired Christ child, no voices comforted her, no miracle brought her back to life. She was dead, as dead as Alice would be.

The priest blessed her, forgave her sins, and made the sign of the cross on her forehead. She was ashamed to tell him she didn't understand what he was doing, that the act was meaningless to her.

Sometimes she didn't sleep for days. Sometimes she slept around the clock. She never knew, when she went to bed, whether it would be dark or light out when she woke up.

If it was dark, she would find Antonio. If it was light, she would sit in her room while the maids came and went, reading poetry her husband had given her, the long love poem to everything on the planet, and dreaming of the garden she would make when the spring came.

She wrote Truitt a letter and told him she was coming home, and was deliberately vague about whether she was bringing Antonio along. She told him she hoped his son would be with her, that he seemed to be coming closer to her point of view. She apologized for being away so long. She hoped his health was good, and asked after Mrs. Larsen. She said that she had eaten nothing in Saint Louis half so good as Mrs. Larsen's cooking, which was, at least in a way, true. She felt as though her life, her old life, were going up in flames in front of her eyes. Then she wrote to Truitt and asked him to send the railroad car.

When the railroad car was waiting in the station, she made the walk one last time through the dusk to Tony Moretti's. The air had lost the sharp heart of its chill. Winter's back was broken.

She knocked on Tony's door, and she found she was trembling, shaking with an old familiar rage. Where was the miracle? Why was she always on the tightrope caught between the beginning and the end?

He was sleek as a tiger, ready for his night. He loathed her. He pitied her. He needed her. He was struck by her calm, the simplicity of her beauty, which he had not noticed before. But she looked full of something, something new.

"I've come to tell you something. To ask something."

"You better come in. At least that."

It was so simple, and she didn't know how to tell him. He was the closest she had ever come to having a sweetheart, and she felt an old fondness for him. She saw the open closet, her useless finery still hanging, the hats and bags, the extravagant dresses, and they seemed like things she had worn a long, long time ago. In another life lost to her now. The dresses were just sad reminders, like the dirty plates from a dinner she had relished.

"Release me from my promise. I can't do it. I won't."

"Won't do what?" He lay back on a long chair, so lean, so muscular and beautiful, his shoes polished and elegant.

"I won't kill Truitt."

He smiled. "Yes, you will. Listen to me, Catherine. You mean a lot to me, but not as much as you think. There was a time you were the moon and the stars. Remember? Coming home at dawn, sleeping until the afternoon and making love as the sun went down? My body, your body, bathed in the glow of twilight and Chinese lanterns. You found me in that bar, a tough little boy, and you made me feel graceful and sweet and wild with love. We could have that again. We could have it forever. And we will. Out of this filthy city, away from these cold and foulmouthed people. We will have a life of music and luxury and endless delight. You made a promise. For us. I hold you to it."

"I can't. He's a good man, Tony."

"So you love him now?"

"No. I don't know if I love anybody, but if I do, I love you. It seems I've loved you forever."

"Then why?"

"He went into this with an honest heart, and he doesn't deserve it. Come home. He'll be good to you. He's good to me."

"I don't care. That house and his money are worthless to me while he's alive. I'm not going to wait until he dies. I'm not going to wait while you sleep in his bed. He killed my mother. You don't shake hands and forgive. You don't forget."

"We've lived the lives we've made. I've lost. You've lost. This memory you have. It was sweet for such a short time. We've behaved badly. To each other. In the world. It's over. We're over. It's got to stop."

"And it will. It'll stop the moment Truitt is dead. The minute you send me word Truitt is dead, this whole life is a history at an end. I'll be sweet as a lamb. We'll have everything."

"I have everything. I have more than I deserve."

He jumped up from the chaise. He grabbed her by the wrists and looked at her with iron fury. "I don't give a damn what you have. You come here all contrite, awash with remorse, changed you say like some country moron who's seen the face of Christ in a potato, and you think you can go to Wisconsin and be the little wife in a town that's named after my father's father, and none of this will have happened. You think you've bought your freedom. As long as I'm alive, you'll never be free, and you'll do what you promised. You'll do what I tell you. You know why?"

She knew. She knew exactly, but she couldn't stand to hear it. She twisted her wrists from his beautiful hands; she walked across the room and stupidly felt her dresses, the fabric of her old life, as though it were an exhibit in the Japanese Pavilion. She couldn't look at him.

"Because if you don't, if you don't kill him, I'll write him a letter. That's all it will take. One letter. You think he wants to hear this? You think he wants to hear about his wife in bed with his son? The filthy details? You think he wants to hear his wife is a common whore who's been doing the same thing over and over and over from the time she was fifteen? Where does his kindness, his goodness go then?"

"I can't stand this. I'll die."

"You haven't died yet. You won't die now. You don't die from being ashamed."

"I'll stay here with you. I'll never go back there."

"And live in this filth? This filthy life? I wouldn't have you. Not now. Not ever. No, Catherine. You'll go back up there, you'll pretend to be everything you're not, a virgin, if that's what he wants, a duchess, a believer, and you'll drop poison in his food, just like you said, and he'll be dead. I can wait. I've waited all my life. I despise you, but you'll lose everything and you'll end up in the gutter."

She knelt on the floor, pulling a dress from the closet behind her. "I beg you."

"Get on your fancy train and go home to your fancy husband and get rid of him. Dead. That's the only way he means anything to me."

"I beg you."

"Some promises can't be broken. It's gone too far. We're too close now, too deep in the water. Get up off the floor and get out of here. I don't want to hear from you until he's dead."

"I—"

"Not one word, Catherine. You haven't earned the right to beg. There's no freedom for you. No place to go. You ruin everything you touch. I'm leaving. I don't want to find you here when I get back. I don't want to find you anywhere in Saint Louis."

She rose from the floor. He was right, of course. There was no way out.

He turned before leaving. His voice was almost kind again. "It's true. I have loved you. I could love you again. We both knew what we were getting into. We got into it out of love. You knew from the start."

When he was gone, she wandered his rooms. Her mind could only plague her with the old thoughts. There was death by poison in her deep bathtub. There was arsenic, laudanum, muriatic acid. There was the silken cord from a sturdy beam. There was the long fall, like a black bird, from the window of her quiet room at the Planter's Hotel. She would set the bird free. There was death beneath the wheels of a train car, death by syringe and razor and bullet.

Then there was survival. There was going on, as she had always gone on, without much joy, against her will, against her instincts, without the stomach for it, but on and on and on, without relief, without release, without a hand to reach out and touch her heart. Without kindness or comfort. But on.

Forced into such poverty, imprisoned in such despair, there was only one thing she was sure she could do. She could survive.

❧ *Part Three* ❧

WISCONSIN. WINTER INTO SPRING. 1908.

CHAPTER SEVENTEEN

———❦———

H E LIKED TO HAVE a glass of clear, cold water by his
bed when he went to sleep at night. The glass was tall
and straight and etched with vines, and Mrs. Larsen
washed it every morning and filled it every night from the cold
tap and put it by his bed. It was a beautiful glass, brought from
Italy, and the light shone through the water and the glass with its
frosted sides in a way that pleased him. When he was alone, when
he was alone for those twenty years, night after night after solitary
night, lying in immaculate sheets, he would sometimes swing his
legs over the edge of the bed, put his feet solidly on the floor, and
take a sip of the clear cold water. He sat up straight because he was
afraid he might choke, alone in the big old house at night with no
one to hear him.

The sheets of his bed were changed twice a week, and he sometimes looked with sadness at the other side of the bed, seeing the
pillow where no head ever lay. He felt embarrassed to think of Mrs.
Larsen taking the sheets off his bed twice a week, to see them so

little used. It was one of the ways his loneliness was made visible to
the world, and he was ashamed.

The glass of water comforted him, and he clung to the habit
with tenacity. The water meant nothing in itself. He was rarely
thirsty. The ritual meant everything, a moment to close the day,
the moisture on his dry lips like a soft kiss.

He could smell his clean white shirts in the armoire, soap and
bluing and starch. He could see the day's clothes, neatly folded in
a chair, waiting for Mrs. Larsen to sponge and press them fresh in
the morning. Everything he owned was clean all the time. He could
smell Mrs. Larsen's industry in the still night air, the laundry, the
furniture polish, the floor wax, and he was grateful for her, that she
looked after him so well. It was a comfort. Even though he paid
her, and took care of her and Mr. Larsen well, it was a kindness.
He paid many people, and not one felt it necessary to be more than
cordial.

He had never called her by her first name, a name he must have
known once, but had long ago forgotten. Mrs. Larsen had been
only a girl when he first knew her, Jane, Jeanette, something, un-
married, not pretty, and she had grown into middle age learning
his habits and making his life comfortable. He presumed she never
liked Emilia. She showed no sorrow when she was gone.

He thought of the endless meals she had cooked and served
to him. He thought of the shirts and the trousers and the shoes
polished and the tears mended and the mud scraped off his boots,
and he loved her for her kindness. So little was done to tend his
creature comforts, and these comforts, in the absence of passion,
had meant everything to him. She had witnessed the terrible sadness, the betrayal, and managed to treat him as though her heart
went out to him and, at the same time, as though the past had never

happened. She knew his awful solitude and didn't pay notice. She cooked enough food every night for four or six, since the sight of the food pleased him, and then she and Larsen ate later, after he had finished and gone to his study. He had asked, but they had never sat down to the table with him. It wouldn't be right. They wouldn't have been comfortable.

He had meant to be so many things. He had meant to be a poet. He had meant to be a lover and collector of art, to encourage young artists and have them gather around him. He had meant to live his life in an orgy of sensation, according to the sensual rules of attraction and seduction. He had meant to be a father, to have children to inherit his love of the arts and the flesh. Instead, he had lost his heart's deepest passions; one day he woke up and realized they were gone, amputated as surely as an arm, cut off by the death of his little girl and the infidelities of his wife, the intractable rage he felt toward his bastard child. His affections and obsessions had been replaced by clean shirts and half-slept-in sheets and polished boots and clear soups. The world of the body and its pleasures had closed over, as a scab closes over a wound.

Catherine Land had stepped off the train from Saint Louis, softer, warmer in her face, unexpectedly beautiful, and the wound had opened and filled him with its pain. Antonio was not by her side, and neither one of them said a word about him.

Standing in the station, he had felt that something in him would break forever if he didn't touch her. He reached up and shyly fingered the collar of her coat. That was all. That was enough. He was lost in hope and desire, as lost as he had been in his first days with Emilia. Catherine was everything. She was not a woman; she was a world. She might wound him, she might lie to him, and still he would do anything to hear one word of kindness from her lips, to feel his flesh touch her flesh without humiliation. He was willing to take the chance. And all this because she had stepped from the train with a small scarlet bird in a cage, and she was coming home to him, bringing a fluttering life. He was at last waiting for someone whose name was known to him. People saw her come home to him, people in his town. She smiled at him, and he knew then that he would die for her.

His skin was soft as a clean chamois. He was strong, he was lean. But he was not young. His heart had for so long been open only to bitterness and regret, but now his sexual passion, buried for so long, was once again wild in his heart.

She looked solemn, almost stricken. The bird sang sweetly. She kissed his cheek gravely and there she was. She was home.

The snow still lay around them as they rode home, and neither one spoke. His heart pounded in his chest. He wanted her. He wanted to know about his son, but he couldn't speak or make a move. He wanted to say something, to remark about the difference between her first arrival, so wild, and this, so calm and peaceful. He wanted to be affectionate and familiar, but he couldn't form a sentence. He fingered the faint scar on his forehead and stared straight ahead.

At home, they sat across from each other in front of the fire. Her dress was new. Her hair and her face had softened. He knew her news before she spoke it, because Antonio was not with her, and because he could see in her face that she wished it were otherwise.

"He's not your son. He swears he's not your son."

"What do you think?"

"I think that what he says is all we've got to go on. Any more . . . there is no more. He says his name is Moretti. He says his parents run a restaurant in Philadelphia. He says he's never seen you or heard of you or been closer to Wisconsin than Chicago. Malloy and Fisk say he's not a nice man, without scruples or morals or decency. I . . . there wasn't any farther to go with it. I tried."

"What does he look like?"

She was careful. "He looks Italian. Exotic. He looks refined, like an aristocrat of some kind."

"How does he live?"

"He plays the piano in . . . in a music hall, a cheap place. I never saw it. He likes it. I went to see him, to where he lives, to offer him anything to come home. He simply said it was not his home, he didn't know what I was talking about. His rooms are done up like a circus tent. He dresses like a dandy. A fop."

"What did his voice sound like?"

"Malloy and Fisk say he's a useless, pretty object, good for nothing. They've followed him for months. They say he's not worth the finding."

"What do you think?"

"I think he's your wife's son and Moretti's. I don't know. He's whatever you want him to be. I think he's lying. I think he can't forgive you and won't come home. Not now. Not ever. I think he's a lost cause. I wish . . ."

"Wish what, Catherine?"

"I wish I could have done more. I tried. I went to him. I saw a flicker on his brow the first time he heard your name, something that gave him away. Or so I thought. And I knew he was lying, and I went to him and offered him money. I talked to him for hours. I told him about your regret, that you were sorry. That you had never forgiven yourself. He doesn't care. I gave him the ring from my finger. Your ring. He asked for it and I gave it gladly, instantly, but he laughed and handed it back. He won't be persuaded. Even if . . .'"

"Even if what?"

"Even if he is your son."

"And you say he is."

"I do. He doesn't."

"Andy."

"He calls himself Tony."

"He asked for your ring?"

"I gave it to him. He was teasing."

She could see the agony on his face. He wanted the thing that frightened him the most, and the pain was terrible, worse than the wound on his forehead when she stitched him up. She hoped he believed her. She counted on it.

"We'll move to the big house. We'll move next week. Give this place to Larsen and his wife."

"We don't have to. There's no reason. Now there's no reason."

"It's been ready for him for years. Malloy writes that he's greedy, that he never has any money. He'll come when everything else has failed. We'll move in and we'll wait."

She thought of her garden and the delight it would bring her. She thought of the high halls and the crystal chandeliers and the portraits of people unknown to her. She thought of herself, skirts trailing, walking the long halls of the upper galleries, and she knew it was what she wanted, that he was doing it for her after his own hope was gone.

"I've been happy here. We could go on."

"I want a child. I won't die without having a child. If you're willing. If God is willing and you'd be so kind, I'd be grateful."

"Of course."

"It's a house for children. A palace of adventures and secret stair-cases, and . . . I was a child when I built it, a spoiled, willful, stupid child. We go on, as you say."

They ate dinner in silence, Mrs. Larsen bringing and removing the plates. They ate little. Even after her long train trip, Catherine respected Truitt's sorrow, and her appetite seemed nothing to her. How could her heart not go out to him, knowing what she knew, steeled as she was?

He had no mechanism to discuss his sorrow. He had not had a single unmitigated joy in twenty years, and now a real sorrow had hit him, without explanation or protection, and he was just as mute. His lost son. The dream of his life, to save something out of all that terror, his own terrible behavior, and now even that gone.

And she, over coffee growing cold, she couldn't resist speaking of it, as much as she felt for him.

"We saw him. In a restaurant. We heard him play."

"How did he sound?"

"Charming. Sad. I'm no judge."

"You play beautifully."

"I'm no judge."

I've lost everything, he wanted to say. I have denied myself and tortured myself and done every single thing that has been expected of me, and it was for nothing. My shirts are clean. My behavior is above reproach. And it means nothing. He was caught in the softest places of his heart, his gaze at her face, the beginnings of a fond-ness for her, because she came home and he was glad to see her, a bird in its cage, singing, and his anguished memory of the cruelties he had shown this boy who now denied his existence. It was too much. And he was struck mute.

The coffee was cold. The dinner was over, and it was late. When they went up the stairs, he asked her gently if she would like to sleep in her own room.

"Whatever for?"

"You must be tired from the trip."

"You're my husband."

His glass of water was by the bed, a good night gift from Mrs. Larsen while they had lingered over their sad cold coffee. He went into the bathroom, to give her time to dress for bed, and knelt on the floor with his forehead on the cold commode until his fever had cooled. When he came back to the bedroom, he neatly undressed and folded his clothes for Mrs. Larsen to take care of, then turned back the sheets, shocked and aroused and touched to see that she was for the first time naked in bed, ready for him, waiting naked, knowing his need.

He made love to her with a ferocity that surprised him, that caused rivulets of sweat to run down his back and chest, his mouth on hers, his hand on the soft curve of her thigh, the thrill of his weight supported on his arms, his hands everywhere. Making love to her was like bathing in warm water. She washed over him. She was pliant and helpful, not forward, but helpful, and he was pleased that he could please her even as he pleased himself. To feel the action and passion and flesh of his body, his own sweat, his own manipulations of a woman's desires, beyond speech, so that he became, in the end, pure movement, pure desire, obliterating his body and his business and his terrible agony and even her face and body until his own body and his need and his own mute sorrow were the only things in the whole wide world. He heard her soft moan of pleasure, and for a moment, for one moment, he felt at peace, his breath coming in long slow sighs, his hands stilled, his angers forgotten and his passions dissipated. He held her in his arms, his weight fully on her now. He smoothed the wild hair back from her forehead.

"Thank you," he said, and she turned her head and said nothing, and he knew that it was the wrong thing to say. It was the kind of thing he had said, long ago, to wanton women in hotel rooms. It was not even what he wanted to say. He wanted to tell her that his heart was finally broken, broken beyond repair or solace, leaving only his sorrow and his rage to hold him upright. But Ralph Truitt couldn't speak of the workings of his heart, it wasn't his habit. So he thanked her and instantly regretted it, regretted also the tears he could not shed over his son. He wanted to weep. But having shed not a single tear after all these years, he had no tears now. Not for himself. Not for Antonio. Not for his wife who would, in the end, bear the awful burden of the man he would become. And she would sleep beside him, and she would know and she would be helpless and he would come to hate her, hate her helplessness.

It had returned, of course, this agony over this boy who was not even his own flesh and blood, and he wondered, with so much within reach, with this woman in his arms and under his roof, why he needed to get Andy back. Yet it was a dream he had held in his heart for so long that nothing could replace it, nothing made up for his loss and his desire for restitution. This boy, this child whom he had betrayed, whom he might have loved and watched grow into a man, a man who might have rebelled and gone away even so, but who might have come back as Truitt himself had done, to run the businesses, learning the ways of production and accounting and the endless management of the people who worked for him, their stories, their hardships, their small victories. Antonio. Andy. Tony Moretti. A stranger, now grown into the handsome, careless man he tried to imagine. This man whom he did not know, whom he had beaten. His wife's son. His own prodigal, to whom he would have opened the doors wide.

Catherine slept beside him. Her slow breathing filled the air with sweetness. The dark surrounded them, and she slept on the side of the bed that had been empty for twenty years. Mrs. Larsen would see the evidence of their lovemaking, the stained sheets, and know that he was not alone anymore. She would smile. The thought made him shy. They knew so much from such small details.

It was no use. He sat up and put his feet on the floor. His naked body shivered with the cold. However strong his body, however smooth his flesh, he was no longer young. He couldn't get it back; too much was behind him and too little ahead. He felt at that moment the end of his life had begun. He felt it in his heart. He felt it in his bones. He heard it in his labored breathing. His blood rushed with pleasure, and his mind dwelt on death. He would be in the ground, beside his parents. He would be in hell, living forever with his mother, with the pin through the soft part of his hand.

He felt, with Antonio now irretrievably gone, that something in him had ceased to live, had given up the hope that had kept him going through all the loneliness and all the years. He didn't understand it. He had so much, and he didn't understand why he had invested this one thing with so much importance. The advertisement and the wife who was not what she pretended to be, the detectives and the money and the hope and the waiting, it was for one single reason, for the dream of Antonio, and now he knew finally that he would never come home again.

The moonlight shone through the window. The faint blue light caught the glass of water by the bed, and he suddenly felt so thirsty he thought he would die. He reached out and held the glass in his hands for a long moment. He smelled it and paused, but only for a second. Then he drank the water, drank all the water, and with the first sip, from the faint smell and the bitter aftertaste, he knew the water was tainted. He looked into the bottom of the beautiful Italian glass. He looked at his lovely wife, sleeping peacefully as a child in the moonlight. He remembered Florence, his days of indolence. He knew he was being poisoned.

And he didn't care. He just didn't care anymore.

CHAPTER EIGHTEEN

I T WAS EVERYWHERE. Arsenic. Inheritance powder, the old people called it. It was in his food, his water, on his clothing. It was on his hairbrush when he brushed his hair in the morning. He smelled it. He tasted it on the back of his tongue and in his throat. Not all the time, not every day, but always there. At first, the effect was tonic. He felt marvelous and strong. His skin looked ruddy and clear. His heart beat solidly in his chest. His hair was glossy and his eyes blue and clear and piercing. People remarked on his appearance, people who never made a personal remark to Ralph Truitt told him he looked ten years younger. They thought his new marriage agreed with him.

Whatever his desperate sorrow, he kept on as before. He was cordial and well mannered and evenhanded with the workers, and he was dying and he knew he was dying and kindness seemed to be all that was left.

Catherine was extremely tender. She listened intently when he spoke, and he spoke to her often, about his business, about his plans to expand. He never spoke about Antonio, never told her how his heart was heavy and dead. He never said that he wanted to die but was afraid of death, of the long painful process of dying. He wanted to tell her it was all right, he wanted to tell her she would have everything when it was done, he had made a will while she was in Saint Louis, not believing that Antonio would ever come to claim it, but he couldn't. He was shocked by what she was doing, of course. Yet he couldn't speak to her about it. He was complicit. He was her only accomplice.

Her voice was like music to him.

"I've never had a minute's peace until now," he said. "For twenty years. Not a minute's happiness. You have given that to me, and I'm grateful. So grateful, you couldn't know." They sat at the long table, their dinner done.

"I'd do anything to make you happy. Give you things. Say whatever you wanted to hear. You know that." He took her hand.

She knew the words he was saying were true. "What else would I want? You're exactly the thing I waited for. I don't want anything else. I thought I would be disappointed. I thought I would want to escape. I made plans. I had some foolish jewels. I lost them that first night when the carriage ran away. They were what I would have used to run away. I didn't know then that . . . How could this come to be? From an advertisement." She laughed, and it was like water falling from a great height. He laughed, thinking of his foolishness.

"I could have chosen someone else."

"I could have sent you my own picture and not India's, and you would not have chosen me. Were there so many?"

"Dozens. All virtuous. Some widows. Some young. Practically children. Younger than you. Some gold diggers."

"Then why me?"

" 'I am a simple, honest woman.' You wrote that. A simple, honest face. I knew right away. There wasn't anybody else, after that."

"It wasn't my face."

"As it turned out, no."

"Do you have any regrets?"

"Not anymore."

"What did you do with the letters? The other letters?"

"I burned them, in a big pile in the yard."

They moved into the grand palace through the woods. Truitt had modern bathrooms installed throughout the house, as a wedding present to his new wife. He had the house wired for electricity, and sent for lamps from Chicago. He had the chandelier wired. He put in a new kitchen for Mrs. Larsen, although she said she didn't need one. Everything else stayed as it had always been.

They packed the pieces of fancy furniture from the farmhouse into wagons and hauled them the long way to the big golden house, restoring the chairs and the tables to the spots they had occupied twenty years before. Truitt gave the farmhouse to Larsen, signed the deed over to him.

The big house was reborn, and they sat close together at one end of the long table in the frescoed dining room, a fire blazing against the chill as the wind howled outside, and they spoke of love and practical matters in low voices. She changed her dress for dinner. She played the piano for him. She read Whitman to him in the yellow salon, by the great fireplace, big enough to drive a wagon into.

They gave dinner parties, small, solemn affairs attended by men who needed Truitt's influence. Doctors came, and lawyers and judges with their mute wives. The governor came. He wanted Truitt's money, and Truitt gave him some as he left. The dinner parties were not amusing. The food was superb.

They picked out their bedroom with care. It was not the grandest, not the ornate one he had shared with Emilia. It was a large, simple, blue room with a view of the walled garden. They installed his father's big bed, and he would lie with his head on the soft pillows at night, while her scarlet bird sang sweetly and she sat in the window seat before they made love. She described the splendors that would come with the summer, the roses and the clematis and the calla lilies and the cheerful dark-eyed daisies. She cataloged the Latin names she had learned. She described the rich fragrance that would come in the night air through the open windows. She would paint every leaf, every flower for him in color, and he would lie, eyes closed, and wonder if he would live long enough to see it. It was lovely, in her description. It was the garden that Emilia had never had the patience or knowledge to create.

She had asked Larsen to dig through the snow, to uncover the ruin of the plants that had not been cared for in twenty years, and she would stare into the cold moonlight at the tangled naked vines and the overturned statues, the empty lemon house and orangery. She would speak to him of the life she would bring to the earth, with her own hands. She would tell him of her long days in the library, of all she had learned.

The house sheltered them against the late snows. The moonlight came through the window. She was alive beside him, and he could not believe that his desires could be so strong as his body turned to poison, while his sorrow for Antonio grew more and more terrible.

The house was too much, too large for Mrs. Larsen, and they hired two girls from the village, and an extra man, so that everything was always clean and there was wood enough to keep a fire going in every fireplace in the evenings, so they could choose any room they wanted to sit in after dinner.

In late February, Ralph's bookkeeper went suddenly insane and murdered his wife of twenty-eight years for no reason. Mr. and Mrs. Truitt attended the funeral, standing solemnly in black clothes while the grown children wept for their lost mother.

"Why do they do these things? These terrible things?" Catherine asked as they rode home in the carriage.

"They hate their lives. They start to hate each other. They lose their minds, wanting things they can't have."

Ralph attended the brief trial, watching as the husband wept for his lost wife and tore at his clothes. The children stared on in horror and hatred.

Ralph, however, understood. He knew that people suddenly woke up one day and reason was gone, all sense of right and wrong, all trust in their own intentions. It happened. The winter was too long. The air was too bleak. The cause was unknowable, the effect unpredictable. The bookkeeper was sent to an insane asylum, where every day he would mourn his beloved wife, and ask if she was coming to see him.

Ralph wanted to believe that Catherine was drugging him to inspire youth and vigor, the way a horse trader would dope a horse to put shine in its coat, fire in its eye, to fool an unsuspecting buyer. He believed that she had brought the poison from Saint Louis, from Chinatown perhaps, bought with some flimsy excuse, that in her long days without him, she had conceived of this plan to give him tiny doses of a poison that would make him young again. If only for a little while. A little while would be enough. In Florence he had sometimes used such poisons so that his lovemaking could go on without stopping for hours, and he had used it to cure a case of the clap he had gotten one summer. He felt oblivious, then. He felt divine. There were reasons. There had to be reasons. It was possible.

Her ardor matched his own. He no longer cared that her skill in sexual variations far exceeded her descriptions of her former life, her narrow, missionary life. She seemed wanton to him, without limits, like the women he had loved in his youth. He loved her, he wanted her, and she was always there. She had gone away to Saint Louis shy and distant, dressed in plain straight dresses, and she had come home a different person, softer, lighter around the mouth, in simple clothes that spoke of quiet good taste and old money, someone he had never expected to find again in his life. She was his dream.

He struggled every night to get through dinner without touching her, to wait until time to go to bed. He struggled to make conversation to avoid her gaze, to listen to her sweet voice as she read to him, the soft strain as she played the piano or they played cards while Mrs. Larsen cleared and cleaned the dinner things.

Catherine lay in his arms every night, and every night the sweat that ran off his back would collect between her breasts, leave them both soaked. She would bring a clean linen cloth, and gently dry his back, his chest, his legs and feet. Every night she slept beside him, every night he drank his crystal water until there was nothing left, and every morning she was there when he woke already hard from his troubled dreams.

Poison. It was the poison of pleasure, the poison he had known would kill him. His mother knew. He still had the scar on his hand to remind him. This was the poison his mother had seen in the flecks of his eyes even before his eyes had looked at a woman's naked body. This was wickedness, and it was fatal.

He dreamed about women. His sensual life, so long ago, came back to him in his dreams, finely detailed, lusciously intoxicating. Voices called to him. He lay naked in open fields, the wind ruffling the hair of a young girl who lay next to him, her dress open to the light, her breasts in his hands. He lay in courtyards, in gardens while water from the fountains played over marble statues and the air was rich with the scent of gardenias and jasmine and rosemary, and the soft voices of women whispered in his ear, while their fingertips pulled at his clothes. While their fingernails, clean and sharp, tore at the flesh of his back. Dreaming, his eyes roamed behind his lids over the luxuries of sex.

He dreamed about men who were not himself and women he had never known. He dreamed about his mother and father, lost in the mute, loveless passion that had created him. He dreamed about the men and women of the town, so religious, so strict and secret and fertile. He dreamed of young lovers and the first kiss, the first ribbon untied with trembling adolescent fingers while standing by a waterfall, a crystal stream, a place he knew.

He dreamed about large house parties. They were gay and filled with good things to eat and well-dressed men and women from twenty and forty years before. In these dreams, he was a child among grownups. There was laughter and pleasure and the unspoken signs of desires fulfilled. They were not people he knew. They were not houses he recognized. The houses were enormous, and filled with many rooms that opened on to one another so there was a constant flow among the guests from room to room, from gaiety to gaiety and partner to partner. They had beautiful skin and musical voices, and he loved them, loved being among them. In these dreams, where he sometimes saw his mother and father happy, he did not have sex, but the air was so redolent with desire that he became sex itself, and walked with strength in his legs, with a pride unknown to him.

He never dreamed of Catherine. He never dreamed of Emilia. They were never present. He dreamed of Antonio, and the sight of Antonio with woman after woman. These dreams embarrassed him and filled him with shame but also with longing.

He smelled flowers, in his dreams. He smelled almonds. He smelled his own flesh dying.

The dreams vanished before dawn, and he awoke anxious and disturbed, to find Catherine already there, reaching out for him.

"You were restless in your sleep. I could feel you moving."

"I had dreams."

"Was I there?"

"No."

It didn't matter that her hair was tangled, her breath stale, her nightdress around her knees. It didn't matter who she was, who she had pretended to be. It didn't matter the atrocity she was committing. What she was doing to him. He reached out of his dream and took her into his arms, wanting more than any woman could possibly give, and getting more than he ever thought could come to him.

He knew that this moment, this feeling of well-being, these gorgeous dreams of gross desire and easy fulfillment, he knew this was a momentary thing. The drug's erotic effect would end soon, and the horror would begin, if that was what she wanted. And the fact of it didn't appall him as he thought it should. He wouldn't stop her. He wouldn't save himself. He loved her. He loved her and she wanted him dead, and his son was lost forever to him and that was fine, too. That was what his life had led him to. This was what he had lived twenty years of solitude for, to see what would happen, to see how it would all turn out.

"Before you came, life was terrible."

"You have so much."

"I have whatever's left from the things I've broken; my wife, my child . . . children."

"Those things weren't your fault. Your wife was terrible to you."

"She did what she was made to do. She made me miserable because I was blind, because I wanted to be made miserable. It wasn't her fault. I was ignorant."

"You were generous."

"I almost killed my son. My own boy."

"He . . ."

"He was all the son I had. He was son enough. And he was innocent. Like Franny. Innocent and sweet and stupid."

"The boy in Saint Louis . . . Mr. Moretti."

"What?"

"He might change his mind. He may be your son. I think he is."

Ralph's hand took hers. They stared at each other across the snowy linen.

"Then he's a liar. He'll never change his mind. Everything has failed. It was all for nothing."

He had made his efforts. He had hired detectives, strangers, to find his son. He had placed a shameless advertisement in the newspapers in Chicago and Saint Louis and Philadelphia and San Francisco and he had received and answered the many letters and he had made his choice. His son had turned out to be a phantom.

His illegitimate son, he was aware. His wife had turned out to be the person he had waited for ever since the day he had driven Emilia away. Poison. The life he had was the life he had made, no more, no less, and he wouldn't struggle anymore, wouldn't try to change the course of events.

"What will you do today?"

"I feel so lazy, like a cat. I'll read. I'll sew. I'll ask Mrs. Larsen if she wants any help and she'll say no. I'll wait for you."

"And does that make you happy?"

"It's all I need. It's all I ever wanted."

When she was in the bath, he looked for the poison. He looked in her sewing basket. He searched the pockets of her dresses. He looked through the few contents of her dressing table. He never found anything. It was like a giddy game to him, an Easter egg hunt, and he didn't really care whether he found it or not. He felt it was his duty to look. He would never have confronted her, no matter what he found. He was agitated when he woke, and he wanted to find something, anything, that would prove what he knew to be true. Nothing would matter. She would do as she liked. She wanted everything, he supposed, the house, the money, everything, and he would have given it to her, all of it, if she had asked. He would have lived alone with nothing, if she had wanted. And he would die, if that's what she required.

Mrs. Larsen told him Catherine was restless during the day. Mrs. Larsen assumed she was bored, confined in the big house with nothing to do. Nothing was holding her in. She could go to town now, buy odds and ends, visit ladies she might have met. But she rarely went out, except to the snowy garden. She sometimes walked the road, in the thinning snow, peering into the ruts here and there as though she were trying to find something, but she always came home empty-handed.

Larsen found them in the end. Coming home with rabbits over his shoulder, he looked down and saw a glitter through the mud and picked up her little jewels and rubbed them with his finger until they sparkled in the sun. He brought them home, went straight into Catherine where she sat playing the piano, the dead rabbits still hanging over his shoulder, his muddy boots on the rug from France. He held out his open hand; she took her things.

"This is it, ain't it? What you been looking for?"

"They are, Mr. Larsen. They mean nothing now. But I thank you. I'll put them away. I wore them once, in another place."

Truitt knew it. He heard it before darkness fell, from Mrs. Larsen, but he never asked, and he never saw the trinkets she had brought with her. Women's things, jewelry, rubies or glass, they were all the same.

A widow in town took strychnine, the poison scalding her blood, the bile spewing from her mouth as she lay on the kitchen floor, a cake cooling on the kitchen table. A young man threw his only daughter down a well and smoked a cigarette as she drowned. Such things happened.

Ralph didn't go to the funerals or the trials. He couldn't stand the idea of being in a crowd of people. He couldn't stand the idea of being looked at. He felt the winter would never end, just as each day he couldn't wait for the hours in his office to be over. He felt he would go crazy until he sat again at the long table, listening to the soothing voice of his young wife.

Every death was the death of Antonio. Every crime was the disappearance of his boy. He wept during the day. He wept on the long ride home from his office. He wept every morning as he woke up. And Catherine was the only thing that could ease his sorrow.

Such things happen, he would think as he drove home, the road ahead blurred with tears. The winters were long and life was hard and children died and religion was terror, so he would weep for these sad people, and weep as well for his own Antonio, his own child down the well. He would weep because there had been no trial, no retribution, no one to protect or save the boy from his father's terrible anger. He had escaped unscathed, and Antonio had run away and been lost in the brutal world, while he rode home in his clean clothes to be poisoned by his beautiful wife.

And so he wept.

She got up to change the sheets in the middle of the night. Her arms flew out, and the linens flew across the bed like great birds. Her hands smoothed the sheets, her arms stuffed the pillows into the cases and she piled them, pillow after pillow, on the great bed.

She put on her nightdress and lay beneath the covers. Mrs. Larsen would find the ruined sheets in the linen closet. Catherine patted his side of the bed, and he lay his head on the pillow and stared into her beautiful, calm face. She looked so far away. She was so beloved.

His heart pounded in his chest. His hand reached under her nightdress and lay along her thigh.

"I know what you're doing. I know what's happening to me."

"I . . ."

"Don't say anything. Don't speak. We'll never mention it again. I just wanted you to know that I know, that it's all right. I don't mind. I forgive you. Just . . ."

Her hands were frozen still. Her eyes were wide in the moonlight. They spoke in whispers.

"I don't know what you're saying, what you're talking about."

"When it gets worse, if that's what you want, make it go quickly. I've waited so long to see what would happen, and now I know, and it's fine, it's fine with me, but I want it to go quickly. I don't want to suffer."

"You're tired. Sleep now. I don't know what you're saying. I would never want you to suffer."

He could feel the blood pulsing through the vein of her leg. He could see her eyes dart away from him, dart toward the moonlight. She put out her hand and closed his eyes. She kept her cold hand over his lids, her breath shushed him in his ear, as one might calm a child to sleep, a child who had waked from a nightmare.

"I'll never talk about it again. You are free."

"This doesn't make sense. I don't know what you're saying. I love you."

She had never said it before. No one had said it to him for more than twenty years, yet he believed her. She loved him, and she was the thing that was bringing his death, an end to his torment. She was the angel of his death. And he loved her with all his heart.

She didn't want to do it. She didn't want to watch him die. She truly loathed the idea of him suffering or sickening or any of the things that were about to happen. But she knew that, any day, a letter might come, a letter that would end it all. Love and money—she had promised herself these two things, but she realized more and more that maybe one person got only one thing, and she would not, could not be ruined. She would live in the gutter, Antonio had said. She would grow sad and disheveled, and eventually she would die. But whatever happened, she could only save herself.

A man ate an entire dictionary and died. Larsen cut off his own burned hand with an axe, believing the burn which would not heal was the kiss of the devil, the ineradicable mark of sin, while Mrs. Larsen watched and screamed. As a boy of fifteen, he had fought in the Civil War and come home without a scratch. Now he lay, a drooling idiot with one hand, in an expensive Catholic hospital in Chicago, paid for by Truitt, while Mrs. Larsen never mentioned him again. Such things happened.

Catherine Land, a young wife of Truitt, Wisconsin, set out to poison — slowly, with arsenic — the husband who loved her, whom she herself loved, to her surprise, the man who had saved her from a life of destitution and despair.

Such things happened.

CHAPTER NINETEEN

I'M COLD. I'M COLD all the time." Ralph Truitt said, as he
sat and shivered in the evenings.

Catherine hesitated in her purpose. With the medicine
dropper in her hand, her courage wavered. She put away the poison.
She stopped for a week. He was a good man, honest, decent, good
in his bones, and he didn't deserve this. She knew that, and she felt
in some way, for the first time, that these things mattered. The idea
of goodness had never crossed her mind, and now it seemed very
real. There was a reason people did things; there was a reason some
lives turned out well, others badly. It had never occurred to her. As
though goodness itself were some perfect heaven, and she might
have constantly judged her distance from it, had she ever stopped
to think. Now it haunted her.

She could change her mind, she supposed, would have to, but
the thought of Antonio hung on her like a noose. It was not an
idle threat. He would write, and it would all be over. Antonio was
love to her, or all of it she had known until Ralph. What Antonio

wanted, what she had promised him, would have to be done, some-how. And so she started again.

Love, even bad love, was a glittering lure that could draw her attention, if only for a time. The idea of Antonio dangled in front of her mesmerized eyes. It was just a drop, after all, a drop in his water, in his soup, a drop on his hairbrush. It was clear and icy and almost without odor. She knew how awful it would be. She knew how he would die. She couldn't stop now.

True to his word, he never spoke of it again. He never asked her to stop, never complained of the changes beginning to affect his body, his life. He became anxious. The dreams that had enchanted his sleep turned terrifying, and still he never complained.

He would wake at two or three in the morning, covered in the sweat of terror, and he would turn to her and she would dry him and place him beneath the covers where he would lie until dawn, shivering with the cold. She felt his forehead with her hand. He was burning up. She felt a tenderness she had never felt for any man, a tenderness that went beyond love.

He looked haggard. His clothes began to burn his skin. Any sound, any noise, began to scrape at his ear until he couldn't stand it.

After dinner one night he spoke in a soft voice, reciting a poem:

I wander all night in my vision,
Stepping with light feet, swiftly and noiselessly
     stepping and stopping,
Bending with open eyes over the shut eyes of
     sleepers,
Wandering and confused, lost to myself, ill- assorted,
     contradictory,
Pausing, gazing, bending, and stopping.

She didn't know what he meant. She didn't know where the words came from. There was no reproach in his voice. She assumed it was the beginning of a dementia that would at least make him oblivious to much of what would happen to him.

Depression, morbidity, followed by death. These were the words she had read in the library. She knew everything that was to happen, the sores, the spots in his vision that would turn the world yellow and green, the bilious pustules, the haggard eyes, the dark hollows. She knew and she had thought she was ready.

"It's wrong," said Mrs. Larsen. "I've seen sickness, plenty of it, in Truitt, in . . . in the world, and this ain't no sickness I've ever seen."

Mrs. Larsen began to watch her. Catherine sat and talked to her.

"I don't know what it is. We'll call the doctor. He'll tell us what to do."

A doctor would find nothing, would suspect nothing. A man Truitt's age might develop eczema and rashes. His hair might fall out. He might develop a visionary mind, an acute hearing, a ringing in the ears, an irrationality. Anybody might. Such things happened. Truitt, while he wasn't old, wasn't young either. But Truitt wouldn't have the doctor. The poison was his fuel. He was not unhappy. And he loved his wife. She was the beautiful, lethal, insinuating spider he had waited for all his life. She was the final knife in his heart. He opened his shirt to her with gladness.

Mrs. Larsen watched Catherine every minute of the day. Truitt was her life, and she felt her life slipping cruelly away, as so much else had gone. Gone into madness, into incurable awfulness. And she knew, as she had known before, that it wasn't natural.

Ralph could not bear to be touched. His skin was so raw he

couldn't stand the feel of the softest nightshirt next to him. He slept naked, under smooth sheets that Mrs. Larsen now changed every day.

He could not bear to have Catherine's skin on his skin, and yet his desire for her was undiminished. He shivered with the constant cold. His skin felt raw, the sheets felt like icy nettles in the night. The anxiety he felt before going to sleep could be lessened only by sex. Gently he led her, taught her to give him pleasure without touching.

When he had come, he could sleep for a while, but he woke from terrible dreams. He would sit on the edge of the bed, shivering and burning up with itching. She would undo her hair and let it fall on his shoulders and slide down his back, to ease the itching. She would do it for an hour, back and forth as light as breath, her silken hair, while he closed his eyes and dreamed. He was like her child. She was gentle past belief.

He didn't understand her sorrow. This awful thing was not happening to her. She was causing his death, and he wanted death, so he forgave her. He felt his life slipping away without regret, along with his houses, his businesses, the people he had known and the memories he had harbored for fifty years. Everything had been a burden to him. Losing it now made him feel light. He let it go without regret. Only the bitter image of Antonio, the face he might have known, refused to leave him. But he felt no sorrow, not anymore, while she seemed to grieve deeply. It was deep and private and she had no way to tell him, and he would never have asked, but he wondered and she nursed and dried him and led him like a blind man to the dark bed where she pulled the soft sheets up to his chin and sat in the moonlight as he slept. She was his assassin and his nurse.

"There is iron and oil," he would say. "There are cotton fields and cotton mills. There is the railroad. There are wheat fields as far away as Kansas," explaining the empire that would be hers. He was losing money, losing money every day, Truitt who had spent a lifetime acquiring it, and he didn't care. There was a lot of money.

"I love you," he would say, his hands caressing her breasts in the dark. "These are the things you need to know. To watch over. You will have so much to take care of. I thank you," he said, and now it had a different meaning.

He would sit in the shadows of the great hall and think of killing people. He dreamed of killing Catherine. He was worried he would kill Mrs. Larsen, or innocent people in the town, even though he hardly ever went to town anymore.

"I'm afraid," he said.

"Of what?"

"I'm afraid of killing Antonio when he comes."

"He's not coming," she said softly. "He's never coming."

Mrs. Larsen was out of her mind with worry and suspicion. She wouldn't let Catherine in the kitchen. She made different foods for him, the things he liked from his boyhood. He wouldn't eat them. She insisted he call the doctor. She had never shed one tear for Larsen, never mentioned his name, but she couldn't look at Truitt's blistered hands without crying.

There was no need, and Truitt didn't want it. Mrs. Larsen begged him. Catherine went to town and begged the doctor to come. She lied. The doctor came. Cancer, he said. Cancer of the blood and the bones and the brain. Cancer everywhere. Cancer caused from breathing the fumes of smelting fires. High in arsenic, he said. Could be that. He had seen so much putrefaction of the flesh, such sepsis of the blood, in the workers of Truitt's foundries, men who died at thirty-five and left widows and children and he was unmoved. Prepare yourself, he said. Prepare and wait. He gave Truitt morphine for the pain.

"It's cancer," Catherine told Mrs. Larsen. "We have to make him comfortable. We have to wait. There's nothing we can do."

"I don't believe him," Mrs. Larsen said. "Something is happening. Something not natural." Her kindness toward Catherine turned to suspicion and a maddened wretchedness. She could do nothing. Truitt couldn't eat her food. He couldn't sit at the table.

Truitt began to go to the churches, each in turn. He had a profound fear of other people, of being touched and looked at, but he went. Catherine went with him, sitting in plain dresses among the Calvinists, the Lutherans, the Swedenborgians, the Holy Rollers, and snake handlers. The ministers left off preaching about the fires of hell, looking at Truitt's blistered face, and spoke softly about the redemptive power of love. The fires of hell had burned out, leaving only mercy. It was difficult, but Truitt sat straight, avoiding the staring eyes, and spoke gently to his neighbors and workers after the services. No one touched him. No one remarked that he looked less than well. The ride home, the jostling carriage in the rutted roads was an agony. Truitt was afraid, he was afraid that the horses would shy. They had done it before.

He would wake in the night and the room would be filled with dead people, all the dead people he had ever known. His mother and father, Emilia, sweet Franny. Larsen with his bloody wrist would be there. Standing beatific in the midst of them would be Antonio, his eyes white as marble, his face a blank. Truitt would call out their names, as if they could speak to him their terrible secrets.

He would hear the poet's voice:

It seems to me that every thing in the light and air ought to
    be happy,
Whoever is not in his coffin and the dark grave let him
    know he has enough.

Catherine would wake. She would move around the room, her arms aloft like white wings, her nightdress billowing around her feet, until the dead were gone, leaving only the blue moonlight. Then she would quiet him, and he would sleep for a while.

Every night he would drink his water, while she turned her eyes away and wept. He felt an enormous sadness, a particular sensation of loss, but he never wept anymore, and he never spoke of it.

Some days he wouldn't speak. He would wander restlessly from room to room, through the many rooms of the grand palazzo, picking up small objects, turning them this way and that in the light, trying to remember where they came from and what they were for. He would ask her the names of things. He would ask her where they had come from. She didn't know. From Europe, she would say. From Italy. From Limoges.

She stopped. She started again. She wanted to walk into the woods and throw the arsenic away where no living thing would find it. But she didn't throw it away. She kept it, in its blue bottle with a Chinese label.

She knew there was a point at which she could stop and the poison would fade. He would be left weak and haggard and scarred from the deep blisters in his skin. He would live, but he would die early. Still, he would not die now. He would not die at her hands, while her hands bathed his skin. He would not die in agony. There was a point at which he could live, and there was a point beyond which nothing could be done for him. She knew she was approaching that point, and her anguish grew every time he forgot a name or sat up suddenly in his chair and moved to another, every time she bathed him with warm water to alleviate his chills and his fear.

Mrs. Larsen had grown to hate her, knowing somehow that Catherine was the cause of whatever was killing Truitt, that she was killing him as Emilia had tried to kill him. But Truitt knew it was his youth, the dissipations of his youth that had brought him to this.

Luxe, calme et volupté, the poet had written, and Truitt had taken it to mean a life of endless indulgence, a life in which beauty and sensation were all that mattered, a life in which there were no consequences. When Emilia had betrayed him, when Franny had died, he had vowed that his days of indulgence were over. He had given up drinking. He had led a sober life. He had learned nothing. He loved Catherine with the sensuality of his youth, he longed for Antonio as he might have longed for a lover, and it was killing him. He had forgotten the poison, had forgotten that this was being done to him. He thought he had done it to himself, long ago, an illness he had contracted in his youth, the rancid sexual contagion of his childhood, knowing it was fatal and was now, after years of denial, finally showing its vengeful teeth.

He looked on his life, on the part of him that was living and that had once been whole, with awkward tenderness. He tilted his head toward it as one might toward a baby, afraid to hold it, to pick up such unblemished beauty. He had once moved and talked like other men, been comfortable in his clothes, held women in his arms. He had been a father. His child had been an idiot. He had been a husband. His wife had been a charmer and a beauty and had ruined his life. He couldn't remember her face. He hadn't seen Antonio since he was fourteen, twelve years ago. Where had they gone? What would his face look like now? His mind turned all day long like a plant toward the light, toward questions that had no answers.

He moved into the old house with Mrs. Larsen. He moved into the bedroom he had as a boy, the narrow iron bed, the overhanging eave, and the one gabled window to the stars. He was afraid of the ghosts in the big house. He thought he could escape them.

He woke up every morning anxious for his wife, and came the long way back to Catherine, offered up his days to her, so that she might patiently explain the things he forgot, so that she could ladle soup into his mouth and bathe him in the warm baths which took away the chill for five minutes. He came back so that she could inject him with morphine and drop poison into his food and onto his hairbrush and onto the clothes he could no longer bear to put on his body. He remembered how it worked, in certain lucid moments. He had, for the most part, forgotten what it was that was being done to him. He never found her at fault.

After he had gone back to Mrs. Larsen's, after dinner and the reading by the fire which warmed the nights, after he had been bundled in shawls and lap robes and Mrs. Larsen had driven him slowly away with a look of hatred that pierced her to the heart, Catherine would walk through the dark, the long way through the dark fields, and climb the stairs of the old farmhouse and sit outside his door until morning. If he woke, she would hold his hand, rub his forehead with a soft warm cloth, she would recite for him the names of the dead and the living who peopled his nights. And every morning, before the sun came up, she would wrap her cloak around her and walk the long way home to sleep for an hour before he came into the house, not knowing where to be, not knowing what chair to sit in, or who she was some mornings.

At last he was ready. He wanted to die. But still she could not do it. And, finally, she knew she could not do it.

He was sitting in a chair in the music room. She had put cotton in his ears, because any noise drove him into a frenzy, and she came to him, she knelt on the floor. She finally couldn't bear his suffering and her own wickedness, or his patient acceptance of what was happening to him. She knelt on the floor and lay her head in his lap and she spoke softly, looking up into his tired face.

"It's over," she said. "I can't do it."

"Do what?"

"I can't do it. Can't do it to you. You're all I've known, all I will ever know, and I can't do it. I love you so much it makes me ashamed when you look at me, to have you see me. But, there, take my hand. It stops now. You'll live. I will make you well."

He looked at her, his face a realm of kindness.

"If you die, I would grieve for you all my life. I'll grieve for you if they hang me, if they put the rope around my neck."

"I wanted to die. It seemed I did. Do."

"You don't. You think you do, but you don't."

"Antonio . . ."

"Will come. I promise. He will come. Until he does, I'm here. Live for me."

He reached out and touched her hair. He caught a single strand between his thumb and forefinger and rolled it back and forth.

He loved her. He would live.

Perhaps there was to be some light, in the end. Maybe, after all, there was a way out of the darkness. She hoped it was true. She was so tired.

Chapter Twenty

—◦◦◦—

She sent a telegram to Antonio. "Come at once," was all it said.

She nursed Ralph with all the care she could give him. She wrapped his hands and body with gauze dipped in liniment, the sores had become so terrible. He itched and burned, and the salve seemed to soften the torment. She covered his face with salve and gauze, his face, where the skin was falling off in sheets. She closed his ears and covered his eyes with cotton, she put her dark glasses on him. The sound and the light had become piercing to him, the smallest footfall an agony. She wrapped her shoes in wool so that her feet barely made a sound as she walked through the marble halls. She drew the curtains against the light and the sound, and she tied him with velvet and cotton cords to a chair when his restlessness and dementia would not let him stay still. She drew the curtains, and the white world went away for a time.

She burned the sheets, his clothes and shoes and bath towels. She burned and buried anything he might have touched, anything that might contain the slightest trace of the white powder. She threw away his razor, his father's, and his silver hairbrush from Italy. She burned the rug, the heavy silk bed hangings. She burned her own nightgowns, knowing as she did that the smoke from the fire was full of the same poison, that everything he had touched she had touched as well, that he had drunk his icy water and kissed her on the mouth.

The blue bottle she took into the woods and poured the poison over rocks, away from water, away from where sheep might graze in summer, or birds might come to nest. No more harm would come to any living thing.

She fed him nothing but warm milk, to make him vomit and to still the tremors of his chill. She gave him limewater to soak up the poisons. She covered him with furs and blankets and held the bowl for him while he vomited into it. She never flinched.

She called on Mrs. Larsen. "I don't believe the doctor. He is, has been very ill. We can make him better. We did it once before."

"What's wrong with him?"

"I don't know. I don't know. But the doctor doesn't know either. He's wrong. This is no cancer. My father died of cancer and this is different. He knows what's going on around him. My father knew nothing. He lost his mind, at the end. It's not his brain. I don't know. My sister was ill once. We gave her milk and egg whites, to make her vomit. Give it to him. He's freezing cold. Keep him warm. What else can we do?"

"The old people . . . there are herbs in the field for the sores. For drawing out the boils."

"Then we'll ask the old people. We'll get what we can. It's still winter. There's not much. You'll watch him. I'll go to Chicago and find a doctor, a real doctor. I'll ask him what to do."

She went to Chicago, to visit poor, sad-faced India. India who

looked like her picture. India whom rich Ralph Truitt had chosen
out of the whole world, who might herself have been wearing silk
and walking the marble halls. She would never know where her
picture had gone. She would never know she might have been loved
and respected, the mistress of those high frescoed halls. And Truitt
would have found happiness with her, a thin happiness. He would
not be dying now, if India had been the one.

Catherine had always loved India, had loved her plain shyness
and her lack of prospects. She wanted to tell her that Ralph Truitt
had loved her; she wanted to say he had chosen her picture and
loved it, because then, when she entered a room or walked down
the street, she might be able to do it differently, knowing that she
was loved.

It was easy to lie to her. It had been easy to say that she had always wanted her picture, a remembrance, a sentimental keepsake,
and to persuade shy India to sit in front of the photographer's
plate.

Now it was easy to tell her only as much as she needed and lie
about why she needed it. India had spent a lifetime watching other
people's lives, looking in shop windows, watching life through the
plate glass of her own indifferent looks, and she had noticed everything and stored it away, her only treasure. It was her only furniture
of use; her protection against the loneliness that never left her and
the ugly men and the sad, sad life.

India embraced her. India held her hand. India listened, nod-
ding, and then she got her hat and coat and said the only things
she had said, through Catherine's long and lying story. "Let's go
downtown."

Chicago outdid Saint Louis in brawl and confusion. They went
through big streets and tiny streets, and came to Chinatown, to a

small shop with dingy windows. Inside, a Chinaman bowed with elaborate courtesy and listened to the version of the story Catherine told. At the word *arsenic*, the air in the room stopped moving for a moment. Catherine thought she would cry, would howl with guilt and terror, but she went on as though nothing were happening. The air began to move again. India breathed, and the wheels started turning, the clock began to tick.

The Chinaman bowed again, smiled broadly, and began to move hastily around his dark shop, pulling phials of powder from one shelf, milky liquids from another, collecting the ancient and secret reversals of terrible and vengeful substances. Now and then he stopped and smiled as though he were telling a joke.

"Brandy," he said. "Keeps his belly warm."

"Opium," he said, "to calm the stomach. Make him happy. Make bad dreams go away." He cut out opium in tiny, waxy balls.

"One every day, until his dreams are clear and clean. Fresh dreams."

When he was done, there were eight bottles, and they cost a lot of money and Catherine paid, carrying the bottles and jars in a plain brown sack from the store. She buried it deep in a big black bag she was carrying, and offered India dinner.

They ate at a grand hotel, Catherine never saying that she would sleep the night in a room upstairs. India was ravenous, her eyes wide, the huge menu in front of her like a shield. She ate oysters, lobster thermidor, a cold soup, and a guinea hen. She drank a great deal of wine. Catherine ate little and drank no wine. She had no taste for it.

"You look different," said India, waiting for the smooth waiter to reappear. "You look like a lady. Like . . ." she nodded her head. "Like one of them."

"He likes a simple way. They're simple people there, not like us. I try to be what he wants me to be."

"And he gives you money?"

"Yes."

"A lot of money."

Catherine was embarrassed. "Yes."

"Give me some. You have a sweetheart, a husband for God's sake, he gives you money. I want money."

"Not here. But, yes, of course, whatever you need."

"I need a lot of things. I need some twenty-eight-year-old man with white teeth to fall in love with me. I need a winter coat and a little dog to sit in my lap. Bet you got a little dog."

Catherine smiled."No. But I have a winter coat. You can have it if you want. I'll get another. Or we'll get you one you like."

The waiter came with dessert, a huge mound of whipped cream and cake and fruit. "You think that's the answer. You think it'll make me pretty or get me a sweet man? It'll just give me the idea, on cold nights, that I could have one of those men, that my face was pretty like yours, that it wasn't all so goddamned endless and stupid and boring. Money. That'll be enough, for now."

Catherine had spent so much of her life on the other side of the glass, the India side, the Alice side. She found it extraordinary to be the one who had the things people wanted. And she, now, wanted only one thing, and the way to that thing lay in her black bag.

Catherine walked plain India the long way home, tried to give her the black seal coat she was wearing, but India refused it, saying it would make her look like a fool. She gave her as much money as she could, knowing India wouldn't spend it on drugs or foolishness or fripperies.

She spent the night in her narrow bed in her plain room in the grand hotel. She thought of Truitt, of Mrs. Larsen sitting up by him all night, nursing him through one more grief. Mrs. Larsen who never once had a bad dream, she said, even after she watched her husband chop off his own hand for no reason at all.

Catherine dreamed of Antonio. He was like a spider, everywhere at once. His skin was in her skin, his organs were connected to hers. Her heartbeat was his heartbeat, the flutter of her eyelids moved above his drugged terrible haunting black eyes. He was her passion and her violation, and it brought her sharply awake.

She smoked one opium ball from the Chinaman and fell asleep into bliss, into cool water and her mother's arms and the water trembling on her mother's hair, the lilac blooms in May. She fell into a dream of her garden, of how it would smell on summer evenings, the jasmine trees white with bloom, the koi darting in the pond when she bent over to sprinkle bread crumbs on the water, Truitt sitting in a white chair in a white suit, playing with a child.

Catherine woke up, and she knew she was pregnant. She felt luxuriously tired, although she knew she had slept.

At her mirror she pulled her hair back tightly, put on her simple traveling dress, and sat on the train for hours. As she ate her lunch, she wondered if she could see the remains of her red traveling suit. She stared out the window, but nothing was there, nothing left that she could see. When she had finished her lunch, she vomited it into the bathroom sink, washed the sink out with a cloth, then threw the cloth from the train. It fluttered away like a stiff heavy white bird. She felt light-headed. She felt grateful. She was beyond gratitude, beyond any understanding of it, and lost in a bliss the opium could not have produced, in a sense of being in the right place, a feeling she had never known. There was, at last, a chair for her to sit on, and Truitt would live.

At home, Mrs. Larsen ran to the door.

"He's quiet, now," she said. "He had a terrible night. Screamed with the pain. Screamed from what he was seeing when he was asleep. I forgot where I was. He slept all morning. I had to tie him down." Mrs. Larsen looked terrible and old, shaky and bleary eyed.

"Go home now, Mrs. Larsen. Go home and sleep. I've brought medicine."

She walked through the long sunroom, the glass conservatory. The first roses had arrived from Saint Louis, tagged with cardboard tags, roses and orange trees and jasmine and fuchsia and orchids, waiting to be put into the enormous terra-cotta pots that lined the hallway. It was hot here, hot and damp, although the snow still lay in its blinding blanket outside, less pure now, more pocked and dirty, but endless.

He sat quietly in a high-backed chair, a lap robe over his legs, her sunglasses on his face. His eyes were shut.

She knelt beside his chair. His hand strayed idly through her hair. "Hello, Emilia," he said softly. "Welcome home."

"It's Catherine, Truitt," she said. "Catherine Land. Your wife. You were dreaming."

"Of course. Catherine. I was . . ."

"You were dreaming." She reached into her black bag, gave him one of the opium balls. "Swallow this," she said. "Swallow this and dream some more."

For days the two women ministered to him, sleeping in shifts or not at all. For the second time, they bathed him together, holding him in the steaming water until the chills had passed, rubbing his stomach endlessly so that the terrible cold would go away. He was drunk on brandy, sedated into joy with opium, and he was getting better.

They sat together in the nights and watched him roll in his sleep.

"Larsen cut off his hand because . . . because I asked him to stop." It was the first time she had said his name.

"Stop what?"

"Just stop. Ten years ago. To leave me be. He couldn't stand it."

"You miss him."

"He was all I ever knew. I miss him, yes."

"You never go to see him."

"I wouldn't. It's my fault."

They sat through the long night in silence. Mrs. Larsen had said about her husband what she needed to say. In her own quiet way she had driven her husband, also, into the far reaches of madness and death. She had known because she had seen it before, she had done it herself.

Catherine took the dark glasses from Truitt's eyes. They were still fierce blue, but ringed with deep, haggard shadows. They were unfocused and wandered unhitched inside his head. His forehead was a mass of pustules that had begun to heal. There would be scars. He looked ten years older, as though some boundary had been crossed and he would never again be young or completely well. She had broken his youth and left him floundering on the shore of old age, his power gone, his ambitions stilled.

His hands, when she unbandaged them, lay quiet in his lap. He was neither cruel nor kind; he was simply waiting for whatever the next thing was. He grew less cold, his dreams became softer and subtler, more filled with shapes that embraced him. He described his dreams to her in the morning when he woke up, and she listened patiently, although the dreams did not make sense and he had the same dreams over and over. They were memories of events he hadn't described to her yet. They were ideas he had had but never acted on. They were dreams.

He no longer scratched his sores. He no longer felt as though his clothes were on fire. He drank the soup and ate the herbs. The women salved his wounds, and they could feel the change in him. They moved him upstairs to his bed in the blue bedroom, and sat together, taking meals with him. Mrs. Larsen finally, after all these years, consented to eat with Truitt.

He wanted oysters, and they sent to Chicago for a barrel of them. Mrs. Larsen kept them in the cold cellar, and fed them brine and cornmeal. Every night, Truitt had a dozen fat oysters and a glass of brandy, Truitt who hadn't had a drink in years, amazed that he wanted these things, amazed that they had gotten them for him. The women didn't eat oysters. The women didn't drink brandy.

Catherine couldn't tell him about the baby. She couldn't bear to tell him about it when he was so ill. She hoped the baby was his. She felt sure, and she hoped she was right, because she couldn't bear the thought that, because of her, Ralph Truitt would have to raise two children not his own. Hadn't he, when she first came home, made love to her while she was showing blood? She believed so. She believed, in the way she had of making what she wanted into the truth, that there had been no other man but Truitt, that the days in Saint Louis had not been.

He had made love to her while she was bleeding. She remembered. It couldn't be Antonio, he never came inside her, his fear of encumbrance was too great. It must be Truitt. He had made her new; her life had begun in a new way when she left Saint Louis, and nothing from that life could grow in her now.

She had never been a kind person. In the past, she had thought of others as no more than a way to get what she wanted.

Truitt was different, had made her new, and she could never go back. She washed his blisters and rubbed his feet and put salve on his forehead, and ground bark into a paste to spread on his hands. His hair came out in clumps when she brushed it, and she sorrowed for that; her guilt was overwhelming.

She could grieve for herself now, finally, for her wandering, wasted life. She lay on a wicker chaise in the sun of the conservatory, with her new roses beginning to show leaves in the warm, damp afternoons, and she wept for herself, she wept for her father and her mother, for her sister, and for every moment lost and forgotten and broken into bits on the long way from where she had been to the place where she sat. It was so fragile, a life, and she thought she had been tough enough to believe differently. Now everything was tender to her, tender as a new wound, her own memories, the dark wharves of Baltimore and the ordered grandeur of Rittenhouse Square and the sex and the stealing and the lying and the angel descending from heaven, the angel who had not carried Alice to the grand capitals of the world so that she might be dazzled by the splendors. As though it were all, the good and the bad, one long endless scar, up and down her arms, across her breasts, and she was applying medications to her own skin as she was nursing Truitt.

Hers was a sickness of the soul, but it was not incurable; she had to believe that there was still innocence inside her, somewhere, and hope, and a person who might have a life altogether different from the one she had had. The scars, her scars, would never go away, she knew that. She would never be whole, as Truitt would never again be young. But new skin would grow over the scars; they would whiten and fade and be barely noticeable to a child.

Truitt had seen her in a new way. And his vision had made her over, had caused her to turn into the kind of woman he wanted. He deserved no less. Catherine, for her part, had led a life in which kindness was neither expected nor given. Battered as she was, she didn't know the difference between happiness and dread. She didn't know the difference between excitement and fear. She felt a knot in her stomach every hour of the day and didn't know what to call it. Her hands shook. She vomited in the mornings, in secret, but she felt that, finally, the end of the tightrope was in view, that the slamming doors and the hostile, mercantile sex and the demented nights in the opium dens were behind her.

She had been adept at the beginning and the ends of things, and now she saw that whatever pleasures life had to offer lay in the middle. She could find some peace there.

Then one day he could speak, his voice no longer a harsh and burning rasp. Then one day he could walk, could dress himself, could carry on a conversation, could imagine going back to work to repair his fortunes, to meet the anxious eyes of the town that depended on his being well. He was changed, of course. He walked like an old man, as though each step were a learned and torturous act. His hair had turned stark gray. When he drank from his glass of brandy, his hand moved to his mouth in a series of distinct, static movements, like flashing photographs.

They sat at the dinner table. He had asked for beef and potatoes and pudding, the food from his schoolboy days. He was reading her the daily disasters from the paper as they ate.

His fork clattered on the plate when a knock came at the big front door. It was far away, and Catherine offered to go, but Ralph was already on his feet, unsteady.

"No. I want to go."

He walked the long way, lighting every light as he went. He

opened one of the big double doors, and a man stood on the terrace in the darkness, looking out over the steps and the snow. He turned, and Ralph could make out his shape, but could barely see his face.

The man held out his hand. "I am Tony Moretti," he said. And then, after a pause, "I am your son."

And even though they both knew what the man said was a fiction, Ralph stepped into the dark and opened his arms.

CHAPTER TWENTY-ONE

S ONS CAME HOME to their fathers, even to men who weren't their fathers, men who had beaten them senseless. Sons came home, malevolent with revenge, home to fathers who could not forgive themselves for the cruelties they had committed. Such things happened.

He had brought everything he owned, the fancy suits, the extravagant Paris neckties, the pristine shirts and the silver-headed walking stick and amber colognes from London. He was penniless. He was like a swan, long-necked and useless except for beauty, and everything he did, every gesture he made and every word he spoke seemed out of place, too exotic, too mannered. He played the piano after dinner, and even that seemed excessive, as though he were playing for a fancy crowd in a rococo concert hall. Truitt preferred Catherine's simplicity of feeling, her lack of expertise.

Catherine and Truitt lay in the big bed in their blue bedroom. Antonio slept far away from them, in a bachelor apartment he had devised out of his mother's old rooms. A dressing room. A magnificent sitting room for which he had taken bits of furniture from all over the house, for which Truitt had ordered an ebony piano. And a bedroom, which was large and grand and hung with tapestries.

They could feel his eyes on them in the dark. A new quiet had entered into the way they treated each other, a simplicity of manner. It was, Catherine supposed, love. It was what normal people had when passion had run its course. They spoke quietly after making love. They spoke of small matters, his business, Mrs. Larsen and her silent sorrow, the husband she would never see again, his care paid for by Truitt, the garden for which the plants were arriving daily. They never spoke of Truitt's illness, as though it had never happened.

"He reminds me so much of Emilia. Her eyes and mouth, that dark hair. An Italian."

Catherine sat up in bed and stared at the pale light of the new moon coming through the window.

"How did she die?"

She could feel his stillness beside her. He remained weak, and continued to have moments when he did not know where he was or who she was or where they lived. His body was covered with scars, a silent reminder of her iniquities and her consolations and his forgiveness.

"I killed her."

The moon seemed so far away. The winter had been so long, she could not remember a time when it had not been winter. She could not remember her life before she stepped down from the train and into the gaze of Ralph Truitt. Would not remember or want to, except for the presence of Antonio, moving like a cat through the house, watching her day and night.

"I can't believe it. I don't."

Truitt sat up in bed and took her hand. "I will talk about this one time. When I've told it all, her name will never be said in this house again. I killed her. I let her die.

"She had moved to Chicago with Moretti. She was my wife. There was no divorce, no legal recourse. She was a Catholic and they don't do that. I had her child, her boy, under my roof and she was my wife and I felt pain every time I thought about her, but I always knew where she was, I heard the stories. Everybody in town heard the stories and I was ashamed, but I went on and nobody, of course nobody spoke about it, at least not to me.

"I sent her money. She wasn't destitute. I sent her money and she lived in a style that was despicable to me, but I sent it anyway because she was my wife, because I was haunted by Franny and had her boy and because . . . because I couldn't let her live in squalor.

"Moretti left her. Left her for some rich widow with a big house and a blind eye to his infidelities and his affectations and his lack of talent or charm. Emilia . . ." She could hear the pain in his voice as he spoke her name. "Emilia took a series of lovers, each young, each useless, going around Chicago saying he had had a countess, a real countess, and describing in beer halls the things she was willing to do. She was still beautiful.

"She never wrote to Antonio. She never came to see the grave of her daughter. She could have chosen differently. She could have chosen something other than this parade of young ne'er-do-wells, something with kindness, something with honor, a house where she might have brought her boy and raised him up. She had money. She was intelligent. She was cultivated. She slept with women, I heard. She got drunk in public. She was robbed twice. By men she knew, men who had been guests in her house.

"I went to see her. Several times. Not to ask her back home, I wouldn't have her here. I asked her to stop. Just to stop it. She laughed in my face. She threw wine at me. She told me I disgusted her."

He took her hand and kissed it. "Do you need to know the rest?"

The moonlight was so faint and cold, her skin rippled with the cold. "I need to know."

"She got sick. Consumption, they called it then. Tuberculosis, I suppose. I sent doctors. I didn't want to see her. She was still so young. She had tuberculosis, they said, she had syphilis, she had gone mad with it, and no man or woman would come near her. Her name was up, as people say, in the streets of Chicago, and no one would come to comfort her, all those dinner parties she had given, all those men she had given a moment's pleasure to, and money, endless amounts of money to show off the affectations of the Countess Emilia. She could still barely speak English. The doctors couldn't do anything. She lived alone and there was no one to feed her or clean up after her, and she had never learned to do the first thing for herself.

"I went one more time. I took Antonio to see her, but it was too awful. He saw her, saw her in ruins, and then I made him wait in the carriage. There was a room . . . there was a room in her house where she had thrown everything dirty, her clothes, her under-clothes, and her fancy petticoats, along with plates she had eaten off of once and hadn't bothered to clean. Embroidered tablecloths she had used once, hats she had bought and never worn. It was up to your waist. Jewelry she didn't want anymore. Packets of letters from Antonio who wrote to her, pleaded with her to come and save him. Some of the letters weren't even opened. The curtains were drawn against the light; you had to wade through this disaster, wondering what to save, what could be saved, some token to bring to her boy as a sign that at least his mother loved him. God knows I couldn't. She had left her life, stuffed it away in this rank, dark room on the third floor of her fancy townhouse, which I paid for.

"She was lying in her bed, barely conscious. Probably drugged. Probably crazy. She was still beautiful. She had a refinement, a beauty, even in her madness, that caught my breath. She needed sun. She needed fresh air and a long cure, out west, in Europe. She might have lived, lived for a while, at least.

"She spoke to me. She told me I was a fool, a fool and a liar and a cuckold. She told me I was weak and stupid and that she had duped me and used me from the moment she set eyes on me and she was glad. I knew it, of course. I had known it by then for a long time.

"I left her there. I left her alone to die. She was my heart's first love, and she despised me and I left her. No cure. No more doctors. No more money. She was thrown out of her house, her possessions auctioned in the street. She died three months later in a charity hospital, her wrists tied to the bed, gone blind, her hair fallen out, a pathetic freak who had no one to hold her hand, no priest to say the final prayer over her head, no redemption, no forgiveness from a God who had finally abandoned her too, left her to die without the words, without the invitation to heaven.

"I could have saved her. I didn't. And I don't regret it. There comes a moment when you can't take it anymore. I saw that room with her discarded dresses and the unopened letters and the unpaid dressmaker's bills, and my heart stopped caring whether she lived or died."

There was a long, dark silence.

"You couldn't have done differently. No one would have expected . . ."

"*I* expected. I. She was my wife. Once, she was. Then she was dead. I don't even know where she's buried. I don't care."

"You have to forgive yourself."

He turned violently to her. "You don't know anything. I don't have to do a damned thing. I'll do and think what I do and think for as long as it takes. You asked. I told you. Never mention her name again."

He lay back against the sheets. He pulled her close to him. He drew up the covers and immediately she could feel the warmth of his body against hers. "What I felt for her wasn't love. I thought it was. It wasn't. It was an addiction, a kind of insanity. I so wanted . . . something, I don't remember what. Revenge. My mother. The long years of her rage. I wanted revenge, and she was the instrument. I wanted my mother to have to live with her every day and to feel small and useless and ugly and old. Only it didn't matter for a minute. To her. It didn't change anything. I spent my youth loving a woman who wasn't worth the effort."

He was drowsy. "I hope, I hope in my heart, that the fire is out. It burned too hot. It kills everything. Now. Say your prayers and go to sleep. Antonio is home. You're here. We'll make it work. That's all that matters. Go to sleep now."

He turned away and she lay in the dark, mute and thoughtless. Antonio had lied to her, had lied to get her to believe something about Truitt that wasn't true, had described in detail a horrible, convulsive, murderous event that never happened. She herself had lied, but now it seemed the lie had burned through her, leaving only white blank space behind, white as the landscape outside the window. At that moment, something in her ended and something began. And she lay awake until the thin light came through the windows while she gave birth to the new thing.

Then Truitt stirred. It was barely morning. He opened his eyes, and she kissed him before he was fully awake. Truitt would do. He wasn't what she had dreamed of. He wasn't what she had expected. But he was enough.

Antonio was everywhere. His insolence, his boredom filled the house. Truitt never noticed the hypocrisy, the small insults. He gave him a bank account, a bank account with enough money to keep Antonio for years. He tried to interest Antonio in the business, sitting with him for as long as Antonio could stand it in his grand study, explaining where everything was, telling him how to buy and sell, how to grow rich. He was not a fool. He could see how condescending Antonio was, and it reminded him of his own youth, his own lack of interest in anything except the pursuit of pleasure.

There was no amusement in the town for Antonio. There were no restaurants, except at the one small, sad hotel, and there were no women. He soon exhausted the drugs he had brought, and faced his days with a lucidity that was rare and unpleasant for him. He smoked cigarettes at the table. He spoke endlessly of Saint Louis and its enchantments.

Truitt opened the old wine cellar for him, and every night Antonio got drunk on the beautiful wines that had been laid by twenty years before, vintages of an astonishing rarity and subtlety. Ports and Bordeaux and Burgundies shipped from Europe when the house was filled with his mother's friends. It didn't matter to Antonio. He just wanted to get drunk and say insulting things to his father.

"The house is cold. My rooms are cold. My feet are freezing all the time."

"The house is old, and big. Maybe your clothes . . ."

"And wear what? The trick, Father, is not to change your clothes to suit your environment, but to change your environment to suit your clothes. You're rich. Do something."

"It'll be spring soon."

"And then we'll be warm and there will still be nothing to do."

It went on and on, Truitt patient, Antonio disdainful of every effort he made to be kind. The money meant nothing. Sleeping every night in his mother's gilded bed meant nothing. Seeing his old playroom, his old toys still there, meant nothing. Antonio had no sentimental heart. He was not to be moved. He had come to bring death.

"People who spend their days in business are wasting their lives. We only live for art."

"I felt the same way. I do feel it. I didn't choose this. There was no one else."

"And someday it'll all be mine? I'll sell it and live a beautiful life."

"It has been what this family has done for a hundred years. There isn't a person in town who doesn't depend on it, in some way."

"They're little nobodies."

They might have talked about the things that mattered. They might have sat up at night by a fire, and Ralph might have been able to say what was in his heart, that he was sorry, that for all he cared Antonio could do whatever he liked, sell the business, burn down the house and sow the earth with salt. He only wanted one thing, his son's forgiveness. And that Antonio was never going to give.

He cornered Catherine while Ralph was away in town.

"He's supposed to be dead. He's not even dying. Come at once, you said."

"He needed you here. He needed to believe you would come. It was the only way I could get you to come. If you believed . . .

"So you lied to me."

"Yes."

"I need one thing. I need him dead. Just remember, I can always tell him. Every night, when he wants to have those little chats, every night I am about to tell him, and I don't. I'm kind of enjoying it, actually. He sits there like a monkey, and you can say anything to him and he literally turns the other cheek."

"He wants your forgiveness."

"He wants to sleep soundly at night. Or does he? Sleep, I mean. You sleep in his bed. You would know."

"He's restless. He's restless for your happiness."

The threat was always there. It was always there and it was very real. They had made a plan, and the plan had involved both of them. Now he said that she disgusted him. With Ralph out of the way, he would throw her out and there would be no place for her to go. Nowhere other than back to the life, back to a woman she had ceased to be.

Catherine didn't know what to do. She realized that, while there was in the world a series of people who knew things about her, no one person knew everything. She had told so many lies, had invented too many selves, one for each tableau. She had nobody to turn to, and the situation as it was couldn't go on for long. Not even Truitt's patience was infinite.

Antonio's rage grew as Ralph got stronger. The color had returned to his ashen cheeks; he didn't feel dizzy as he walked up the steep stairs to the house. His sleep was untroubled by the old anxieties. The ghosts were gone.

She read to them at night by the fire, Whitman, the American poet.

"God. This is boring. Do you have any idea how boring this is?"

At night, as she and Ralph made love in the blue bedroom, she thought of Antonio pacing in his rooms far away, drinking brandy, smoking cigars, and she could feel his anger, and knew that it was leading to something awful, something she couldn't picture or describe. She tried to warn Truitt, but he wouldn't hear it.

"He's going to ruin everything. He's a danger to you."

"I was the same at his age. I was restless and bored and hateful. Certainly he is his mother's child. Maybe he'll never come around. Maybe he is my son. I never wanted to stop, either. The disdain. The hatefulness. I have to try."

Ralph took Antonio to the factory, patiently explaining how the ore was smelted, showing him the shapes and variations that could be made from the molten red-hot iron. Antonio insulted the workers, laughed at their efforts.

His only real interest was Catherine, whom he always called Mrs. Truitt. When Ralph was away, when he finally got out of bed and she was sitting at lunch, or discussing the night's menu with Mrs. Larsen, he would creep in like a cat, and suddenly be beside her, in her way, in her mind when she had almost forgotten his presence.

"Mrs. Truitt . . ."

"Please don't call me that."

"You're my father's wife. What should I call you?"

"Catherine."

"I would never. Mrs. Truitt, think what fun we could have. All that money. There's enough wine for years. All those bedrooms, we could fill them up with people we know, with our friends . . ."

"Antonio. There is no we. Not anymore. You have to understand."

"And all you have to do is make him die."

"I wouldn't. I couldn't, in fact. I no longer have the medicine."

"There's more. I'll go to Chicago. The house is crawling with rats, that's what I'll tell them."

She looked out the dining room windows, down the long field toward the river. The ice was already fragile. The children no longer came to skate after school. The winter wouldn't last much longer.

"I won't do it. I've told you a hundred times. He's my husband. You already have everything you could want."

"I'm bored."

"Then go to Chicago. Play with your friends."

"I don't have any friends in Chicago."

"They're the same as the people you know in Saint Louis. There's not a hair's difference between them. They sleep all day and drink all night and gamble and go to whores and smoke opium. The things you like. You could buy clothes. You have money. Truitt has an excellent tailor. You could live like the Prince of Wales."

"It wouldn't be any fun."

"Go to Europe. He did."

"And get lost for five years?"

"He would send you all the money you wanted."

"I don't speak the language. I don't like churches. I've told you what I want."

"And I've told you you won't have it. Not today. Not ever. You'll have to make do."

"Making do is not my way, and you know it."

"I am begging you. For one hour, for one afternoon, please leave me alone."

He would leave her then, but she could feel his presence in the house. She stood for hours in the secret garden, staring up at the windows of her bedroom, hoping for spring, wishing Antonio would go away, wishing she had never started on this disastrous course, wishing she had never seen the light in Truitt's eyes, wishing she had never heard the poet's words: "Those who love shall be made invincible." She didn't feel invincible. She felt like a new wound, open to the air, vulnerable to any passerby. How had this happened? Standing in the ruins of the garden, she could barely remember how it started, but she felt giddy with fear, that she would never escape it. The knot in her stomach said that Antonio was right: Truitt would find out one way or another. She had laid waste to her life, and that life was now a secret buried deep inside her, safe except for Antonio.

She had been to the doctor in town. She had timed it out very carefully in her mind. The child was Truitt's. It lay in her belly like the garden lay in her mind, under the earth, waiting for care. When Truitt was stronger, she would tell him. When Antonio tired of his scheme and realized that everything that was Truitt's was also his, he would go away and spend money until he died in Saint Louis or London or Paris, an aging fop too bored to live anymore. He would move from city to city as he had always done, using people, soiling them like sheets and walking away, to find fresh faces and new diversions. Truitt had loved a person who didn't exist. Surely he would love and find consolation and hope in the person who was going to be.

CHAPTER TWENTY-TWO

E VEN THOUGH HE COULDN'T RIDE, Antonio bought an
Arabian horse, the finest in the whole state, some said.
He hired a teacher, a young farm boy, and took lessons
down in the vast old barn, where Truitt had leveled the floor and
made an indoor riding ring. In two weeks that fascination was
spent, and the horse stood idly in the barnyard, picking through
the thin, icy snow far from the desert sands.

Antonio bought a car that was newer and fancier and far more
expensive than his father's. It arrived on the train and astonished
the town, but he couldn't drive, and the roads were too rutted anyway, so it sat in a stable in town.

Antonio went to Chicago for five days and came home with a
glazed and exhausted look, a trunkful of new clothes and a packet
of arsenic and a ball of opium. He came home with a Miss Carruthers, Elsie Carruthers, a girl Catherine recognized from the theater
and her nights with India, and installed her in a suite of rooms next
to his own. They would spend the nights there, drinking vintage

wine and tearing at each other's clothes. But Miss Carruthers was ignorant and was bored with the long dinners and the poetry, and she and Antonio stopped coming down for them. Ralph said it was what young men did; it was what he had done, although he had traveled three thousand miles to do it. He had never brought his depravities under his mother and father's roof, but he never said a word to Antonio. It was a relief to Catherine to have him out of the way, a relief to find she enjoyed her time alone with Truitt again.

Antonio grew bored with Miss Carruthers, and Ralph paid her a sum of money to get on the train and go back to Chicago. After that, Antonio had nothing to do. Nothing at all.

"Mrs. Truitt, we have the powder. You know the plan. I told you I'd tell him and I will."

"You don't need me, if that's what you want."

"The lost son killing the father? Wouldn't work. I'm a coward. You're not. No, Mrs. Truitt, I will always need you. The sound of your hem on the stairs makes me want you, all over again."

"The past is dead."

"No, it's not. It never is."

"I couldn't do it."

He touched her neck, the beating pulse. "Tell me you love me."

She slapped his face.

He smiled. "You see?"

Antonio was used to being adored and desired and had no place in his heart for the complexities of love. He was never driven by the need for affection; desire had its exaggerated and dramatic pleasures, but he was bored by the endless scenes and recantations. Love was simply the same steady heartbeat hour after hour. It bored him with its lack of event. And, given the chance to have and do anything he wanted, he was filled with a crippling lassi-tude, a despair and anger that made him feel like a tiger in a cage. He looked for the new sensation, the new conquest, and found nothing.

Ralph realized Antonio would never wear a wedding ring. The simple happiness of domesticity meant nothing to him, that his life would be spent moving from woman to woman, from raw pleasure to pleasure, forever, until his looks ran out and his desires failed him, and he would be left with nothing. Love that lived beyond passion was ephemeral. It was the gauze bandage that wrapped the wounds of your heart. It existed outside of time, on a continuum that couldn't be seen or described. Ralph thought of Catherine during the day with a mixture of love and fear, but he found him-self content that she would be there when evening came.

Antonio would never see it. His mother had died for sexual plea-sure, she had debased and ruined her life, and Antonio was the product of her attenuated perversity. Never to give up the primacy of sex was to die alone, in a kind of poverty. It was never to know the comfort of sex without need.

Ralph had found his passion again, so long suppressed. He had found it in a woman who had deceived and lied and pretended and worse, but he woke up every morning with the feeling of having passed the night in dreams of pleasure. He had sought one thing and found another. She was the instrument of his death. She was the invitation to his life. He knew where he stood.

He grew stronger, and he got richer and more powerful. His business, so long a duty to pass the time, to assuage his guilt over his father's lonely death, had become infused with his passion, and his arms reached out, his hands full of money, to buy and to ruin and to save and to build and to own whatever would make his power grow. It was what he had become. It was what America had offered him. It was what Antonio might grow to be.

"It bores me."

"It bored me, too. It was getting good at it that made it interesting. It's life, Antonio. It's work. It's what people do."

"It's not my life. It's not what I do."

"The country, the whole country, Antonio, is building and growing. There's so much of it to own and control. There are people, on farms, in cities, who don't know where to go. All they need is a light, and they'll follow."

"You. They can follow you to hell for all I care."

And still Ralph persisted, his patience infinite, his love vast and unexplored. Antonio was, for him, the one thing he had managed to save out of the disaster of his early life—or at least he was doing what he could to save it—and he would do anything, endure any insult, to make him stay.

He had been willing to die, but now life had come back to him, life and power and passion, and he would never stand unloved and alone in a crowd of people on a train platform again. He would never again be an object of pity to the men who worked for him and their wives and children. He would never again be little more than a rumor.

The house was growing around them. Mrs. Larsen's staff of two had grown to six, including a laundress, a maid for Antonio, and someone extra to help in the kitchen. Catherine had sent to Chicago and hired a gardener who brought the tropics to the conservatory, who made the orange and the jasmine bloom in the hot afternoon sun. It was wet there, and songbirds flew from branch to branch, singing. It made Ralph's bones feel warm, to sit there in the afternoon. It made the pain go away.

The heavy old damask curtains were pulled down, and lighter ones were put up, to let in more sun. The silk bed hangings in their bedroom were replaced with fabrics adorned with Chinese patterns, designs from another century. Their exotic splendor transported Ralph and Catherine into their own Xanadu, a place that was wholly and entirely the kingdom of their own desires.

Seamstresses came from Chicago, bringing pattern books and bolts of rich material, to make dresses for Catherine, nothing excessive. They made Ralph splendid striped shirts with white cuffs and collars and gold collar buttons.

They were rich, and while they felt no need to be ostentatious, they felt comfortable with living the way rich people live. Ralph didn't change his habits, and he stopped drinking again once he had had enough brandy; he ate only as much as he needed and not as much as he wanted. The food was exquisite. The company increased as light was let into the house.

But still he was unable to get through to Antonio. He had gone through so many years of hope in the effort to find him and bring him home, and now Antonio hated the house, he hated the business, he was rude to Ralph's wife and to the servants. But Ralph had time. He had had nothing but time for the long years and it had taught him to stand straight, not to bend into the cold.

Every day the winter thinned. The stubble rose again in the field, the light grew longer in the afternoons. Ice still coated the black river, but it was as though the prison doors were opening and people waited for the first warm day and then, finally, the day when the girls appeared in their summer dresses. There was a future.

Antonio learned to drive the horse and carriage, and immediately, over the muddy roads, he went to town every night, where he took up with a young widow, Mrs. Alverson, whose husband had committed suicide two years before. Her sexual desperation matched his own, and their rendezvous were the talk of the town. It hurt Ralph to hear his name mentioned again as a subject of gossip, to hear of that kind of scandal. He made an attempt to rein in Antonio's behavior.

"Her husband was twenty-five. She has a baby who was born after her husband was already dead. Her heart is an open wound."

"She likes my company."

"She lives on charity. Of course she likes your company. People are talking."

"Your reputation is worthless to me, if that's what you're worried about. You have no reputation, as far as I'm concerned. I'll do exactly what I want to."

"Maybe you should go to Europe. There are many Mrs. Alversons over there, women who have a better understanding of the arrangement. Maybe you'd be happier. I was happy. There are women . . ."

"And leave you and Mrs. Truitt and the fun we're having? Why?"

"Antonio. Because Mrs. Alverson . . . what's her name?

"Violet."

"Because Mrs. Alverson is worth more than this. Anybody is. Because you have no heart for business. The only other thing I have to give you is money. I've given you enough to go around the world, if that's what you want. You'll play it out. You'll come around. The fire burns out."

When he was Antonio's age, Ralph had been forced to give up his dissolute life, to come home and take over the business. He had learned by doing, badly at first, then better and better. It had become his life, and Italy was a distant memory. Antonio had reached an age when the notion of going to a foreign country where he didn't know anybody and didn't know the language and had nowhere to live was overwhelming to him. He had his life in hand, and the thrill of the new wasn't available to him. He had brought his whole life to Wisconsin, and now he had no way back. He also had no way to get what he wanted, and his rage mounted. His old friends would envy him, but his old friends were not welcome here. Here it was all governors and senators and tired old businessmen with cigars and potbellies who came to lick the boots of Ralph Truitt, hoping to get in at the beginning of the next big thing, the next capital investment that would make them even richer.

Antonio retired to his widow in town and his rooms in the vast house, and he didn't care that he was breaking his father's soul, little by little. It couldn't last long, this tenuous balance of hatred and greed. It couldn't last.

Violet Alverson came to dinner. She was painfully shy and gentle, and seemed in awe of the grandeur of the food and the house. Catherine showed her everything, and she seemed most enchanted by the conservatory with its songbirds and its tropical plants. She didn't know which spoon or fork to use, but Ralph talked to her in a gentle, kindly voice about her hopes for the future, a better life, a life of her own, a fine boy who would have an education and be somebody, somebody in business, perhaps.

Catherine asked her to spend the night since it was four miles back to town and the roads were dark and muddy, but Violet declined, and left in her borrowed buggy, whip in hand. She and Antonio had said not one word to each other. She drove home believing that he was going to ask her to marry him.

After the dinner, Antonio got bored with Violet Alverson. She had a child, and she had no conversation. She was not pretty enough to stir his vanity. He wrote to her that he wouldn't see her anymore. He wouldn't even go in person.

She hanged herself the next day from the same beam her husband had used, in the attic of her shabby house with its sad double bed. Her baby was asleep on a quilt on the floor. She had nursed him just before she tied the rope. Her dress was still unbuttoned, her bare breast hanging out. The cries of the baby alerted the neighbors. The local newspaper said she had died due to her continuing grief over the loss of her young husband. Ralph and Catherine went to the spare funeral of this woman they hardly knew. Antonio stayed home and played the piano.

Chapter Twenty-three

——⟨⟨⟩⟩——

THE WIND BLEW WARMER from the south. The nights were still long and frigid, but the earth was visible now. Ralph spent the last light of the days in the barn with his car, making it shine, bringing it to sputtering life again. The winter had gone on too long. He had Antonio's automobile brought out from town, and he taught Antonio to drive on the long drive-way up to the house. It was the first mechanical thing Antonio had ever been able to do well. His automobile was a marvel, leather upholstery and brass and crystal lamps, with bud vases in the back, and he and Ralph drove up and down along the sweeping road to the house. The car brought them a measure of peace. They tried to get comfortable with each other. They tried to talk.

"It was a terrible thing, the thing I did to you."

"You were angry, I suppose."

"I was angry. I was angry and your mother was gone. I had loved her with all my heart. Believe me. I had. When she was gone, everything went black."

"And I was left behind."

"Your sister dead. Your mother gone. You were left, and I turned that grief and rage on you, a little boy, and I will never stop regretting it."

"You managed to forget pretty well, it seems to me."

"I looked for you for ten years. I looked everywhere."

"It must have cost a lot of money."

"I didn't care. After you left, ran away, I knew what an awful thing I'd done. No amount of money can make that right. Being tortured for something you didn't do."

The slow dance of the father and the son, the old song of regret and retribution twined through their every conversation. During the conversations late at night Antonio was usually drunk, Catherine upstairs in bed.

"You married."

"I wanted you to come home. I thought it would help. And I was lonely. Lonely and unloved and sad every day. You don't know what happens to a life without love. To a heart. It withers. It loses reason. I just wanted what people have. I wanted a companion, some company in my heart. Someone other than myself."

"And have you been happy? Happy with the young Mrs. Truitt? What do you really know about her?"

"Her life hasn't been easy. I'm glad to make it better. And she brought you home. She's my wife. Yes. I'm happy."

"She's much younger."

"She'd be a friend to you, if you'd let her."

"I have friends, but they don't live here. You beat me until I was blinded by the blood in my eyes. You kept me locked in a room. You left me alone with no explanation of where my mother was or why your cruelty was so immense and unending."

"I'm sorry."

"Time will tell if sorry is enough. I don't think it is. If you died tonight, I wouldn't come to your funeral."

"You'd be very rich."

"And you would be unmourned, except perhaps for the lovely Mrs. Truitt. Certainly not by me. And not by all those people who live in fear of you."

Despite the vitriol, it was a beginning, some kind of communication between father and son. Ralph went to work every day with a hope that Antonio would come around, would grow to forgive and to love. He was an honest man and he had such a yearning to believe.

For Antonio, of course, he was a fish on the line. Antonio gave and then withheld, leaving the hook in his father's mouth. It gave him pleasure.

Antonio wanted so much. He wanted for most of his childhood never to have happened. He wanted his mother to have been faithful and beautiful and virtuous. He wanted her to have cared for him. He wanted her to have taken him with her when she ran away, giving him more than the idiot sister and the terrifying father who was not his father. He wanted the days of his boyhood to have been different. He wanted, more than anything, for his mother not to have died in squalor, to have lived and stayed with him and kept things from becoming so sadly, wrenchingly wrong. He didn't care anymore about the beatings. They had made him stronger than his father, his real father, ever could have been. He cared about the loss.

He sat drunk by the fire every night after Ralph had gone to bed, to the consolation of sex with Antonio's old mistress. And he cried. He wept for his own boyhood and its simple pleasures. He sat in his old playroom and touched everything, the rocking horse, the stuffed animals and the wooden boats and the tin soldiers and he wept for his own losses in battle.

It wasn't the beatings or the loneliness he was weeping for, sitting with a bottle of brandy on the floor of his unchanged playroom. It was time. It was the time he couldn't get back. Yes, Ralph would do anything, and yes, the future could hold a better life. But he would never get back the days and the hours that might have been something other than angry and miserable and painful. No money could ever change that, and nothing Truitt could say would make it right.

There was an almost sexual pleasure in the boundless sorrow, a comfort he could give himself by letting go, a release not found even in sex for the first time with a woman he coveted. He didn't know why he behaved the way he behaved. He didn't care. Nobody else had lived his life. Nobody else could tell him how to be.

Perhaps, he thought, Ralph was right. Maybe he could change. It wasn't as though his life had given him much joy or peace.

Perhaps weeping in the playroom was his first fearful and tentative step toward some kind of love. He didn't know what love was, but he knew that he had begun to feel differently toward Ralph, to feel something that was not blind hatred. He was a child, and he wanted his father and his mother.

He would wake up in the morning on the floor of his old rooms, his head throbbing, his body covered with the quilt that had covered him as a child, and he would shiver with grief and sometimes with remorse at his own behavior. He wished he could have been another person.

Ever since Truitt had stopped torturing him, ever since he had been strong enough to run away, he had done nothing but torture himself. If Truitt had tried to kill him, then Antonio, for all his sorrow, had done his best to finish the job. The blurred days and nights, the women, the debauchery, none of it had been enough. With the return of Truitt's love, he would have to be his own destruction.

The idea that he could have a wonderful life had never before occurred to him. That he was rich, that he could go to Rome and marry a princess, that he might drink cold champagne at dawn on the deck of a steamer bound for the South Seas, in the company of someone who simply loved him, that he might do anything that would give him joy, that would create a wonderful life, these were phantoms that eluded him.

Love was gone forever, just outside the window, just beyond reach, like fruit on an upper branch. In its place was the sexual attraction of tragedy. He would hang his head and swig his brandy and mourn for his life, for the hours of his childhood, for the kindness of this man who wanted to father him, for the lost beauty of his mother. He explored the extravagant rooms of his father's house, knowing that there was no home for him anywhere. There was no getting there. There was no one there when he arrived.

He wanted nothing more than to lie in a small, dark, warm room in an anonymous house where there was neither day nor night and have ravenous sex with woman after woman until he died. He wanted a drunkenness of the flesh. He wanted the thing he loved most in the world, the soft touch of another human being, to become a torture. He wanted to die in a sexual embrace, the last of thousands.

There was Catherine. She was like the drug, the poison he craved. In the absence of other diversions, she was a woman whose secrets he knew. She was always in the house, sewing, reading the books she had sent from Chicago. She had abandoned him. She had betrayed him, denied him the golden promise.

She slept every night in his father's bed. His father had sex with her, and told her he loved her, a thing Antonio had never said, and would never have meant. It wasn't enough to want all women; he wanted Catherine be all women to him.

She deliberately avoided him. She shut herself up in her room, sewing, when Truitt was away. She sat at the table like a stranger and talked to him as though she had no memory of the velvet cords that he had used to tie her to his bed, of the fire that had burned her skin. His sorrow was infinite. His desire was specific, and immense.

Truitt went to town. Antonio would find her, follow her, would open his heart to her, tell her how coming back to this house had made him different, how it had opened a wound he had thought healed forever. The sight of Truitt, the man who had been so capable of destruction, sitting calm and safe from accusation, even sitting in his own remorse, made him afraid, he said. It frightened him to think it could be different, that things could, from this moment, change.

She advised patience. She advised giving the old wounds time to heal. There was no more talk of Truitt's death. He told her he had arsenic in his room, the arsenic he had brought from Chicago, and that late at night, drunk on Bordeaux and alone while his father slept with his mistress, his creation, he picked it up and sniffed it and held it in his hands and longed for death. He told her that if there were a button in his leg he could push so that he would vanish and never have been, he would push it. She expressed horror that he would contemplate such a thing. He had learned to drive a car, she said. He could go anywhere. His life was waiting. She didn't understand a word he said. She was no longer the woman who had spoken to him for hours of nothing, of amorous nothings.

The silence enveloped him, strangling him. Every morning, his razor was an invitation. Every night, the arsenic was an aphrodisiac. His loneliness was terrifying, but he wouldn't come to town, wouldn't come down to meet the proper young women his father invited from Chicago, to sit at table with their banker fathers, all exquisite manners and musical, sexless laughter. They had no darkness. It was useless, the light, to him.

He wrote suicide notes and stored them in a locked drawer. He wrote letters to his father in which he described Catherine's past in fine detail, letters that would destroy, in a single swift stroke, both their lives forever. These letters he burned.

He was lonely, lost inside himself; he was exhausted from simply sustaining a life he found horrible, from holding his head up in a scornful public, from the pretense of his own narcissism. He said the words over and over to himself, realizing how trivial they sounded. He spoke his heart to Ralph, late and drunk one night.

"I want . . . I wanted to be somebody else. After I left, I wanted things to change. They didn't."

"We all wanted to be somebody else. Somebody braver, or more handsome, or smarter. It's what children want. It's what you grow out of, if you're lucky. If you don't, it's a lifetime of agony. I wanted . . . what? To be elegant, not some country hick, to be loved, to live unharmed and have my way in everything. I never wanted this, never wanted to have anything to do with business.

"I wanted to marry a contessa and live happily ever after. It doesn't happen that way. Play the hand you have, Antonio, that's all anybody expects. And it's a pretty good hand."

"I'm in pain, all the time. I hurt."

"And I'm sorry for that. If there were anything . . ."

"There isn't."

"I know."

It was a road without end, a conversation with no point. If you spend your days speaking to someone who speaks a foreign language, how are you ever to be understood? He could say the words, his father could listen, but the words had no weight for either of them. It was a way of passing the time, the mournful son and the compassionate father.

Let it go, Antonio would tell himself late at night, as he lay on the nursery room floor. Live a regular life, crippled, sorrowful, but sweetly ordinary. Speak to the girls from Chicago. Drive your car so that you can be the envy of the town. Learn the rules of business and give up the dark room and the thousands of women. It was like seeing a distant shore and knowing he would not reach it.

Catherine never left his mind. When he met her, he was a young boy, a young man, and she was an elegant courtesan pursuing opportunities. She had seemed glamorous. She had manners, and she knew things about the world. He knew nothing, nothing at all. She had bought him shirts. She had taught him how to dress, how to eat in restaurants and speak with his eyes lowered. She had shown him the intricacies of his own body. She had woven a circle around him and kept him safe for a time. Then the monsters returned to claim him, and he himself became a monster—cruel, unyielding, and conniving. He had turned on her because she had seen him in his innocence and hope, because she believed in these things, and he had hurt her again and again, and she had allowed it, and for this he felt a sorrow which burned like hot lead.

On a sober morning, when he happened to be awake, he went

and sat by Truitt in the office. He listened and watched as Truitt increased his fortune, as he listened to the complaints of his workers and dealt with them fairly and compassionately. It was like watching a painting. There was no movement; there was no sound. Truitt thought his son was taking an interest. Truitt thought he was coming around to a kind of acceptance, the kind of bargain he himself had made so many years before. The next morning, Antonio couldn't remember having been there, couldn't recall a single word or picture one detail of the office.

His father, his real father had left his mother for a rich young widow. His father was the man who had no face. His father had taught piano, was named Moretti, had given him life. This Truitt was a remote stranger whose death was the only thing Antonio had lived for for more than a dozen years. This Truitt who bought and sold and disposed, who spoke to him in kind tones that Antonio could not bear.

Only Catherine was real, and she had become somebody else, someone unknown to Antonio. But beneath her clothes lay her skin, and, just as Antonio remembered in his skin every blow from Truitt's hand, remembered every word spoken in anger, so there lay, in Catherine's skin, the memory of who and what she had been. She had meant the world to him, and he couldn't let go. Not now.

Not ever.

CHAPTER TWENTY-FOUR

NTONIO FOUND HER in the conservatory. It was late afternoon, and the songbirds twittered from branch to branch and the jasmine hung heavy with scent and the roses had begun to bud in the warm hothouse air. The late light fell through the fronds of giant ferns and palms she had bought in Saint Louis. The windows were fogged with moisture. Orchids grew in Chinese pots. She was sewing, folds of fine dark blue, almost black wool covering her lap, billowing out onto the red marble floor.

He sat at her feet, like a dog, patient, benevolent, longing to be loved. He was ashamed of his willingness to be humiliated. She showed him the picture of what the dress would look like when it was finished. It was almost done, a simple dress of elegant shape with buttons that ran from the floor to the neck, with white gauze collar and cuffs. It was pleated down the front to the waist, the pleats held in place by stitches so small they were almost invisible. The wool was thin and expensive, fluid in her hands. She moved the dark cloth swiftly through thin white fingers, the needle flashing in and out, the quiet click of the steel needle on the silver thimble she wore on her finger.

She deftly turned the dress, hauling in the yards of wool to work on the hem. Antonio's knee grazed the fabric, and he was electrified. Beneath the dark blue was her shoe, and her white stockings, and beneath that her fresh skin, the map of her whole body. Beneath were her sweet scents and her secret places, places he had traveled and dwelt.

"Hattie Reno," she said softly. "You had a letter from her. I recognized the handwriting."

"I told them. I had to say something. I burned the letter."

"She's well."

"They're all well. They miss you. She said the theater was filled with dull people. She said the beer had gone flat since you left, all the bubbles gone away. You amused her. She misses you."

"Don't say anything about me. It was another life."

"Was it, Mrs. Truitt?"

"People change, Antonio. People move on."

"I don't. I don't move on."

"Hattie Reno was my best friend. Now I hardly remember her. Not out of unkindness, it's just that things are so different."

"You're pretending."

She put down her sewing for a moment. "I don't think I am. I got tired of being terrible, terrible to people."

"You were never terrible to me."

"We were terrible to each other. It was another time. It was like a madness. Antonio, it's gone now. You have to make your peace with that. You have to make peace with your father." She resumed her sewing, the swift stitches going through the dark hem.

"I'm too tired. I'm so tired, you can't imagine."

She looked at him. "I know it's hard. I know he did terrible things to you. You have to forgive now. Unless you do, he can't forgive himself."

"You tried to kill him."

"And then I stopped. I couldn't do it. Something in me changed. I couldn't hurt a fly, now."

"Once you would have done anything for me. You made me a promise."

"I was another person. Another person made that promise."

"And that's it?"

Her eyes flashed. "What do you need that you don't have? You have his love. You have his money. You have his attention. Make something of that. Make a life for yourself."

He touched the hem of her dress. Fire shot through his fingers and up his arm. He touched her shoe.

"Don't do that."

"It means nothing? Nothing at all?"

"It means nothing. Don't do it."

He got up and walked away, the heels of his shoes sounding on the marble floor. He didn't know where he was going or what he was going to do.

She couldn't mean it. She couldn't separate her long past from her present as easily as that. She couldn't deny what they had been to one another, the things they had done, the plans they had made.

He sat in his room and drank brandy. If he wasn't going to have his father's death, he wanted his old life. She couldn't turn her back on the pleasures of the vices as easily as that. He wanted her. It went off like a gunshot to his brain, and after that he knew nothing. It was all darkness after that.

He walked swiftly back through the corridor and down the long steps. He walked through the great hall under the Venetian chandeliers and into the conservatory. She was still sitting, but she knew he was coming, she must have known, because she had put down her sewing. She sat quiet and calm, waiting for him, her eyes large, the mixed desires she felt written on her face.

He grabbed her hands. She pulled away. He grabbed her arms and pulled her up to him. He pressed himself against her, the full length of his body against the full length of hers, his mouth on her mouth, his hands around her, moving across her shoulders through the fabric of her dress. She was trembling.

She pulled away. "Antonio. Don't do this. I'm begging you."

"I have to. I'm so sorry. I have to."

He kissed her again. He put his hand up along her face, while with his other arm her pulled her close to him. He put his hand beneath her dress, he felt her skin, her warm smooth skin, and the fire was in him and he knew there was no turning back. She wanted this. She had to remember, and she had to want it. He said it over and over to himself.

Then he lost all thought, he lost the ability to think and became pure motion as his mouth and hands took her back to the days and nights in his room in Saint Louis, the days when she had been somebody else, somebody who lived for her body and its delights, somebody who gave herself because she had no care for who or what she was. She had laughed, then, she had been scornful of the ordinary world with its ordinary moral scruples, and he had been part of that, her diversion, her own wild love. They had been twins in their desires, rising and falling on each other's breath, and he had covered her body with kisses, and there was no part of her that was not his.

She was the delight and the agony of his youth, yet she had not mattered, he now realized. She was only the portal to this sensation of being lost, of floating unmoored high above the earth, and he wanted that back again. It was as close as he could come to death.

She was new. She was a stranger. It was as though she had come to him in disguise, the trappings of her old life gone, the dress and hair and clean face of her new life a costume she had put on to amuse him.

She struggled against him. She fought, and this too drove him on, made him feel unbound. He could have her when she didn't want him. He'd done it before. When she was angry with him, he could still have her. When he had been too rude or too drunk or too late, she would still come creeping into his room while he slept and lie down beside him and let him take her, because she had nowhere to go, because she believed that her life was in the gutter and he was the gutter in which she lived.

He tore at his shirt, and her hands scratched at his body, her nails drew blood, and she started to scream, to call Mrs. Larsen. He held his hand over her mouth and lifted up her skirt, tearing at her stockings and her underclothes until her flesh was beneath the palm of his hand. Then things grew calmer. He breathed more gently. For just a second, there was no sound except the twittering of birds, as his hand moved toward her sex, as he covered her mouth and she didn't make a sound.

He took his hand away from her mouth and kissed her, violated her mouth with his tongue and bit at her lips and still she didn't make a sound, still she stood twisting beneath his arms, but soundlessly, only the rustle of her skirt on the floor, only the sound of the flapping wings of the birds and the rustling of the palm fronds where the birds alighted. He kissed her eyes, the skin of her fore-head. He licked her face and bit at the lobes of her ears. It felt as though he were on fire.

He needed her to want him. He needed her never to have gone away, never to have abandoned him in this insane scheme they had concocted, never to have slept with his father. She was his lover. His. She was the desire of his childhood, the woman on the trolley car, the young girl in the restaurant, the whore at the end of the dark street.

He ripped at her dress, and it tore open in his hands, two quick pulls and it was open. He tore at her thin camisole until he could see her breasts, the dark nipples full and erect. He fell to his knees and pulled her forward, her breasts in his mouth, his teeth biting her nipples. He knew he was raping her. He knew this was not her will, not what she wanted, and he found that erotic as well.

He tore at fabric, and he saw the dark triangle of hair. She was still standing, her hands on top of his head. His hair was wild, it was slick with sweat from the exertion of doing this thing he didn't want to do, this thing he had to do to bring himself one step closer to his own death.

She was crying now, and he could hear her breath coming in and out as she cried, and he rose and licked the tears from her face as he undid his pants and pushed himself into her, against her will and he knew it and didn't care. She wasn't Catherine anymore. She was someone he didn't know, and he didn't care if he hurt her or defiled her or made her ashamed. She was the last one; this was the last time. He would never see her again.

She stabbed him twice. She stabbed him with her sewing scissors out of a basket on the arm of the chair. She stabbed him in the back and then she stabbed him in the shoulder when he lurched back in shock. Her dress hung open in the front, her skin exposed; her camisole was a rag around her naked torso, just beginning now to round, to show a fullness. Her body arched forward as she howled in pain and rage and despair.

"Why?" was all she screamed. "Why?" Again and again.

Now he began to cry, blood pouring from his shoulder and his back, he howled in pain for all that was lost, everything that was broken now for good, everything he could never get back. He had wanted something, but now he couldn't remember what,

"He killed my mother! I saw it!"

"He didn't, Antonio. That never happened." Drawing her ruined dress around her, trying to hold it closed with one hand and sweep her hair away from her face with the other, her eyes dry now, her mouth hard and unyielding and her voice hard, too, hard and filled with the truth.

"He let her die. She was sick, Antonio. You dreamed it. You imagined it so much, out of hatred, out of . . . I don't know, out of something, that you thought it was real, but it wasn't. She was sick. She was alone and dying, and he took you to see her and she didn't even know your name, and he turned his back on her and walked away and in that, yes, he killed her, but not the way you think."

"No!"

"Yes. And he has spent a lifetime regretting it, wishing he could have felt otherwise, but he didn't, and he let her die and you have to let her die, you have to let her die in peace and not look to find her, not wonder where she is. She's gone, that's all. She was always gone. Long before she was dead."

He was bleeding badly. He was in pain. He didn't care. He fell to his knees and buried his head in her ruined skirt and wept, wept for himself. And then they heard the sound in the door. They heard

Truitt's footsteps in the hall, but it was too late. Her dress was ruined, Antonio's blood fell to the marble floor and Truitt would know everything that had happened, and know, too, that he had finally been betrayed beyond his ability to endure it.

Then he was standing in the door. Then he knew.

Antonio turned to him, his hands covered with his own blood, his face a mask of pain. "Yes! I raped her. I've been with her, inside her a thousand times. Do you know what she is? Do you know who she is?"

The color drained from Truitt's face. He stood stock still. He saw everything, in frozen detail, the tattered dress, the blood on his boy, the birds, the palms. He smelled the jasmine and the orange blossoms and he saw the dress and the blood and he understood, and he knew he was going to kill his son.

He stepped forward and picked Antonio up by the shoulders and held him in his arms, the son's blood staining his father's shirt-front, wetting him through to the skin.

And then Truitt's hands moved. He fists came down on his son's head, buckling his knees, and Antonio stood while his father beat his face and his body with his fists and he didn't resist, he didn't try to protect himself. It was like a dream of long ago, a memory of his boyhood. He merely thought, said to himself, this is it, this is the moment and then you can rest. If we just get through this, you can finally come home, be at home and rest.

Finally he ran. He turned from his father's grasp, he turned from Catherine, seeing her scream but not hearing it, seeing the last look on her face as she screamed because she loved him and hated him at the same time, seeing her call his name but not hearing it, the voice he had loved, he ran from the conservatory, scattering the tiny

birds, he ran and Ralph followed him, his fists still beating his son's
bleeding back.

Antonio ran into the big hallway, the hallway with the Venetian
mirrors, the long corridor tilting wildly, where he could not get a
footing because his shoes were wet now with his own blood, and he
ran to the fireplace and picked up the iron poker, and when Ralph
ran up to him, he hit Ralph in the face with the poker, drawing
blood, sending his father reeling, his head cracking on the stone
floor. Catherine followed into the hall, she caught at him, tried to
stop him as he ran past her and out the door into the garden.

Catherine ran to Ralph. She lifted his head from the floor. She
saw his eyes open wide in rage and knew that this was not hers to
stop, that it would play itself out to an end she didn't want and
couldn't have imagined. Ralph got to his feet, Catherine begging
him to stop, now, to stop before it was too late, but he didn't hear
her or wouldn't hear her, and he followed Antonio into the garden and beyond, catching and beating him. Antonio never made
a sound. He stood and ran and was caught by his father and was
beaten the way he had been beaten so often as a boy, except that
this time he was guilty and filled with sin and horror, and they
both knew it.

Down the long meadow they fought, Antonio fighting back with
whatever he could find—sticks, rocks—hurting Ralph, drawing
blood from his head. But Ralph wouldn't be stopped, as he used
his fists to beat back the memory of the wife who had used him,
the child who had run away, the days spent in the idleness of love
while his own father lay dying, the mother who had buried the
needle in his palm. In his fury, all the rage of all the years came
pouring out.

Catherine was standing on the broad stone terrace, afraid to go any farther, afraid to interfere, knowing that however it played out, the end was already decided. Mrs. Larsen was standing beside her now, flour in her hair. Catherine could see every detail of what was happening, every detail of the field, the Arabian standing in the short grass, its head down, then up in alarm as the two men passed, screaming and fighting.

They came to the pond, and Antonio skidded out onto the ice and stood like a bull in the ring, wounded, bleeding, tears still running down his face. There was no more fight in him. He had come to the end of his strength, the end of his hatred, the end of his regret, and he stood in the center of the pond, on the black ice, waiting to be killed. He thought of the days in heaven, he thought of his reunion with his mother, he thought of the incredible pain of dying, the physical pain the body could stand before it gave out, until the irrevocable blow was mercifully given and darkness fell.

Ralph paused at the edge of the pond. He was bleeding, too, from a cut on his head, and his hands were broken, the pain shooting up his arms. He found too that his anger had spent itself, that while the unforgivable things were still unforgivable, and the terror still terrifying, he had no more stomach for the rest. He thought of the accounts in the newspaper, the suicides, the murders, and the corpses, and he found that the living were more beautiful than the dead, that in the end, something must be saved, even if that meant it also had to be endured. Antonio would go away. Antonio would never be seen again and would die alone with his guilt and shame and memories, but there would be no corpse to carry to the graveyard, not today. There would be no white, still flesh in his house, not anymore. He would mourn his loss, but he would, in secret, still love his son and send him money, and when he died, the son would be sent for, and would stand by his father's grave and remember this day as though it had happened to somebody else a long time ago.

Then they heard the crack. A white jagged line shot through the black ice and Antonio went down, into the icy water, under the ice. He came up under the ice, no air to breathe, his head hitting, his blood mingling with the black water.

Antonio struggled, but he couldn't see his way out, and he floated into unconsciousness, into the peaceful cold of the black water, his body showing dimly beneath the surface of the ice.

Ralph Truitt howled in pain, and he tried to get out to his boy, but the ice gave way around him and he floundered in the frigid water. He ran to the barn where he found a pole and a rope, and he raced back to the water, trying to save him, trying to save the years and the days, not knowing or admitting that Antonio was already dead, already gone, the plumes of blood now visible under the ice, surrounding his dead body, floating, arms at his sides as though he were flying, head down as though he were looking from a great height on the small earth beneath him.

The pole and the rope were useless, and as his son lay all night under the ice, Ralph was inconsolable. He slept alone. He wouldn't speak. He ate nothing.

Catherine couldn't sleep. She walked the halls of the huge house, looking at the pictures, running her hands over the furniture, finally going into Antonio's rooms and packing up his things in trunks. She stripped the sheets from his bed and smelled in them the rich scent of her old lover, and she wept until there weren't any more tears. Then, finally, she went and lay down on the narrow bed in the perfect playroom and slept.

They had to get men to come in the morning from town and

pull Antonio from the water, his pristine shirt still bravely white over his chest. He was long and narrow and light as a boy. His black hair lay back in the cart as they pulled him away, and it froze to his scalp in the morning light and the warming wind.

Ralph would have forgiven him. He would have taken his son in his arms and said, hush, hush now, it's over now. There is no more to happen, no more that can happen. The story, the old story has come to an end. He would have put his mouth to his son's and breathed over and over until the warm breath filled his son's lungs, and his son's eyes opened and looked at him and trusted him.

But there was no use. There was no point. It was just a story. It was just a story of people, of Ralph and Emilia and Antonio and Catherine and the mothers and the fathers who had died, too soon or late, of people who had hurt one another as much as people can do, who had been selfish and not wise, and had become trapped inside the bitter walls of memories they wished they had never had.

It was just a story of how the bitter cold gets into your bones and never leaves you, of how the memories get into your heart and never leave you alone, of the pain and the bitterness of what happens to you when you're small and have no defenses but still know evil when it happens, of secrets about evil you have no one to tell, of the life you live in secret, knowing your own pain and the pain of others but helpless to do anything other than the things you do, and the end it all comes to.

It was a story of a son who felt his one true birthright was to kill his father. It was the story of a father who could not undo a single gesture of his life, no matter the sympathies of his heart. It was a story of poison, poison that causes you to weep in your sleep, that comes to you first as a taste of ecstasy. It was a story of people who don't choose life over death until it's too late to know the difference, people whose goodness is forgotten, left behind like a child's toy in a dusty playroom, people who see many things and remember only a handful of them and learn from even fewer, people who hurt themselves, who wreck their own lives and then go on to wreck the lives of those around them, who cannot be helped or assuaged by love or kindness or luck or charm, who forget kindness, the feeling and practice of it, and how it can save even the worst, most misshapen life from despair.

It was just a story about despair.

CHAPTER TWENTY-FIVE

—◦◦◦—

THE FUNERAL WAS ONLY the three of them, Truitt and Catherine and Mrs. Larsen. Truitt had dug the hole himself, spending a long day breaking up the thawing earth. There were no tears. There was a minister from one of the churches, and Antonio was buried with the fewest possible words next to his sister and Ralph's mother and father, near the old house.

His coffin seemed so large to Catherine. It was impossible to believe that his beautiful body was shut inside it, locked away from the light and the air forever. "Every thing in the light and air ought to be happy," the poet had said. "Whoever is not in his coffin and the dark grave let him know he has enough." She felt the giddy sense of being alive in the presence of the dead.

Two days had passed. She stood now in the ruins of the garden she hoped to build. The high walls cut off her view of the rest of the world; there was still snow in the corners of the garden, and the fallen statues were glazed with ice. It seemed ten degrees colder here than in the rest of the world, although the back of the house was splendid in the western sun. She could barely remember how all this had begun.

She had wanted something, and she had set out to get it, clear of her purpose and sure in her actions. But it had gotten confused, confused in the mass of the ordinary, confused in the way people live, in the way the heart attracts and repels the things it wants and fears. Her own heart had gone out in directions she never imagined, her hopes had become pinned to the things she would never have allowed.

She wore the blue wool dress she had been finishing when Antonio died. His hands had felt the cloth around her body. She stood, severe and simple, in the middle of an old garden in the hidden back of a remarkable house. Antonio was dead. A whole life was dead to her.

She had no idea how it would turn out. Truitt had not spoken to her since the death, and she had not interfered with his profound grief. They ate together at the long table, but there was no discussion, no reading of poetry after supper, no sumptuous feast of flesh in the dark. She had picked for herself a small and insignificant bedroom, and retired there to weep in private for all she had lost.

She was afraid. She was afraid for the rest of her life. When Truitt disposed of her, as she supposed he would, she would have nowhere to go. She didn't want to end like Emilia, alone in a filthy house. She didn't want to end like Alice, dying in the snow in an alley, remembering how nice it had once been, glad to have the burden of an exhausting life lifted from her, abandoned even by the angels and laughing at the death squeezing her with cold fingers by the throat. She had no one in the world. Her whole world, what was left of it, was here, and there was no way to get back to where she had been before.

The memory of what she had done with her days and nights seemed unthinkable. They came to her, those days and nights, like the pages of a calendar being flipped by a child, a blur of days and months and years. Had she gone to the theater? Had she written coquettish letters in a fine hand, the lavender-scented ink staining the sleeve of a ruffled gown from Worth in Paris? Had she turned away in bed from men so that she wouldn't see the money left on a bedside table? It wasn't possible. Yet she couldn't deny it—every bad memory, every loss of faith, had brought her the long way from where she had been to where she was.

It was obviously done with Truitt, Antonio had seen to that, his last act of cruelty. There was no way to judge what the depth of his sorrow would drive him to do and she stood, knowing she had done wrong but unable to imagine the consequences. He couldn't stay silent. The truth was too blatant to ignore, and he had been through it before. Perhaps it was simple weariness that had kept him from striking her when he turned from the frozen pond, the still meadow and the rearing Arabian and Antonio gone.

She had something she wanted to say to him, not about the life which was growing inside her, stronger and stronger every day, but about the virtues of his heart, about the years he had waited in patient humiliation for happiness to find him, about how he had set out to build a small kind of happiness and been horribly deceived. There was no apology she could make. She had known more than he did, and she had used that knowledge to ruin his life, again, the one thing he had guarded himself so carefully against.

She didn't know where he was in the house. She hadn't seen him since lunch. He retired to his study, or to the blue bedroom, and she had no way of knowing what he did or what he thought about. His silence was suffocating to her, his distance unbearable.

She would die for him if her death would do him any good. But it wouldn't do anything except add to the anguish of events that he had never anticipated.

She had never before had anything to hold on to, nothing to root her to a place or a time, not until Truitt. And she had brought harm to him, in the belief that nothing mattered, that no moment had consequences beyond the moment itself. She had agreed to kill him without realizing that he would die. She had agreed to marry him without realizing that marriage brought a kind a simple pleasure, a pleasure in the continued company of another human being, the act of caring, of carrying with you the thought of someone else. She would, she supposed, never see him age beyond the present day, and found that the thought made her immeasurably sad.

Somewhere, for those other people she so often thought about, there was the comfort of continuance and of habit. She realized it wasn't easy. The winters were long, and tragedy and madness rose in the pristine air. Even in the country the madness of the time would not leave people untouched. Throughout her life, people came and went, some amusing, most not, but their leaving was no more surprising to her than their coming. Truitt had arrived, and leaving him now would be the end of comfort for Catherine Land.

She didn't know what to do with her hands. She wasn't cold, not yet, and the house looked warm as the lights began to come on, Mrs. Larsen moving slowly, room to room. Mrs. Larsen had known Antonio since he was a baby. She had watched him go into the ground next to his sister and turned away as though it were the most natural thing in the world. For her, life went on, dinners got made, lights got turned on, and that was the way you got from one day to the next. Habit saved her from grief, from horror at her own husband's sudden insanity, from the ache of watching a young man die whose sweetness had left the earth long before his body.

It was four o'clock, and everything around her stood perfectly still. The wind died, and the animals in the field, even the gray Arabian, stood to watch as the light slanted suddenly into the prism of evening. The large facade of the house, with its imposing windows and its classical statues spaced along the edge of the roof, lit up golden and hazy and ancient. It was the hour at which she had arrived. Her discarded dress. Her lost jewels, now so trivial. Truitt standing on the platform in a black coat with a fur collar in the howling snow. The startled deer and the runaway horses. Just as everything waited—for the end of winter, for the beginning of spring.

She moved her foot and looked down. The grass under her shoe turned green as she watched, and it grew away from her, grew greening until the whole of the patch where she stood was green and clipped and glowing in the golden light. The green wonder of the world filled her garden and spread out from her feet wherever she walked.

It moved away from her, and she stepped back. Everywhere she placed her foot turned green and lush. The parterre grew rich with the odors of rosemary and sage, clipped into globes between a lover's knot of box and yew, and lavender, the long spikes with their purple heads as still as the rest.

The beds along the old brick walls still lay brown and tangled, but as she walked toward them spreading green from the hem of her dress, the old canes of the roses began to uncurl themselves, the dark waxy foliage began to make its first appearance. The tiny snowdrops and crocus sprouted along the edge of the beds, white and yellow and purple, the hellebores and then the narcissi, the poetic Acteon and the rich yellows and pale yellows of King Alfred. The flowers appeared and the names came back to her from the long afternoons in the library, those hours of rest from her exertions with Antonio.

He was a dessert that was too rich, but she had run to him from the time he was hardly more than a boy, the mixture of beauty and arrogance, the tenderness and charm which cost him so much now stilled forever, buried beneath the black earth, already frozen over again. She wept for how cold he would be. It was not his fault. So little that happened was anybody's fault.

The lilacs bloomed, blue and white, and the air grew soft with their perfume, the gentle swaying of their heavy-headed flowers, and the irises with their sculptured heads, blue and yellow and indigo and brown.

The tulips shot up, the Asian flower, the flower of mania, with many colors and shapes, some with speckled leaves and sharp pointed crimson petals with indigo eyes, some yellow, some white, some pale pink and green, some variations which came only once and never reappeared.

The foxgloves began to appear, shooting up spikes which opened into many bell-shaped flowers that hung their heads along the stems. The peony bushes came into bloom, and then came their rich Chinese blossoms, many petaled, the size of tea plates, heavy with moisture, pinks and whites.

She swept out her hand, over the painted hostas and dianthus and sweet alyssum, the sumptuous Chinese lilies with their splendid colors, suddenly filling the air with a perfume that was like a kind of fainting.

The rose canes unwound and thrived, the glossy foliage giving way to bud and bloom, the old roses, the old names. Mme. Hardy, the sumptuous pure white moss rose, and silvery pink La Noblesse. Old Velvet, the color of blood, of Antonio's blood; Clifton Moss, the resplendent pristine white of his shirt, purity and violence mixed together. The brilliant Fantin Latour rose up and flowered, the old French roses, the double Pellison, the bright crimson Henri Martin, Leda, with crimson markings on the edge of white petals.

There was no sound. There was no shift in the light. Everything was still.

The trellises straightened, and the climbing roses stood tall, twining up and around, mixing the thorny canes with clematis, purple and white.

The statues righted themselves, the classical figures with their sinuous curves, patinaed with age and moss, and the grotesques which hung at the four corners of the garden, which guarded the way in and out.

She had never seen anything so beautiful. The secret garden made her weep with the beauty of all that was living. It would last long after she died. Now and then, one of the roses would release a shower of petals that fell prettily through the golden light, until the ground beneath the climbers splayed against the wall was carpeted with the fragrant petals, the rich sweet and peppery smell filling the air, perfuming even the fabric of her dress.

The garden was perfect. The garden was her glory. It had come from nothing except the earth; it grew wherever she walked, wherever she turned her gaze. It would fill the house with vase after vase of flowers, so that their days would be perfumed. Truitt would ask her the names and she would reel them off and tell him about their histories, of the tulips brought from Asia Minor, to illuminate the sultan's nights, the jeweled earrings and the candled turtles. She would put together bouquets and take them to the town, to girls getting married, bringing them still dewy on the wedding morning, the stephanotis, the white roses and the lilies.

The light shifted from golden to pale yellow and then to gray blue, but the flowers seemed to glow more as the light faded, as though each petal were illuminated from within, until her little square was filled with light and fragrance and gaiety that all of Saint Louis couldn't match. Each rose, each bloom was a perfect masterpiece of kindness.

It was almost dark, and the darkest flowers vanished into the twilight, even as the pale white and palest pink roses seemed to give out a richer fragrance. The first star appeared above the brick wall.

The star brightened and was joined by other, paler stars as the dark deepened into night. She heard her name and turned toward the golden brightness of the house.

"Catherine."

She turned and Truitt was standing on the steps. He was still wearing the black suit he had worn to the funeral, a band of black crepe around his arm. She turned away, her long dress sweeping the ground, and the garden was vanished, had gone away, its beds a mess of old and dying flowers, its branches bare, the roses all thorns and the limes and yews a tangle of ruined wood. The garden waited, as it had waited for twenty years.

She was just a simple, honest woman standing in the ruin of a late winter garden, waiting for the spring.

"Catherine." She turned back toward him, afraid of him for the first time, afraid of his anger and his pain and his disapproval, and afraid also of her own shame. A wasted life. A ruined idea. Antonio dead.

Such things happened.

"I knew." His voice was clear in the darkness, his body a silhouette, his face lost in shadow. "I always knew."

"Knew what?"

"I knew what Antonio told me. Your history. What you've been. The lies you've told me. Who you are. I always knew. Malloy and Fisk sent me a letter. I burned it. It's private, and it means nothing. But I already knew before you came back from Saint Louis."

The garden waited. How could he forgive so much? How could he be so patient? So much depended on her now, on her answer, and she tried to wait as long as she could, still smelling the sweet perfume of the last old Bourbon rose.

"I'm going to have a baby."

He stood for a long time, until she shivered with the sudden cold.

"We're going to have a child."

In the darkness, she could see just enough to know the stillness in his tired face. He reached out his arm toward her. The lights from the house behind him began to come on, one by one. "Well then," he said. "Well then. You'd better come in the house."

She took one last look at the garden. The air had turned suddenly cold, but it was a springtime kind of cold, an evening cold, without threat. It was almost dark. Things wait, she thought. Not everything dies. Living takes time. And she walked toward the golden house and took his outstretched hand in her own.

Such things happen.

BEHOLDEN

The pictures you're about to see are of people who were once actually alive. That's the way it begins. And it never lets up.

I was set on fire in 1973. The blaze in my heart and brain was caused by the first reading of Michael Lesy's brilliant book *Wisconsin Death Trip*. Its collage of words and photographs paint a haunting, cinematic portrait of a small town in Wisconsin at the diseased end of the nineteenth century. We had imagined the cities to be teeming with moral turpitude and industrial madness, and rural America to be sleeping in a prosperous innocence, filled with honest and industrious people. Not so. Lesy unlocks the Pandora's box of country life to show us its dark and ravaged soul.

The portrait he paints has never left me. It had a profound influence on the structure and genesis of *A Reliable Wife*. I set it in Lesy country, frozen Wisconsin in the dead of winter, and played out a complex entangling of three lives against his starkly compelling canvas.

I owe a great deal to Michael Lesy, to his explication of the awful life endured by the mass of people caught between machinery and madness. Read Lesy's book. It will never leave you. It left me changed forever. Such things happen.

SPECIAL THANKS

To Elaine Markson, first responder and a great gardener; Doug Stewart, tenacious and smart agent; Chuck Adams, fine and careful editor; Michael Taeckens and Brunson Hoole at Algonquin; Bob Jones, who saved me more than once—as good as they come; and to those who read this book in its long incubation, and always said the one thing that gave me continuance: Dale Sessa, Nancy Axthelm, Dana Hoey, James Whiteside, Marybeth Hurt and Paul Schrader, faroff and lovely Jodie Tillen—a great heart and a great eye—Daphne Merkin, Jeb and Lexi Byers, Bob Balaban and Lynn Grossman, Everett Kane, Sally Mann, and her fine daughter, sweet Virginia Mann, Alexandra Como Saghir, Lisa Tracy, Suzanne Rice and Elizabeth Greenlee. So many wonderful friends! And to Nell Lancaster and Jim Waddell, to whom I owe a debt of gratitude beyond words.